St. m a

Mc Intyre 15

THE MURDERED HOUSE

Drury 14
Hansen 13   White 3/21
Chunchan 12

SIMATIS "

Robertson 11

Nettleship "
Haverfield 12
Lucas 12
Chapman 12
SN
Relf 12

Tuly 12

PARKVIEW 12

RM 12

Trueman 16

THE MURDERED HOUSE

PIERRE MAGNAN

Translated from the French by
Patricia Clancy

THORNDIKE
CHIVERS

This Large Print edition is published by Thorndike Press, Waterville, Maine, USA and by AudioGO Ltd, Bath, England.

Thorndike Press, a part of Gale, Cengage Learning.

Copyright © 1984 by Éditions Denoël. English translation copyright © 1999 by Patricia Clancy.

First published in France as La Maison Assassinée by Éditions Denoël.

The moral right of the author has been asserted.

The text of this Large Print edition is unabridged.

Other aspects of the book may vary from the original edition.

Set in 16 pt. Plantin.

Printed on permanent paper.

LIBRARY OF CONGRESS CATALOGING-IN-PUBLICATION DATA

Magnan, Pierre, 1922–
   [Maison assassinée. English]
   The murdered house / by Pierre Magnan ; translated from the French by Patricia Clancy.
     p. cm. — (Thorndike Press large print reviewers' choice)
   ISBN-13: 978-1-4104-2423-5 (alk. paper)
   ISBN-10: 1-4104-2423-5 (alk. paper)
   1. Large type books. I. Clancy, P. A. II. Title.
PQ2625.A637M3513 2010
843'.914—dc22   2009046319

BRITISH LIBRARY CATALOGUING-IN-PUBLICATION DATA AVAILABLE

Published in 2010 in the U.S. by arrangement with St. Martin's Press, LLC.
Published in 2010 in the U.K. by arrangement with The Random House Group Ltd.

U.K. Hardcover: 978 1 408 47844 8 (Chivers Large Print)
U.K. Softcover: 978 1 408 47845 5 (Camden Large Print)

Printed and bound in Great Britain by
CPI Antony Rowe, Chippenham, Wiltshire
1 2 3 4 5 6 7 14 13 12 11 10 09

For my sister
Alice Magnan

I

The Alps of Upper Provence
A coaching inn
28 September 1896
St Michael's Eve

Monge was on his guard. It was one of those nights when you know you have to be on the alert in these parts if you want to avoid unpleasant surprises. It was a night when you hold your breath, when anything can happen.

Monge had just come back from the stables where he had been rubbing down the remount horses for the Gap mail coach. They were soaked to the skin. He would have to get up at three o'clock to feed them, for at dawn they would be harnessed to the shafts of the dray that made the Embrun parcel post deliveries.

He had also just provided some bread and sausage for the fellow who was lying on a pile of postal bags among the harnesses.

Spruce as a young lover and carrying the beribboned cane of a journeyman doing his tour of France, the young man had arrived at dusk, at just the wrong time. He was dripping wet and his stovepipe hat glistened with rain, but he had cried out: "Evening all!" to the people who peered wide-eyed into the gloom. Monge had straight away taken him to the stables.

Monge, the master carter and inn-keeper, hung his cloak up behind the door and gazed at the people inside with that strange new look, which lately he seemed to turn on everything. The hanging lamp had not yet been lit: the light from the hearth was bright enough for what they normally had to do. On the plaster walls, mottled with mould, the shadows of the people sitting in the low-ceilinged room were jagged at the edges from the movement of the flames.

The *caquois*[1] was squawking in its cradle on the floor. Girarde got up. She carefully put down a large pile of sheets at the corner of the bread bin. She picked up the *caquois* with her reddened hands, then went and sat down on the other side of the hearth facing the old Grandfather. The child stopped crying at the first rustle of her bodice being

1 *caquois:* the last-born child (Provençal dialect).

8

unhooked. He clung with both hands to his mother's bare breast, and then all that could be heard was the sucking of his hungry lips, accentuated by the crackling of the fire under the soup pot.

The Grandfather stared shamelessly, his toothless mouth wide open, drinking in this scene he never tired of watching. He delighted in this new life, in which he thought he had managed to pass on enough of himself to guarantee some sort of immortality. The old man had a philosophic turn of mind. When he lost the last of his teeth, he stopped chewing tobacco. For fifty years this incessant mastication had blocked out the sounds of the world around him, so that now he heard them with a new clarity, as if for the first time.

Suddenly that evening, he stopped gazing at his daughter's breast. He looked up the wall to the greenish spots of saltpetre. Without moving his head, he called out to his son-in-law in his toneless voice.

"Monge, did you hear anything?"

"What's there to hear?" Monge grumbled.

The old man did not reply but shook his head. He strained his ears with their thick white hairs to catch the sounds. Outside, the sound of the Durance in full flow, washing the unstable banks at Dabisse down to the dyke at Peyruis, filled the valley with a muffled roar that swallowed the moaning of the wind in its wake, and sometimes even the sound of vehicles on the road or a flock of sheep in a fold.

As the noise of the rumbling waters went right through the protective walls, the sly laughter of the two older Monge boys as they tickled each other under the table went almost unnoticed. They were also hidden from sight by the oilcloth.

Monge shrugged his shoulders, but nevertheless went over and stood in front of the small window above the sink. He lifted the curtain. The night landscape he saw in front of him was just as he had imagined it. The sky, which had released downpours of rain for three days, had cleared at dusk, as it had every evening. The clouds, still swollen with rain, drifted sluggishly across the face of the full moon. In this cold light, the river rushed by between its indistinct banks. The water was a putrid colour, thick as mortar but with small crests of waves pushed back by the bottom of the fords.

A fine white jetty stood out behind the road between the Durance and the house, La Burlière. It was the ballast at the end of the railway line, which finished straight ahead in front of him. Tomorrow a hundred

10

workmen would arrive — steaming in the rain — with the clang and the vapour from the locomotives. They would start working again on the track where they had left off the day before. They would add another twenty to thirty metres and continue like that day after day, until they disappeared at the next turn on the horizon. The rails would start to rust in the rain and the wind, and then one day, when they reached Sisteron, and then Gap, the train would go through La Burlière, and that would mean the end of Monge's trade. Even though it could have a dramatic effect on his life, Monge reacted to this prospect the way he reacted to everything after that particular evening: with indifference, almost unthinking.

The man had a bitter taste in his mouth. A single idea obsessed him, ate into him like a cancer. For months now he had been living in another world — since the day when he was coming up from the cellar and, without meaning to, through the crack in the trapdoor that had not been quite closed, he had glimpsed a man's hairy hand quickly withdrawn from Girarde's wrist, where it had been placed in a protective gesture. He had not wanted or dared to find out what was going on. And besides, it happened in a flash. On that day — a Saturday — there had been a lot of vehicles on the road at La Burlière. Carters came, went and drank in large numbers. All that combined to produce a hullabaloo of swearing, shouting, laughing, whip cracking, of people in hobnailed boots coming and going through the courtyard and the house. In all that hustle and bustle, how could he recognize who had risked making that gesture, obviously a welcome one, since Girarde had not taken her hand away. Anyway, he would have had to find the will to do it, and Monge didn't have the stomach for it. He had been taken too much by surprise, and rushing into a confrontation would upset all his plans. So, while he pretended not to have noticed, he had been brooding over it ever since.

Silently, he watched the development of this new woman by his side, even though she was in no discernible way different from the one he knew before. He watched her with a passion, without letting any of the changes in him alter his usual expression. But his pretence had been rewarded. One night, lying beside her, he had been awakened by a strange noise. Girarde was dreaming, crying out softly in her sleep. Was it the cry of a creature in pain? Was it the cry of a creature in love? Monge could not tell which. In any case, those cries were not for him, Monge. They flew over his head, over his body. They were either calling for help or expressing their joy to someone.

That happened several times as the nights went by, while under the eiderdown Girarde's belly swelled into a little hill that drew all the sheets and blankets to it. Monge would light the oil lamp and sit there leaning on his elbow for some time, watching Girarde's full lips moving. They never uttered a distinct word, but the vehemence of this incoherent speech allowed Monge to give free rein to his imagination, and he certainly did so. All this agitation would stop as suddenly as it began. All at once, the sleeping woman's face would become perfectly moonlike, perfectly content again, as if the dream that had been formed in her subconscious was enough to bring her peace.

Girarde was never woken by this intense scrutiny. It was Monge who finally blew out the lamp, as he sat there deeply distressed and trying to find some comfort in the noises outside: the wind in the pines, the sound of the Durance, the ringing of the bell up there in the mountains at Ganagobie, where the friars had bidden farewell to this world of women in double beds who

13

dream out loud.

But as soon as he woke up, he began to brood over it. He got several sharp rebuffs from coach drivers and harness hands when he presented the fresh horses the wrong way around.

He brooded a lot more when Girarde had the baby. When the *caquois* was born, for six hours he had a face no one recognized, a face that had never been in the family. A face that wasn't from around here. At least that is how Monge saw it. He also thought that the midwife seemed very apprehensive when she held it up in front of her in the little side room; that she was trying to get it away from the candle light; that she would willingly have buried it under her apron if she had dared, and once it was there with its head under her arm, she would have smothered it like a fluttering pigeon. What is more, he, Monge, thought that Girarde insisted on keeping her face turned to the wall, using pain as a pretext, as if the child was the incarnation of a glaring truth.

Monge just stood there in front of her, stunned.

Later the *caquois* turned blond and smooth as an angel on a church ceiling. The unknown face had faded away under this seraphic countenance. But Monge had imprinted that first face — perhaps the false one — into his memory. He didn't see the new one. He turned his head away, so that he couldn't see it.

It was while he was turning over these recent memories in his mind that Monge saw the image of the kid at his mother's breast reflected in the window. He turned around and came back to the big table where the older boys were whispering and laughing irritatingly around his feet. He suddenly reached for the drawer, which opened with a creak. He took his time counting the things inside, then pushed it closed.

He went and wiped his hand over the dust in the bread bin. He rummaged through the box of knobs. He took down the handle to wind the grandfather clock, inserted it into the dial and slowly began to raise the weights. He advanced the hands by ten minutes.

"Monge!" exclaimed the old man. "You really don't hear anything?"

Monge did not reply. He shook his head, without really paying attention. He had taken down his rusty old gun from above the hood over the fireplace. He was checking the breech, but his mind was elsewhere.

While she changed the baby from one breast to the other, Girarde observed her husband, her head bent a little to one side. Convulsions that had struck her in the cradle had left her with a slight cast in one eye that tended to make her gaze wander upwards a little; but the other eye, straight and cornflower blue, unerringly followed Monge's every movement.

She had been watching him closely for months. He seemed to change from week to week. They had never said much to each other in twelve years of married life, but at least the atmosphere between them had been calm. Each went about his own business, and as for the rest, the deep sleep of people exhausted by work took the place of tenderness. When she needed tenderness . . . But that was precisely the thought she had to get out of her mind when she was with Monge.

Had he detected a glow of happiness in her straight blue eye? She wondered about that every evening while he sat there brooding.

Monge put the old gun back on the rack and slowly began a tour of his domain. He opened the creaking cupboard door. He went through the provisions and the jams. He counted the pieces of soap piled up in a pyramid on the shelf. Then he straightened the Post Office calendar that someone had knocked.

Since he had withdrawn into himself, he often inspected his possessions like this. You would have thought he was identifying them, weighing them up. Besides, he was not content to look at them. Like a blind man, he felt them. The jugs, the china coffee cups lined up on the sideboard, the demijohns of oil in the dark corners, the set of copper saucepans, the bread basket, the warming pan, the Cornelia sewing machine — he put his hands on all these objects, as if he wanted to preserve the imprint of their shape beneath his fingers.

But also he felt and stroked each wall, each sharp corner, wherever he had grazed his skin since he was a boy. He caressed the spot where a stone, even though it had been plastered, jutted out further than the others. He had hit his head against that stone one day when a kick from his father had sent him flying against the wall. He no longer remembered why . . .

But what attracted Monge most of all was the darkest corner, between the side wall of the hearth and the place where the faggots were kept. There, beneath the hanging spit that was only ever used at Christmas, a rudimentary pine salt box hung on the end of a piece of string. Knocked together for temporary use by some long-dead relative, it had been blackening there for maybe a hundred years. Monge just stood there in front of the box, rubbing his chin with his blunt fingers. More than ever he seemed to be lost in his sombre thoughts.

That night, he suddenly reached out and took the salt box off its hook. He slowly brushed the flat of his hand across the empty space where the box had been. It was lighter in colour and stood out against the black wall surrounding it. As he removed the box, he frowned from some sort of mental effort. Then he pressed his palms hard against the front of the hearth, where the ashes were barely warm. Crushing some bits of charcoal between his fingers, and using his hands like a trowel, he carefully blackened the spot behind the salt box, then hung it up again.

The Grandfather and Girarde had not missed a single one of his movements. When he turned round towards them, they tried to catch his attention, but his eyes had that dull look horses sometimes have.

"Monge! If you can't hear anything this time, you're a blockhead!"

The old man had risen half-way out of his

seat and turned towards the door. The old lock rattled with the battering of the wind. It was as though the house had been released by the land and was escaping from it, floating away on the waters of the Durance, down to the sea. This noise of the river and the tall trees in the wind dominated everything. What else could be heard above all that?

Nevertheless Monge came back to the window to find out. A line-inspection car with its arms lifted to the sky shone in the rain at the end of the last rail that had been laid. Beyond that, the flow of the dense Durance brushed back the twisted foliage of the willows in the opposite direction from the wind. In the moonlight a large fallen tree could be seen floating by on the current, entwining the eddies in its tentacle roots.

In the window pane, the image of Girarde and the *caquois* at her breast, reflected by the flames from the hearth, seemed to float on the surging water. The delicacy and charm of this fragile nativity scene mocked the brutal forces at work in the night. It danced on the whirlpools, whipped up by the wind, that plunged to the bottom of the current with a desolate sound like a hunting horn.

19

Monge took full advantage of the situation to gaze at this fleeting vision, for when he was with her in the daytime he only dared observe the scene surreptitiously, when no one was looking. The firelight, softened by the moonlight through the window, outlined the features of the mother and child in a soft bronze glow. It was then that the features the child had had for a brief moment at his birth returned and reshaped his little face, as if the two sources of light from the hearth and the moon had converged specially to reveal a truth that Monge had refused to accept. It came to Monge in a flash that between himself and the road, between himself and the inspection car, between himself and the Durance, the faint image of an unknown man's face floated on the current.

Monge was so bewildered by all the torments he was wrestling with that he had almost gone to see Zorme that very afternoon to ask his advice. Now Zorme was a man you didn't normally want to see. He was silent and menacing as a raven. He would suddenly appear at your side without you knowing it: you just turned around, and there he was. People put on a brave front when they were with him. You had to keep your anxiety to yourself. If he thought you were afraid of him, he became very domineering.

He was a man who lived, and lived well, without working. The grass grew free on the path that led to his house. He could leave the key in his door, his wallet on the table, the stew on the fire, a litre of wine opened. The routes followed by gypsies, which crossed radially between Peyruis castle and the rocks known as the Penitents of Les Mées, deliberately avoided the area around the house, indicated by runic crosses cut into certain stones. The circumference of the detour they had to make was a full kilometre.

No one knew precisely the cause of this fear. But if someone happened to let the name escape from his lips, he would try to catch it, like a butterfly, and pull it back in again. If a child asked an innocent question about him, he was rebuffed and told to eat his soup. Even the clerk at the registry office would swallow hard before writing the letters of that name on a certificate.

This was the man who had come to La Burlière in the pouring rain at around four o'clock that afternoon, as he often did, unannounced and for no particular reason. He didn't even say anything, just waited for others to speak. He had been coming there like that for the past few days — just by chance, he said — since the Durance had taken on that dismal, polluted river colour. He prowled around La Burlière looking like an anxious crow — head to one side, hands crossed behind his back, fingers working. His big black moustache had been trimmed to put people's minds at ease, making him look a little more good-natured.

Monge was filled with dread whenever he was there. While the rain was falling that afternoon, he felt him hovering and sniffing around him, breathing over him. Monge had watched him as he left with his big red umbrella. He had seen him from behind as he climbed over the brand-new railway ballast, walked around the line-inspection car, stared at it for a few seconds, then ran down the other side towards the river, on a level with the bank of the fast-flowing, swollen waters. He saw him lean over and touch the water, then draw some into the palm of his hand and feel the weight of it as it flowed out. After that, he had scanned the overcast horizon from which the torrent gushed forth as if it had spontaneously surfaced there behind the low, rain-soaked mist. And then Monge could see Zorme with his hat pushed back, under the umbrella, talking aloud as if

22

he was speaking to someone or asking a lengthy question. He was frowning anxiously.

While he was recalling Zorme's bizarre behaviour, Monge noticed that he had unconsciously placed his outspread hands against the window panes, to block out the vision of Girarde and the child, so intimately linked by that softly rising breast.

Suddenly he turned away. Girarde looked at him with her strange wandering gaze. She got up to put the *caquois* back in its cradle, then came back to her seat, placing her hands flat against her thighs. The Grandfather's head was leaning to one side. He had obviously not stopped listening to something else besides the annoying laughter of the two elder boys under the table.

The house shuddered as the force of the storm lashed the walls. Sounds of the nervous remount horses rose up from down below in the stables. But the old man was probably right. Despite the elemental din of the river and sky combined, it did indeed seem that a furtive sigh — the presence of a man — had managed to slip beneath the howling of the wind.

Monge came back towards the hearth. Once again he put out both hands as if to unhook the salt box, but decided against it.

Then he walked with heavy, deliberate steps towards the table. Once again he opened the drawer, but this time he did it silently. The two older boys under the oilcloth stopped laughing.

Seen from outside, shining in the moonlight and still wet with the recent rain, La Burlière was a house with few windows and straight walls built with pebbles from the Durance. The stables underneath extended further than the main building, out into the sulphurous zaffre rock from which they had been excavated. The horses inside were bathed in golden light from the oil lamps.

The only doors in this house were coach doors where waggons, drays, timber carts, and double carts drove in, or hayloft doors where the forage was stored. Everything was arranged for the comfort of horses and carriages, and nothing for people. When you looked at it on a night like that, with its blind wall stretching to the turn in the road, it had the narrowness and sharp angles of a coffin. At the corners of the stone-paved courtyards stood four ancient Italian cypresses, gleaming in the rain like enormous green candles.

At least that is how they seemed to the three men crouched in the shadows between the harness shed and the carriage cemetery, with its broken shafts and rimless wheels: wrecks of former vehicles that had faced the terrible hazards of all the mountain roads, and had been brought back here to rot in peace. Through the openwork of this rampart, the three men watched the small window — the only one in the front wall of the house — where a dim light shone fitfully.

They had been huddled together there for quite a while. Their heavy clothing smelled of rain and of the giant box bushes they had silently crept through to get here, for they had not come by the road. They had followed the banks of the feeder canal and crossed the ruined Roman bridge, coming out above La Burlière, where they had remained for some time crouched behind the juniper bushes. At nightfall, before the sky was cleared beneath the moon, they had quickly scrambled down the slope and hidden themselves there between the shed and the old carts. Since then, they kept their courage up by whispering to each other.

"Do you think they'll ever go to bed?"

"Yes, eventually."

"How will we get him to talk?"

"Like the others in our trade. We'll warm up his feet for him . . ."

25

"Have you taken a good look at Monge?"

"What do you mean, taken a good look? He's got feet like anyone else, hasn't he?"

"Well, you haven't looked hard enough, if that's what you think. I've seen him . . . One market day, when he was having a tooth pulled out by the Greek."

"The one whose daughter plays the drum?"

"Yes, indeed! That's the one. In Monge's case, she didn't have to play it to cover the sound of his cries. He didn't cry out at all! All he did was feel his cheek afterwards — and then only for a moment . . ."

"There's a world of difference between a tooth and a hot coal. He's not made of iron, the *Uillaou*[2] . . ."

"I'm not so sure . . . One day I saw him punch a stallion in the head. It had just bitten him. I've never seen a horse come to attention like that . . ."

"He's right. Monge has an iron heart. The three of us know all too well that he's got an iron heart . . ."

"Quiet! Shut up, both of you!"

"What's up?"

"Don't you hear anything?"

"What's there to hear?"

2 *uillaou:* lightning (Provençal dialect).

Crouching on the ground out there in the open, without the protection of the walls, you couldn't hear a thing, except if your stomach was tight with anxiety. The torrent that ate into the mountain and ploughed it down to the sea was tearing through the corridors of the night. Its noise even dominated the howl of the squall that whipped up the holly-oak forests from the slopes of Ganagobie to the Lure foothills, over there on the Mallefougasse peaks. You could only guess what was happening from seeing the foliage on the trees being suddenly sucked up towards the moon as if they were raising their arms to heaven.

The three men were whispering. They could just as well have been shouting. No one would have noticed they were there.

"I tell you, I can hear something!"

Even though that was hardly likely, the three men crouched even closer to the ground. You could tell they were ready to hear anything. Sometimes one of them glanced over his shoulder like a frightened rabbit, but the only comfort that gave him was the sight of the anvil-shaped top of the Ganagobie plateau, which seemed to drift beneath the moon like a stone ship. It was hard to tell whether it portended good or ill. That tribunal of rugged cliffs, concealing its dangerous nature under an innocent-looking holly-oak forest, reserved its judgment for all eternity. As always happens when men suspect that a mountain might be prone to turbulence, a sanctuary had been built on top to bring it under control. And from here, in the courtyard of La Burlière, you could make out a faint gleam of light like a dying ember. It must have been the last of the monks in the brotherhood praying by the light of a single candle before going to lie down on their wooden boards.

"Now you know I heard something!"

A cold shiver went down the backs of the three men. A black shadow suddenly appeared and walked towards the house with his back to them. There on the rounded cobblestones of the courtyard, someone coming from the road was battling against the gust of wind that made his trousers and jacket balloon out, blurring the outline of his body and making him impossible to recognize. The only thing you could tell was that he was tall and that he kept his arms slightly bent and his hands open, like someone getting ready to seize an opponent bodily.

While this person was approaching the low door, the squall increased in ferocity. The wind turned and blew the sound of the torrent down towards La Burlière, as if wind and water were joining forces to break down the walls. The man was now standing in front of the entrance. He raised his hand to knock on the door, then changed his mind and gave a sharp tug on the latch string. The door opened with difficulty, as if it had trouble turning on its hinges, and then closed again behind the man.

The trio hiding behind the wheels never took their eyes off the window. It was the only indication they had of what was happening inside. From time to time, the shadow of a hand or a head blocked out the source of light coming from the hearth. Sometimes a whole body stood longer in front of the light. They waited, not saying a word.

Suddenly the door opened, and this time it opened wide. The large body of the person who had gone in earlier blocked it completely, but only for an instant. He rushed out as though he had been pushed from behind, as though someone were throwing him out. Nonetheless, he pulled the door to and stood in full moonlight in front of the three men. But, in spite of the moonlight, he was too far away for them to be able to put a name to the face.

The squall, that had not abated in the

slightest, once again swelled the trousers and jacket of the man who was walking towards the well, with his arms slightly out from his body and his fists tightly shut. Although he was moving forward with measured steps, he seemed to be standing still, with the gawkiness of a scarecrow about to collapse on the ground. They saw him walk around and past the horse trough, grip the marble rim of the well and lean over. Thinking that he was going to throw himself in, they gripped each others' arms tightly, to prevent anyone from stopping him. But he didn't throw himself in. He stood up straight again. A cloud crossed in front of the moon, and in the darkness he passed so near to the men lying in ambush that they caught his smell of cold tobacco, and recognized him.

He stumbled in the ruts of the track the carts had made in the paving stones over the centuries. He crossed the road, buffeted by the wind. He went over the railway ballast, clung on to the line-inspection car, climbed on and began to pump the handle, his clothes billowing out around him like a flag. Riding on his ghostly trolley, he disappeared like a nightmare into the storm near Lurs station, all shiny white and new, down there by the turn in the railway track.

30

Then an amazing sound came through the roar of the water as it swept its gravel downstream. Piercing the storm that was wringing the branches of the pines and holly-oaks with its doleful moan, the bell in the priory high above on the Ganagobie plateau began to ring for matins. This simple ringing of a bell that could cut across the raging elements reminded the three men that they had no time to lose.

Then, pressed close against each other like one single body for mutual strength, the three of them rushed towards the house. The bee-keeper's hoods which hid their faces gave them square-shaped heads like incomplete foetuses. In the moonlight, the blades of their cobblers' knives seemed to be carried by a single arm.

Through the window, the last flames of a dying fire flickered in the hearth.

II

1919

Maître Bellaffaire, the notary at Peyruis, considered the young man in front of him: he had the look of an archangel, but with pectorals that swelled the faded vest he wore in place of a shirt. The notary marvelled that during four years of war, when there must have been so many occasions for it to happen, such a broad chest had never stopped a single bullet. It was really extraordinary how the trenches could have kept anyone in such good shape. He had trouble making the appearance of this survivor coincide with everything that had been said about those infernal places where you should avoid being sent at any price. How could anyone survive it with those supple muscles, that Easter morning complexion, that smooth skin without a single wrinkle . . .

From his side of the desk, Séraphin

Monge looked at the notary in that special way orphanage children look at people. He had begun life with no trust in men. The Sisters of Charity had not taught it to him. He was afraid of men, just as they were; the chaplain, the Bishop, the bursar, the benefactor . . . They spent their lives bowing down to them and had accustomed Séraphin to do the same. As for God Himself, they feared Him as they feared men and expected no quarter from Him. They had succeeded in making Him powerfully credible to Séraphin, by portraying Him as quick to anger and quite pitiless.

After his orphanage upbringing, four years of war had hardly improved this attitude to life; it even lent a certain attraction to the constant prospect of death. Anyway, this mistrust of his neighbour wasn't much good to Séraphin. Although he understood men's minds, he was no better equipped to defend himself against their actions, which is why he was listening to the notary with an angelic smile on his face, while the latter bamboozled him with pages of lawyers' accounts.

And what was the notary saying? He was talking about the war. He gave a little sigh.

"Of course, I should have — we should have — sent you accounts . . . before . . .

but unfortunately there was a slight contre-temps . . . Earlier of course . . . it wasn't possible to have a board of guardians from members of your family, for the simple fact that you had none. We had to deal with the situation as quickly as possible: get you a wet-nurse, help, shelter, and then, an education . . . Yes, indeed! Whatever people might say, the Sisters of Charity aren't cheap when you have property . . ."

Wetting his finger, he noisily riffled through the papers he was examining over the top of his glasses.

"The land, of course, was sold. Unfortunately, the house . . ."

He put on a contrite expression.

"We weren't able to sell the house . . ."

"Why?" Séraphin asked without thinking.

"Why? But . . . because . . . Well, surely you know why?"

"No," Séraphin said.

"What? You don't know? But you've read your family record book, haven't you?"

"I know that I'm an orphan . . . ," replied Séraphin in a low voice, as though he were ashamed of the fact.

His lawyer's sense of prudence made Maître Bellaffaire break off the subject at that point and simply lie by omission. It's what his father would have managed to do, without the expression on his face changing in the slightest. But, when a certain image takes hold of one's mind, it's very difficult to have complete control over one's feelings . . . He spoke in a deliberately emotionless voice:

"In those far-off times, you know, I was ten years old and I was a boarder at Saint-Charles in Manosque . . . So . . ."

His white hands, adorned with oversleeves, made a graceful but half-hearted gesture like a bird's wings.

"But what does it really matter to you now? The past is the past!"

For the first time during the interview, Séraphin raised his eyes and looked at the notary, who quickly averted his in the direction of the filing cabinet.

"Were you brought up by the Sisters of Charity?" Séraphin asked.

"N . . . no!" Maître Bellaffaire spluttered. "Of course not!"

"I was . . ." Séraphin said quietly.

"In short!" The notary brought the subject to a close. "There are 1,250 francs 50 centimes remaining from the sale of the land, livestock and chattels . . ."

He patted the money that had already been counted out and sat on the desk to his right. He spoke volubly of the absolute

honesty of all those involved in these painful circumstances. He waved the bundle of
papers in which everything was set out in
the beautiful writing of some scrupulous
law clerk. According to him, everything was
in order. There was nothing underhand. (He
pronounced the word very firmly.)

"In short! We declare: 1,250 francs and
50 centimes! Plus the house, and here's the
key!"

Having declared it, he put the object down
on the desk beside the money. It made a
sharp sound like the crack of a whip on the
oak desktop. Séraphin looked at it intently.
It was a big, twisted key, obviously very
worn, and attacked by pustules of oxidiza-
tion spreading over it like lichen.

The notary got up and walked to the other
side of the desk. He slipped the notes and
cash into the envelope already prepared to
this effect, which he handed to Séraphin
with the key.

"There you are," he said. "Go through
your accounts! And if, by any chance, you
find fault with anything, do let me
know . . ."

"Oh . . . I'm sure they're correct . . ."
Séraphin said in his slow way of speaking.

The notary became aware that his client
was feeling the key all over with his large

fingers, examining it with great attention. To tell the truth, Séraphin found it strangely cold, coming from a place as snug as a desk drawer, in the notary's office, on that spring morning . . .

He stood there, in the way, not making a move to leave.

"Is anything worrying you?" Maître Bellaffaire asked.

"Tell me, sir . . . I'd like to ask you . . . When I was at the front . . . almost every month . . . I received a parcel from here . . . Do you know who sent it to me?"

"A parcel? No . . ."

Then he corrected himself: "It must have been my poor father . . . He was such a generous man."

Séraphin shook his head.

"Your poor father . . . I believe he died in 1916?"

"Yes . . . Yes . . ." Maître Bellaffaire admitted.

"Well, it couldn't have been him. I received them right up to the end . . . up to last month. Just before I was demobilized . . ."

"But . . . Was there no sender's name?"

"No. Never."

"Well then, it must have been some kind soul . . . You see! The world is full of decent

37

people."

He tried to put his hand on Séraphin's shoulder to hasten his departure. That was no good. He had to raise his hand too high and the gesture did not look at all protective.

"They've found you decent work, I hope?" he asked.

"I've got a job as a road worker . . ."

"Road worker!" Maître Bellaffaire exclaimed. "That's fine! You'll never be short of work with the Highways Department. And what's more . . . You'll have a pension!"

He didn't say "lucky devil", but he thought it so much that you could read the words on his lips.

When he had closed the door behind him, Maître Bellaffaire went and stood with his hands behind his back at the solidly-barred window. Holding back the heavy curtains, he watched the orphan walk away.

This quiet hulk of a man had made quite an impression: he moved about in silence and you couldn't even hear him breathing.

The lawyer's office looked on to a small square with a fountain shaded by plane trees. Séraphin walked over to it. He seized the copper spout with both hands and bathed his head beneath the jet of water. This movement made the faded vest rise up towards his armpits. The muscles that emphasized his ribs rippled like rope, while other muscles tensed to support the hollow of his belly. As he twisted his body backwards to get his mouth under the grotesque mask on the end of the spout, the vest gaped, revealing his prominent sternum.

On the other side of the carved pillar with its erotic scenes, the *pêchier*[3] a young girl was filling overflowed. She stared wide-eyed at him, admiring the glow of his face with its eyes closed and its mouth almost biting the water on its way down his throat.

Old Burle, after sticking a plug of tobacco behind his back teeth, appreciatively observed the strength of Séraphin's movements as he raised the rammer. They were both repairing the turn at the canal bridge where truck tyres had damaged the road. It was already summer, but that evening a black dust was creeping into the distant sky above the Durance. It did not look like the usual clouds: it was diffuse and light. You had to look at it for some time to realize that it had replaced the blue sky and was already moving across the sun.

"Son! There's going to be a storm!" Old

3 *pêchier:* pitcher or jug (Provençal dialect).

Burle predicted. "We'd better make for the cabin."

Séraphin put down his rammer and turned towards him.

"What if Monsieur Anglès comes along? He told us to get this turning finished."

"Oh, Monsieur Anglès . . . Monsieur Anglès . . . The storm won't come down on his back! It won't help Monsieur Anglès much if I can't stand up for a fortnight afterwards!"

Séraphin did not reply, but went on working while Burle took his time bringing him one or two shovelfuls of crushed stone.

"Those trucks with their solid tyres," he cursed, "they'll be the death of us road menders!"

He sank his spade into a heap of stones on the side of the road, spat a bit of tobacco juice into his hands, and looked warily at the sky again.

"Y' see, son, when Les Mées is that colour, it means that all hell will break loose! You'll see it! There's going to be a mighty storm!"

His outstretched arm pointed to the procession of rocks called the Penitents, that looked as though they had been turned to stone by an evil spell just before they reached the Durance. They dominated the

40

village, over there on the other side of the river, and the dismal aspect of those huge monks with their heads hooded in pointed cowls did not augur well to Old Burle.

"Just look over there, son. It's not often you'll see Les Mées that colour! What's your name again?"

"Séraphin."

"Séraphin? Oh! You're called Séraphin?"

Old Burle stopped chewing his tobacco for a moment, his arm still pointing to the Penitents. He seemed to be searching his memory for something that name reminded him of. But he didn't spend much time thinking about it. His attention was too much engaged in what was going on about him.

"Look, Séraphin! Look at the Bléone valley. You'd swear that dust was flowing down it instead of water! It's already over Le Couar! It's coming towards us! In five minutes' time . . ."

He didn't finish his sentence. There was a small flash of lightning further away over the reeds of the Iscles[4], and immediately a strange noise descended on them. It was as if their ears were deafened by a load of

4 *Iscles:* the little islands and clumps of water-willows in the Durance river.

41

gravel someone had tipped out right next to them.

"Hurry, Séraphin! Let's get out of here!"

Burle threw his shovel on to the pile of pebbles and ran off. It was too late. Hail-stones as big as cherries whipped around his ears.

"Up there!" he shouted.

He pointed to two big cypresses, twisting and turning in the gale, that all at once sank out of sight. Séraphin put his tools down on the roadside and dashed off after his work-mate.

"Wait for me! Where are you going?"

But Burle was already scrambling up the slope as fast as his short legs could carry him. The lightning was literally pushing him from behind. It ricocheted along the ground with that awful noise of tin pots being dragged over pebbles, a noise only recog-nized by those who have had a narrow escape. Drawn there by the air currents, it rushed into the green tunnels of the holly-oaks, literally encircling the two men. Whipped about the ears by the solid deluge of hail, they opened their mouths choking, wanting to cry out in pain but not daring to.

Burle was already at the top, in front of the two cypresses. They had served as a landmark and were bent over in the wind like sickles. He was standing on the raised paving stones of an old haulage yard, getting his bearings. Dilapidated sheds, collapsing on the skeletons of carts and agricultural machinery, offered no shelter. Burle stumbled across a blind wall, barred by a solid oak door, which didn't budge when he kicked it.

"Séraphin! What the hell are you doing? *Tron de pas dieu!* Come on, for God's sake!"

He saw him emerge from the hailstones like a drowned man, his fair hair hanging down around his head, but walking in the deluge with the same deliberate step. At that moment the lightning flashed so close to them that the thunder following immediately afterwards nearly deafened them. In that blinding light, Burle suddenly saw the essential features of Séraphin's face etched differently than in ordinary daylight.

"Good God!" he exclaimed.

However, when you've had a cartload of hail blowing in your face for five minutes; when the hailstones have gone down your shirt collar, well past your waist down to your underwear, where they have piled up forming a nest of ice just where your balls sit, you hardly have the leisure to reflect at length on certain thoughts that cross your mind.

"What are you up to?" he shouted. "Come and help me knock the door down!"

Séraphin loomed up in front of him, dominating him with his large frame, but not making a move. He stared at the door, as the hailstones rained down on him. It was closed off by two old black wax seals, linked by a hemp cord in perfect condition. But what Burle saw in particular was that Séraphin was handing him an old key, large, twisted and worn. He took it and turned it in the lock. The seals gave way with the sound of a veil being torn.

Burle rushed in through the wide-open door and turned around. Séraphin remained on the threshold as if rooted to the spot in spite of the hailstones that whipped about his ears.

"Well? What the hell are you doing?" Burle shouted at him. "Do you want to catch your death of cold? Come on . . . come in!"

"No!" Séraphin exclaimed in a low but determined voice.

Burle rushed forward and shoved the inert mass of the man. Séraphin was pushed, punched and kicked into entering the den. He let himself be manoeuvred like a big, lanky, awkward puppet. A lingering smell of salt, cold hearth and beaten iron caressed his face, as familiar as the smell of a home-coming. Musty traces of curdled milk and powdered savory still floated in the air.

"I'm Séraphin Monge . . ." Séraphin mur-mured.

"What of it?" said Burle wiping his face with his handkerchief. "Do you think that'll stop you from catching your death of cold? Take off your jacket, take off your shirt. Strip off completely! Take a look over there and see if there's still some wood. Just a moment till I see if my matches are dry . . . Just as well I've got a rubber tobacco pouch . . . There! Shove that firewood on top of the ashes, it'll catch all right. You see . . . During my goddamn life, I've known three men die of double pneumonia in July . . ."

By the time the fire started to crackle, he was already down to his long underwear, standing there with his white chest hair, bow legs and short thin arms that scarcely had any muscles. He turned his back to the fire.

"It gets you first down the back, son. You're solid, but don't set too much store on that! The stronger you are, the more transparent your lungs are . . . In my god-damn life I've seen two of them, two road workers nearly as solid as you . . . After

45

something like what we've had today, they only lasted eight days. And — this is to give you some idea — it took six of us to carry their coffins . . ."

He stood up straight, then took hold of his trousers by the belt and shook them hard. The hailstones that had piled up inside showered on to the floor with a sound like marbles.

Outside, the storm raged on. Sometimes hailstones ricocheted in the chimney. Once Burle had warmed up again, he prepared a fresh plug of tobacco.

"Do you realize, son . . . The wood burning there . . . It was cut twenty-three years ago . . . Twenty-three years . . . It's quite dry . . . What are you doing? Are you listening to me?"

"I'm looking around," said Séraphin.

The tall flames from the firewood that was crackling in the hearth had chased the shadows from all the nooks and crannies.

"Push the door closed!" ordered Burle. "If ever the lightning finds a draught . . ."

Séraphin obeyed. Behind the leaf of the door, hanging on makeshift pegs, were two cloaks that for some reason the moths had left alone. They hung next to a carter's whip and a dark lantern. A whiff of the stables still clung to their folds.

"So . . . Your name is Séraphin Monge?"
said Burle.

"Yes."

"So you're the one they took away to the
Sisters of Charity when you were three
weeks old?"

He slapped his thigh.

"What a dreadful business that was, my
friend! You see, they couldn't find anyone.
Wet nurses squawked with fear . . . Oh,
there were some who tried! They said that
their breasts became icy cold when you put
your mouth on them! They couldn't take it!
They had to pull their breasts away. Then of
course you screamed . . . What a business!
They finally found you one near Guillestre.
She had a goitre — and even then the priest
had to lecture her about the sufferings of
Christ . . . So, you're Séraphin Monge?
Hell! You've grown up all right!"

He bent down. A flash of lightning hit the
courtyard. The light from it made the
firelight in the hearth grow pale, in spite of
the closed door and the shutters over the
small window.

"Bloody hell! The son of a bitch'll get us
in the end! We'll have escaped the war and
Spanish flu, only to end up killed by lightning!"

Burle waved his open hand towards the

storm outside, raging on a level with the Durance. Sitting naked at a corner of the hearth, Séraphin did not shudder at the flashes of lightning or the crashes of thunder. His eyes were taking everything in, taking possession of the objects in the room. They went from the bread bin to the cupboard with the smoke-blackened door. He noticed the clock in the furthest corner. The pendulum could not be seen behind its filthy window, but the face had remained quite clear. It said 10:40 — the time when the mechanism had run down, the weights lay on the floor, and the clock had stopped ticking.

Séraphin looked over to the demijohns lined up on the flagstones, the sink with its red tiles, the set of saucepans, the Post Office calendar hanging askew on the wall. He spent some time gazing at the table surrounded by benches and chairs. It was covered with an oilcloth with dark stains and a great tear in the middle. The edge of this table led his eye to a small piece of furniture under the sideboard tucked between the shallow baskets used to hold the olive pulp for pressing. It was a cradle on rockers, scarcely fifty centimetres high, that had been placed on the ground. The dancing flames were reflected like red daggers on its bars, while the glow from the hearth lit up the rays around the deeply carved rosettes that decorated it, in spite of the grey dust that had gathered in them. Séraphin looked at it tenderly, completely enthralled.

"They simply removed the bodies," said Burle, "and then they took you away. Apart from that and the three inches of dust, the last time I set foot in here — that's twenty-three years ago, exactly your age — everything was like this . . . !"

He made a sweeping, circular movement with his arm.

"Only, back then . . . phew!" he said. "Talk about clean! Everything shone in Girarde's place. What a woman she was!"

He put out his hand with his fist closed and thumb up.

"Girarde?" asked Séraphin.

"Your mother!" he told him.

"My mother . . ." Séraphin said thoughtfully. "My mother . . ."

The word fell slowly from his lips and he repeated it several times as if he was counting gold pieces one by one. His legs began to feel weak beneath him, so he sat down on the flagstones of the kitchen stove, at the corner of the fireplace. Burle, who was standing, could at last put his hand on the young man's shoulder.

"No one's dared tell you about it?" he asked.

"No," replied Séraphin, "no one."

"Do you want to know?" Burle asked.

"Yes," replied Séraphin

"All right, I'll tell you . . ."

He noticed an old straw-bottomed armchair. He had the impression of seeing it for the first time since he had been in the room, even though it took up a lot of space in front of the hearth. The seat was out of shape, giving the impression that someone still occupied it. It had a commanding presence that was difficult to ignore. When Burle finally sat down on the creaking straw seat, a new burst of the storm made him start, and he had the distinct impression that he was sitting on someone. He began to speak hurriedly to get rid of the disturbing impression.

"Right!" he said. "It was the carters coming from Embrun who fetched me. I was on the road, as I'd been for forty years past. They were running and had also collected the construction teams working on the railroad track as they passed. As a result, when we got to the door you see closed over there, there were about fifty of us . . . standing glued to the spot . . . speechless . . . On that morning, there were only two sounds

50

in this room: the clock that was still working and a baby crying its head off. That was you: you were hungry. The rest . . . well . . . What I remember . . . was the smell. Since then, son, I've never been able to *ajuder*[5] anyone to kill their pig. It smelled of blood . . . of warm blood. A smell of blood flooded the house . . . You have no idea."

"Oh!" Séraphin sighed, "yes . . . I can . . ."

Burle looked at him, taken aback.

"Ah! Yes . . . That's true . . ." he said. "You'd know that smell now . . . But I hadn't been to war — I've never fought in a war. So I didn't know the colour blood can be, when there's so much of it . . . It was everywhere! Everywhere you can see dust, there on the ground, was full of bloody *piades*[6]! Feet had walked in it. It was on the bread bin, the cupboard door — you'll understand why in a minute — on the clock. The clock over there! If you dust the glass front, you'll find it splashed with black spots . . . And then . . ."

Burle got up from the chair, which he looked at warily. He pointed to the place where he had just been sitting.

"There!" he said. "There, where I was sit-

5 *ajuder:* help, assist (Provençal dialect).
6 *piades:* footprints (Provençal dialect).

ting, that's where the Grandfather was —
your mother's father. His eyes were wide
open. The blood . . . had made a big red
beard on the front of his apron . . . It was
as though someone had tied a red cloth
around his neck to give him his soup."

With a movement of his hand around his
own face, he outlined the beard as he
remembered it. He swallowed noisily, as if
something was sticking in his throat.

"And there!" he went on, dropping his
voice a little, "collapsed against the wall,
with one hand in the ashes was Moungé
l'Uillaou, Lightning Monge, because that's
how quick he was! Short, thin, wiry, but
sharp . . . cunning . . . He was so tight-fisted
that if you threw him up in the air, he'd
cling to the ceiling. A . . . hard-hearted
man," Burle added and then stopped speaking.

"Moungé l'Uillaou . . ." repeated
Séraphin.

"Your father . . ." murmured Burle.

He turned and pointed to a precise spot
on the side of the hearth.

"And then his hands . . . His hands! They
had left red marks around the salt box!
Look, you can still see them! There, around
the salt box, those black marks."

He turned towards Séraphin.

"No one has ever worked out how he could have reached it, because . . ."

He strode towards the table.

"The killer hadn't finished the job. His throat had been cut like a pig's too, but not completely. He must have fought as though someone was trying to take a bag of gold from him . . . Look!"

He pointed to the tear in the oilcloth.

"Look carefully at that table: it's made of oak! In your poor father's time, it was already more than a hundred years old, and oak hardens with age . . . Well, just take a look! Do you see that hole? Do you see the black marks like spilt wine around the hole? That's your father's blood here too. The killer ran him through with the spit that was hanging over there . . . And your father, your father . . . With that spit through his body, still managed to drag himself over to the salt box . . ."

His finger remained pointing at the object for several seconds, as though he were accusing it.

"We've never known why!" he concluded.

Slowly, heavily, as though he were about to collapse with each step, he covered the distance which separated him from the spot where Moungé l'Uillaou had fallen. He mimed the scene as if words were incapable of expressing it, clasping both hands against his chest, as though clutching an invisible spit. He heard a sound of wood being struck. It was Séraphin who had collapsed into a chair.

"Do you want me . . . to stop?" Burle asked.

"No," replied Séraphin.

So Burle went over towards the dark cupboard at the very back of the room, beside the trapdoor that led to the cellars and the stables. You could still make it out in spite of the dust, because of the big iron ring used to swing it open, which for some reason had remained raised up out of its groove.

Burle tugged the knob of the cord which worked the cupboard latch. Then, in spite of the din made by the thunder and hail, there was a rustling of lace as all the spider webs tore at once, and the door hinges, rusty from lack of use, gave that desperate sound of things that have long since ceased to function.

Burle opened it wide and kept his finger pointing to the dark interior.

"Your two brothers . . . were huddled there at the back . . . Their throats were cut too . . . Like your grandfather and your father. They'd been dragged there, I don't know why. The traces led straight from the table to the cupboard . . ."

When he said "throat cut", he traced the cut on his own throat with the outer edge of his hand. His short arms and expressive fingers described the lightning speed of persons unknown as they fled. Twenty-three years later, they seemed like ghosts who were still encircled by the shadows in the restricted space of that room. The very thought made Burle's voice tremble with nameless terror.

It was after the cupboard that he showed some reluctance to go on. He stood there in the centre of the room with his arms dangling at his sides, staring at the layer of grey dust that covered the flagstones at his feet.

"And then, there . . ." he said hesitantly. "Well, I think it's there . . . Yes . . . right across there . . . Yes, it must be there because we had to — afterwards — make a detour to open the cupboard where your brothers had been shut up . . . Yes, it was there. There was Girarde, lying on the floor, with her skirts raised . . ."

He heard the chair into which Séraphin had collapsed creak loudly.

"No, no . . . Don't worry . . . She hadn't been raped!" Burle said hurriedly.

"My mother . . ." Séraphin said in a toneless voice.

"Yes, your mother," Burle confirmed. "Oh! Mark you, she had her throat cut too, from ear to ear, only she, d'you know? She was the only one who had her eyes closed. All the others still had their eyes open looking at you."

"Had she . . . suffered?"

"With her skirts up like that . . ." the old man continued. "We all turned our heads away. And like I said, there were about fifty of us. But that poor dead woman lying there . . . for all to see . . . You couldn't . . . You didn't have the strength . . . And yet, you saw it all the same . . . I can tell you one thing: she'd been feeding the baby . . . so her breasts were out of her bodice . . . And on the tip, there was still a drop of curdled milk . . ."

"That's enough!" Séraphin shouted. Once again he was speaking while the thunder roared, but this time the clamour couldn't drown out his voice.

"You wanted to know . . ." Burle said apologetically, shrugging his shoulders.

He shook himself and continued.

"And then!" he exclaimed. "There, beside the bread bin, beside the cupboard, there you were! In that cradle!"

He gave it a gentle push with his foot, and

straight away the cradle dutifully began to sway on its rockers with a little spinning-wheel hum, as if someone was still rocking the babe that had been in it.

"That's where you were!" Burle insisted, his arms hanging limply by his sides.

He looked at Séraphin who was putting a log on the fire to hide his face. He looked at the cradle as it slowly stopped rocking. His face was a picture of disbelief, as it must have been twenty-three years earlier.

"We don't know if they hadn't seen you. You were partly covered by the sheets your mother had folded. They'd fallen on top of you . . . and, I might mention, they were also splashed with blood . . . But in the end! All the same! We saw you! And then! You must have been wailing! Well, we don't really know . . . If they hadn't seen you . . . If they wanted to spare you . . . What we do know is that you were the only one left alive!"

He came back to the hearth and sat down heavily in the Grandfather's chair. And this time, he no longer had the impression that he was sitting on someone.

"If you'd seen all that . . ." he said. "And the worst of it is that you did see it! There was a neighbour, taking pity on you, who carried you to the cemetery behind the

57

funeral cortege of the whole family. That caused an almighty stir . . . it was heard as far away as Paris! There were maybe two thousand people. Even those who didn't like your father — and there were lots of them . . . There were gendarmes on horseback, who listened to everything, who watched everyone, who said that a criminal always goes to his victim's funeral. And the likes of that funeral, my poor young fellow, had never been seen in Lurs . . . They had borrowed hearses from Les Mées and Peyruis . . . And your two brothers, they were carried to the cemetery on covered stretchers . . . Two hearses and two stretchers. Then came your neighbour, all alone, dressed in black, behind all those bodies, carrying you dressed all in white, wailing. It was the only sound to be heard when the priest wasn't chanting . . . And you were wailing as if you knew what had just happened to you."

Séraphin got up from his chair. He looked huge to Burle, as he stood there, looming over him.

"And . . ." he said.

"Sit down again! Sit down!" Burle exclaimed hurriedly. "You make me dizzy! Hey! Before you do, just turn over the shirts and trousers, so that they'll dry on the other side. Good, that's the way! I know what you wanted to ask me. Yes, of course they eventually caught the killers. It seems there were three of them — workers on the railway line that had just been completed as far as here . . . It seems they were found dead drunk, with four opened bottles of your father's brandy next to the miserable beds where they slept. They came from over there, a hell of a way, some country or other, I think they call it Herzegovina . . . They didn't speak two words of French, and it was the devil's own job trying to find an interpreter . . . As well as that, their boots had tramped in blood. The footprints that had been discovered on the flagstones at La Burlière were exactly the same size! There was blood between the hobnails on the soles. There was blood on the bottom of their corduroy breeches . . . No doubt about it . . ."

He spat a stream of tobacco into the fire.

"You know," he continued, "around here, whenever you shove a pair or two of suspects who seem as guilty as hell in front of twelve jurors, it hardly ever happens that they don't all give the thumbs down . . . Because, well . . . You understand . . . All the doors around here lost their keys long ago, and those by chance that still exist, well . . .

Everyone knows that they're under the big stone at the foot of the stairs, so . . . It's too easy to get in and cut someone's throat . . ."

"It's too easy . . ." Séraphin repeated automatically. He was still staring at the spot between the bread bin and the cradle, where his mother lay dead, with her skirts raised and her throat cut, twenty-three years ago . . .

"They were guillotined," Burle said, "on 12 March at six in the morning, in front of the prison at Digne. We wouldn't have missed that for all the money in the world. I don't know how we found out, but there were around two hundred of us . . . some from Lurs, some from Peyruis or Les Mées . . . there were even some who came from Forcalquier or from Château-Arnoux. It seems people thought they were going to have a great time. As it happens, we didn't see a thing! It was snowing so much that we didn't even hear the blade fall. The only thing that could be heard was the prisoners shouting something — that they were innocent, it seems, but they were shouting it in Herzegovinian, and well . . . you can imagine . . . Nobody was bothered by that . . . Especially as the policeman who was holding us back — with about twenty of his colleagues — kept repeating that they all protest they're innocent . . . that by protesting it so much, they start to believe that they are innocent . . ."

Burle got up.

"Well, there you are!" he said, slapping his thighs.

By now the storm was growling further away.

Although he had not taken off his shoes, Burle tried to get into his long underpants, which he thought were dry enough.

"There you are," he repeated, "that's what happened here three weeks after you were born. Do you know now why everything is still intact? Why, in twenty-three years, no one has come and stolen even a gram of salt from that salt box over there? Do you understand why the house has never been sold? And it's not for want of trying! Five times they put up the yellow notice on the stable door! Five times, and not a soul came! You see, this is a marked house — it bears not only the sign of murder, but also, and above all, it bears the sign of the scaffold. They'd have given La Burlière away, if anyone had wanted it!"

He handed the other pair of dry trousers to Séraphin, who put them on, his mind elsewhere. Burle took his pouch from his jacket pocket, opened it and started working on a new plug of tobacco. He shook his head for a while as he listened to the last moans of the storm.

"But," he said at last, "as far as I'm concerned, it didn't happen like that . . . *It can't have happened like that* . . . You see, there was too much mystery in Monge your father's past. First of all, he was just a master carter. Don't imagine that the La Burlière land was good for anything more than a bit of livestock and hard wheat. Besides that . . . And yet . . . Girarde always had new blouses; your brothers, new shoes and school bags at the beginning of each school year. He had three horses, did Monge, three beauties . . . And when they went to the Manosque fair, they always came back with their cart full of things . . . There was something wrong there!"

He chewed his tobacco for a while, his eyes fixed on the hearth as if it were a mirror of memories.

"And then," he continued, "if you'd like to know . . . When I arrived with the fifty others — but I was there first, I'd run so quickly — I was the one who barred the door with the shovel I was still carrying. Now, one thing struck me straight away, and it struck me in spite of my *estomagade*[7], in spite of my horror. It suggested cold anger, anger kept in check for a long time . . . Apart from the bodies, there was no mess — except for the sheets that had fallen on your cradle; except for the salt box that your father had knocked sideways as he fell . . . except for the Post Office calendar askew on the wall. Someone had closed and latched the cupboard door on your dead brothers. In short, it was tidy, they didn't search for anything . . . And another thing: the wounds, the lips of the wounds! The blood had stopped flowing long ago, and the edge of the wounds was quite visible: it was white, clearly drawn, a perfect line, like a razor cut . . . but straighter, you see . . . I said to myself right away, 'Jean, there's only one thing that can make wounds like that: a *tranchet*[8], a well-sharpened *tranchet!*' And there was no sign of *tranchets* on the three men from Herzegovina! The barristers said it: *that kind of knife comes from these parts!* And it's true: we use it to cut grapes, open walnuts, skin a rabbit and even, if we're in a hurry, make the hole in the pig's neck . . .

7 *estomagade:* shock (Provençal dialect).
8 *tranchet:* a paring knife with a slightly curved blade, such as a cobbler's knife.

And this kind of knife, it seems, doesn't exist in Herzegovina. The barristers showed the knives they have there, and they're not our *tranchets*. As for us, there's not a man from fifteen to forty-five, who wouldn't have one on him, a *tranchet* . . ."

He had bent over, absent-mindedly raking the ashes on the hearth with a spade he had taken down from the wall, shaking his head all the while like a stubborn mule.

"Oh! . . . In the end I stopped saying anything, because I'd have been in trouble with the people around here . . . But I said it, I said: it can't have happened like that . . ."

"And I suppose you'd know, would you, you stupid clod! Just how it happened!"

The voice that said these words didn't surprise them straight away, as it spoke during the rumbling of the storm. Nonetheless they turned around slowly to see where it came from. A man was standing there in the shadows, in front of the door that had closed again behind him. In the flickering light from the fire, you could see that he was dressed entirely in black. He was a man with impenetrable black eyes, an old man, but one who didn't look old. He held his head a little to one side under his battered hat. The only thing about him that suggested age was his big black moustache. You couldn't place him, for his clothes came from another time, and his appearance was such that he might have come from any century. He wore a watch chain across his waistcoat, which was neither gold, nor silver, nor even iron. It was dull and undistinguished. By contrast, something shiny, probably made of gold, dangled at the end of the chain: it was a charm in the shape of a skull, its features worn away with age.

The man must have walked there in the hail during the forty minutes of the storm. His big red umbrella, faded with the years, was now reduced to tatters around the spokes. He had been hit on the forehead and the nose by gusts of hailstones, as had the two road menders, and like them, his ears were bleeding. His impenetrable eyes were fixed on Séraphin, who was taller than he was by more than a head.

"I was sure," he said, "that one day you'd end up opening this goddamn door!"

Burle spread his arms.

"We had to find shelter . . ."

"Shut up, you! What did you tell him?"

"Everything . . ." Burle said.

"Everything?"

"Well . . . Everything that could be told."

"Because you know it all, I suppose? What

can and can't be said!"

With a sweeping, tragic gesture, he pointed in Séraphin's direction.

"You've ruined his life! That's what you've done!"

He turned round suddenly, opened the door and strode away, kicking at the hailstones that crunched underfoot like gravel. In a fury, he lashed the air around him with his tattered umbrella, until all that could be heard was an indistinct growl as he retreated like the storm.

The two road menders, somewhat cowed, went out after him.

"Who's he?" Séraphin asked. His voice sounded hoarse.

"It's Zorme," Burle said. "He wasn't pleased I told you . . ."

He closed the fingers of his right hand around the thumb of his left.

"He has a power . . ." Burle murmured nervously.

"Quiet!" Séraphin exclaimed. "Listen! What's he saying? What's he talking about?"

He was already far away from them. At the foot of the tallest cypress, whose branches had been battered out of alignment by the hail, Zorme had turned around to face the two men and was shouting words they couldn't hear, flailing the air with his red umbrella all the while.

"Don't bother!" Burle exclaimed. "Don't try to understand! He says a lot, but it's not for us. He's arguing with the devil! Whenever he opens his big, black toothless mouth at us, we all go and hide! Don't look at him!"

But he was talking to empty space. With that impressive step that never changed speed and always seemed to be crushing something underfoot, Séraphin had set off behind Zorme, who was more than two hundred metres away and still retreating.

Burle wanted to call him back, but his bones suddenly felt deathly cold as he looked at the valley in front of him. Surprised by Zorme's sudden appearance, he hadn't had the time to look at it.

"My vines!" he whispered.

He immediately pictured them under the rich wedding white that had spread everywhere over the battered countryside. A stunned silence reigned over the buried olive groves, as if around a new tomb. Except for the small stream of water that wound between the banks of the fords, the bed of the Durance was white as a winter morning. Petrified with cold, Burle was beginning to gauge the extent of the disaster, when a sparrow owl flew out of the woods and fell dead in the middle of the carters' yard. The wing on the side of his body that had stuck in the ice seemed to make a sign to the heavens, like the raised arm of a drowned man.

A soft and gentle evening had suddenly and surprisingly fallen on all that green devastation. The air smelled of crushed wood and sap. You would never have thought that the calamity that had just struck the valley could have come from a sky so clear.

"Séraphin!" Burle shouted.

He wanted to have someone by his side, now, to witness his desolation. He wanted to proffer a few well-chosen words regarding divine goodness, but not alone, not into empty space. But Séraphin had disappeared and you couldn't even make out his or Zorme's footprints. Scarcely five minutes ago a deathly cold had covered the earth, but now from that same sky, the summer warmth was blowing, taking possession of the valley again. The ice was breaking up so quickly you could hear it collapsing. The sound of running water filled the fields at the same time; it filled every hole and gathered in muddy furrows. The Durance began to flow more swiftly.

"Séraphin! What the hell's he doing?"

Burle began to run, and run quickly. He picked up the owl by its wing in passing, to show to his grandson, who couldn't believe that nature was cruel or life was fragile. He rushed down the slope towards the road, the La Burlière road, which was strewn with broken green branches. He wanted to catch up with the two men if he could. The roadway was streaming with water and the holes they had been filling were now even deeper than before. Burle gave a dispirited shrug. He passed the brambles flattened by the weight of the hail, that hid the side of the road where they had been working before the storm.

Then he saw Séraphin, collapsed across the pile of sharp-edged stones used for the railway ballast. He was sobbing so hard that his whole body shook. Burle would say to his family that night:

"I'm the only one who saw him cry."

It wasn't true. A passing truck driver stuck his head out of the cabin window and shouted over the noise of his heavy vehicle:

"What's wrong with him?" pointing to the sturdy body with its arms around the pile of ballast stones.

"Nothing!" Burle shouted back. "Drive on!"

But there were also two cyclists who

passed, on their way to find out what damage had been done to their own vineyards. They were wild-eyed and white as a sheet. Seeing that strong body prostrate on a cartload of stones, they stopped to help.

"Hey, Burle! What's wrong with him?"

"Nothing," Burle replied. "He's mourning his mother."

"His mother?" the two cyclists said in chorus. "But . . . that's Séraphin Monge! His mother must have died more than twenty years ago!"

"Yes," Burle said sombrely, "but he only really lost her five minutes ago . . ."

As they could make no sense out of his reply, apart from the fact that there was nothing more serious happening than tears, they got on their bicycles again and went on their way.

Burle was about to put his hand on Séraphin's shoulder, but he stopped halfway. Something deep within him had just given him a huge jolt.

"Zorme's right! You stupid idiot! If you hadn't told him anything, he wouldn't be crying now!"

Filled with a kind of apprehension, he looked at the colossus of a man brought to his knees by a few simple words. The old man was overcome with impotent rage.

"Mother! Mother! Mother!" Séraphin moaned.

He beat his fists even harder, bruising his enormous hands against the sharp stones. He felt no pain.

III

1919 was a dismal year in our part of the country.

The only people you met in the fields that were being worked were poor widows dressed in full mourning merging with the burnt trees in the distance; children dressed in black; sad old men with crepe bands in their caps ploughing the fields, although they were well past working age. They had scarcely enough strength to push the plough in front of them, and instead of yelling at the horses as they used to, they could only berate them in low, quiet voices.

Whenever a young man happened to pass within their field of vision, they observed him suspiciously out of the corner of the eye, as if he had stolen something from them, as if it wasn't fair that he should be there.

Those who had died in the war weighed heavily on the living, like a wound that wouldn't heal. Not a week went by without the Paris-Lyon-Mediterranean train repatriating one or two servicemen's bodies free of charge at Peyruis-Les Mées or La Brillanne-Oraison stations.

Séraphin was present at all these transfers. Surrounded by old men, he was a head taller than anyone else there. The young people stood in front: survivors clustered in a group around a gold-fringed flag, which they hoped would bring them in some money. Séraphin expected nothing. He had been given a road worker's job and lodgings in a narrow municipal house, where the stairs between the three floors took up half the space.

When he returned, he never thought that a more tormenting vision could wipe the war from his mind. And yet an hour's storm and an old man's tale had been enough to replace that obsession with another. His hands had remained bruised for three days after beating his fists against the ballast stones on that day. Every night since then, before falling asleep, the narrow confines of the kitchen at La Burlière filled his mind instead of nightmares from the war. On Sundays, he went back there alone and spent hours wandering from the hearth to the oak table, from the bread bin to the cradle.

No matter what he did, the image of his mother with her skirt raised and her throat cut, lying at the foot of the table, was always there before his eyes. Exhausting himself with work was useless: there was no rest for him at night. Although he visualized her death over and over again, the thing that tormented him most was the fact that his mother had no face. No matter how he tried, he couldn't manage to give her one.

Old Burle was one of the last to die of Spanish flu. It only took a few days. Séraphin went to see him before he died to ask him to describe his mother's features.

"What's the use?" Burle said to him.

He wasn't afraid. He looked like an eagle tethered by the foot, and he still had the strength to spit his tobacco at the stove, where it hissed softly as it dried.

"Don't worry about me . . ." he said finally. "And be sure of one thing: Spanish flu takes no time to say . . . I wouldn't be in this situation if I'd told you nothing. But it doesn't matter . . . I did the right thing. And remember, it can't have happened like that! Do you hear me? It's not possible!"

At first Séraphin tried to live like everyone

74

else. On Sundays he was there under the Chinese lanterns and garlands from the victory celebrations. Lots of girls there danced together or had to sit on the sidelines. They were the same age as the war casualties who had left them without anyone to hold. Several had begun to walk towards Séraphin without thinking, as they would have approached any man. But one step, one look was enough: the sight of him stopped them in their tracks. They became helpless and silent in front of him. Several of them whispered little secrets about him to each other. "He's too good-looking! No, it's not that he's too good-looking . . . He chills me!" — "Do you know what happened to him? Do you know what my mother told me?" — "Who doesn't know?" — "I just couldn't do it! I'd always be feeling that his dead family was lying beside me! And yet, it's not fair! Just look how handsome he is!"

Some girls didn't go dancing. Firstly those whose fathers or brothers had died at the front and who were still in full mourning for years on end. But there were also those whose families tried to keep a distance between them and the common run of mortals. There are families like that everywhere. They want to be *comme il faut,* so they have to keep a tight rein on their

75

daughters. If the girls are ugly, the words "beyond reproach" are very successful with the timid ones, and as "the top has preserved the bottom" as they say, some suitable match always turns up. But if they're pretty, they're treated like saints' relics in a shrine. People say: "They think they've got a real princess" or "She's the apple of their eye."

During those years, "two apples of their eye" took pride of place between Peyruis and Lurs: they were Rose Sépulcre and Marie Dormeur. Rose Sépulcre . . . no matter how long you'd known her, you were dazzled every time you saw her. She had a triangular face that broadened into a stubborn forehead, softened by her raven's-wing hair — black at nightfall, but almost steel blue in daylight. People wondered where her almond eyes came from. Her two little breasts begged to be imprisoned by a hand. You hardly dared turn round as she passed by, in case you missed the way she swayed her hips, artless and alluring at the same time.

She was born in the permanent warmth of an olive oil mill. Her father, Didon Sépulcre, boasted about bearing the name of the locality. It was a godforsaken little hamlet on the banks of the Lauzon called

Saint-Sépulcre because of a chapel which was now little more than a grassy mound. "We're called Sépulcre because we're as old as the chapel."

This man was prosperous and well-known. He dreamed of seeing his two daughters well established. He had also increased his domain — an action generally disapproved of — with the best land of the Monges, which he had bought when that entire family had been removed from the land of the living. As he wasn't superstitious, he would have liked to buy La Burlière as well — it was going for a song — but his wife was against it. "If you buy La Burlière," she had said to him, "you can live there on your own. I'll never set foot in it. I'm sure La Girarde must still creep around the walls at night. And I'm also sure," she had added with a shudder, "that she must be looking for her baby to feed."

Now that the war had ended, Didon Sépulcre began to worry as he counted the relatively suitable boys who still had not been accounted for. At every new marriage he pulled a bit harder on his lower lip with his thumb and forefinger. All the more so because Rose was becoming hard to control. She was slipping through his fingers like wet soap. Her mother had given her a bicycle with the cheese money, and since then, Rose's feet scarcely touched the ground. They had to trust her to do the right thing. She took two hours to get bread from Lurs and fetching her grandmother's shopping in Peyruis took a whole afternoon.

While this girl from the banks of the Lauzon transported her beauty around on two wheels, two hundred metres above the valley, in the village of Lurs, another "apple of their eye" was preparing to defy fate. People were often mistaken about her beauty: it was really due to her radiant good health. When Marie Dormeur strode around, she was like a force of nature, cleaving the air around her. Her face was like a harvest goddess's, to be admired now before it faded away. She was the first beauty in her family.

Her father Célestat had eyes of different colours and was thin, bony and as dark as a Saracen. He had the habit of sucking in his cheeks. People could never understand how this sixty-kilo baker with arms like a cricket could ever knead by hand batches of dough that weighed more than he did. Her mother, Clorinde Dormeur, as tall and white as a leek, had long pigeon-toed feet that always stuck out from the counter and made her stumble over all the sacks in the bakery-cum-grocery. Every time she went into the room behind the store and happened to catch sight of her reflection in the mirror, she would say "misery me!" as her cheeks and chin were pitted with pockmarks. People said, "But she's got a heart of gold."

So everyone thought it some sort of miracle as they watched Marie Dormeur cross Lurs, cutting through the wind before her, always carried along by an irresistible momentum, even when she was not going anywhere or intending to do anything in particular. She was simply full of life.

At that time, Marie Dormeur and Rose Sépulcre had one thing in common — they were afraid of nothing and no one. They were going to need it.

Shortly after Burle's death, Séraphin went home after nightfall. Like everyone else around here, he never locked his door. When he went into the kitchen, he found someone waiting for him. A silhouette was outlined in front of the window by the light from the street lamp that lit the little square below. He heard the gentle swish of a dress as someone moved rapidly. A girl emerged from the shadows, so close to him that her breasts touched the bottom of his ribcage every time she took a deep breath. She had a strange perfume of wild roses and he could see her face in spite of the dark.

"Don't turn on the light!" she whispered. "They'd see me from outside . . . and tell my father . . ."

"No," Séraphin replied.

"I saw you at the fountain, the day you came out of the notary's office. I was filling my grandmother's *pêchier* . . . Since then, you're the only one I see . . ."

She spoke quickly and gave the impression of having repeated it all to herself time and time again for nights on end.

"No," Séraphin said.

"I'm Rose Sépulcre. You've seen me. You can't possibly not have seen me!"

"No," Séraphin said.

"Oh! You might say no now, but just wait!"

He felt her place her hand flat against his belt and slide it slowly down his belly. She began to caress him through the material. He heard her whisper.

"You see . . . You see . . ." her moist lips hesitantly whispering a suppressed but intense desire for what he could give her.

In the darkness where he was usually shut up alone, his eyes wide open, it was a strange sensation to feel his member rise under the caress of that little hand, and yet not be able to banish from his memory the frame of that dark red picture he invariably

80

stepped into as soon as the shadows fell. It was a picture in which he walked amid faceless bodies — since he had never seen them — always following the same path. With that slow walk of his, like a man uncertain of living, he went towards the cradle he would have loved to creep into again, even though it could scarcely have accommodated half of one leg. But it was a picture that had a smell to it, the one described by old Burle, who could nevermore go near anyone who was killing a pig.

Faced with all these tortured but faceless bodies forming a barrier between himself and her, what could Rose Sépulcre do, armed only with her beauty and desire?

"No," Séraphin said without raising his voice.

She felt the young man shrink under her hand, which she immediately removed.

"Why no? What do you mean by that word you keep repeating?"

"No," Séraphin said.

She pushed him to one side, beating on his chest with such anger that his ninety-five kilos were shaken as though by a storm.

"Let me pass!" she shouted and rushed down the stairs.

He heard her wrench open the front door, then run out into the street. He opened the window and leaned on his elbows. The sound of the four jets of water pouring from the fountain did its best to calm Séraphin's anguish. A sparrow owl hooted in a tree. In the distance the music of a viol leading the end of a dance filtered through the pines on the hills, carried by the rise and fall of the wind.

But in Séraphin's head the only noise, the only murmur that he was able to hear, was what Burle's story had planted in his imagination: the sobbing sound of blood spurting from a severed artery. "Her throat was cut," he had said.

He had worked out from the position of his mother's body on the stone floor, as described by Burle, that as her life's blood flowed away she had tried to reach the cradle where he was lying.

Leaning on the window-sill, Séraphin kept his hands pressed to his face for a considerable time, as if the picture that haunted him had taken place in front of him in the quiet Peyruis street or on the barren land of the Iscles of the Durance, down there behind the dyke.

"As long as that stays in your head," he said to himself, "you'll never be able to live like anyone else."

No doubt that was the night he made his decision.

IV

"Clorinde! Hey, Clorinde! Come out here! Just listen to this!"

In the sudden gust of wind that blew up the street and swirled the dust around her, old swarthy-skinned Tricanote seemed to appear out of thin air, holding her stick like a lance as she tried to gather in her goats. They were jostling each other, horns up, chest to chest. As for Tricanote herself, the wind ballooned out her skirts so that she looked pregnant, indecently so, as she was all of seventy-four years old. But she was still strong, with a well-arched back above her skinny legs and bony bottom.

"Clorinde! Hey, Clorinde!"

Clorinde Dormeur was rubbing the pans of the scales with sabre polish. She appeared suddenly, with the cloth in her hand.

"What on earth are you doing, shouting like that! Célestat's having his siesta."

"Say, Clorinde, have you heard?

Séraphin!"

"Which Séraphin?"

"Séraphin Monge! He's gone crazy! He's burning his furniture."

"What are you talking about? Séraphin Monge, the one who . . ."

"That's the one! He's down there at La Burlière. He's burning everything!"

"How do you know?"

"There's a man . . . He's just come back! He was hunting just above La Burlière. Suddenly he sees the chimney smoking, so he does what we'd all have done. He goes down and watches what's going on behind the little window. Well, my girl! That's where he said to me, 'I saw Séraphin. He was trying to break up the table with a sledgehammer! And there were pieces of the kneading-trough burning in the fire!' "

Clorinde Dormeur had clapped her hand to her mouth, as she could easily picture this carnage of furniture and it pained her as though it were her own.

Marie was upstairs, behind the open window of her bedroom. She was cleaning the little long-necked Dresden vases that her godmother had given her for her first communion. As she wiped them one by one, she was thinking something through. Séraphin had been in her thoughts for a while now. She had met him when she was delivering bread to Paillerol on her carrier tricycle. He was stripped to the waist, holding his sledge-hammer above his head, just before bringing it down on a large piece of rock that had come away from the embankment. All his muscles stood out with the effort.

She had been saying to herself for some time now, "If I don't throw myself at him, that slut Rose Sépulcre will get him . . . She's capable of anything, that one with the name that sends cold shivers up your spine. Bessolte's already told me that she saw her go into Séraphin's house one evening."

That's why Marie shuddered that day when she heard Séraphin's name mentioned. The horror of the sacrilege he was committing made her drop what she was doing and rush down the spiral staircase. She dashed across the shop floor and out into the fresh air in front of her mother and Tricanote, who stood there stunned. She flew between them like an arrow, and with the same speed grabbed her carrier bike from against the wall, turning it towards the road before she jumped on.

"Marie!" Clorinde shouted. "What are you doing? Where are you going?"

But Marie was already disappearing behind the humpback. Clorinde came back to Tricanote, who had managed to gather her goats together.

"But where's she going?" the old woman asked, quite concerned.

"You tell me! The girl's crazy! She'll be the death of me!"

Marie sped down the winding road towards La Burlière and the smoking chimney. She pedalled the jolting tricycle like a maniac, with all the strength of thighs that had grown powerful by continually cycling up from Peyruis to Lurs.

Burning furniture that has a history is no easy matter. The bread bin, apart from the lid, was the first to go. It was full of borer holes and the legs were already crumbling, but it groaned like a living being as he broke it up with his sledge-hammer. It was as if with one blow he were destroying the thing that made those warning creaks and groans for the whole of its life — for more than a hundred years — and after that, during all that long lonely time in the cold farm where even the smell of bread, that lingered in its borer holes, had finally disappeared. The bin seemed to weep for a long time as the fire consumed it.

The table did not give way. The top was

six centimetres thick, and as it was four metres long, it could not be put into the
hearth. Even with his sledge-hammer,
Séraphin could not hammer out the mark
of the spit that had lodged in it after piercing his father's body.

He unhooked the salt box and threw it in
the fire. The lump of salt that remained in it
burned for some time sending green flames
shooting up among the red. He stared at
the marks around the empty space that old
Burle had pointed out to him. The blood-
stains had seeped into the slaked lime, age-
ing with it but never dissolving into it. Now
that the salt box was no longer there, you
could see that as he tried to get at the box,
the dying man had left the imprint of his
hands around the edge of the empty space
where the lime was freshest.

Séraphin stood up with a sigh. He caught
sight of the clock crouching fearfully in the
darkest corner. With two strokes of his hammer, he had demolished the whitewood cas-
ing, splitting it in the middle of the naive
painting of a bunch of flowers that had
originally been there. He had ripped out
the mechanism and the pendulum, and laid
them on the table that was battered but still
standing. He thought he could just as easily
smash the cradle with his foot. However,

the first kick jarred his bones right up to the thigh; at the second, better directed kick, it suddenly turned over on its yoke-shaped rocker, the sharp edge of the rail hitting Séraphin full on the shin. Furious, he sent it flying against the wall, but the cradle bounced back into the middle of the room, as if made of rubber. It rocked defiantly, humming like a spinning wheel.

Luckily the hearth was big enough to take it. Séraphin lifted it up from the ground and was about to throw it in.

Marie Dormeur, out of breath, suddenly opened the door. She saw what Séraphin was going to do, rushed forward and gripped the bars of the cradle with both hands.

"Get away!" growled Séraphin.

"Just a moment! Have you looked to see who I am?"

"Yes. You're the baker's daughter . . . I said, get away from here!"

"No one's ever spoken to me like that!"

"That's the way I speak."

The strong man and the robust girl struggled with the cradle as it swayed and twisted between them. Each of them took several hard knocks from their violent pushing and pulling.

"Aren't you ashamed!" Marie shouted.

"Burning this cradle when it could be used for your children!"

Without stopping the fight to get his piece of furniture back, Séraphin shook his head and replied calmly.

"Never. I'll never have children."

"But I want them!"

Taking advantage of Séraphin's surprised reaction to her reply, she pulled the cradle so hard that it stayed in her hands. She immediately wrapped her arms around it, clutched it to her chest and retreated towards the wall, determined to defend it with fists and feet if necessary.

"Who's stopping you?" Séraphin said.

He took hold of one of the benches that were placed around the table and threw it into the fire.

"All right then. If you want it so much, take it!"

"I certainly will!"

She turned her back on him and ran out with the piece of furniture in her arms. She opened the box on the tricycle and placed the cradle in it. She went straight back, however, and closing the door behind her, she looked Séraphin up and down.

"Now," she said, "you know what I want . . ."

But suddenly she raised her hand to stifle

a cry. She had just seen the eviscerated body of the grandfather clock lying on the floor. She groaned.

"My God!"

It seemed to her that he had just committed just as irreparable a crime by demolishing the clock as by trying to destroy the cradle. She noticed the mechanism and the pendulum left lying on the table. She rushed at them.

"You can't burn that!" she said.

She grasped the top of the clock with the floral frame and carried it off like a thief, placing it and the pendulum in the bottom of the box as carefully as she had the cradle. He had followed her out and was shaking his head as he observed everything she did. He gave a deep sigh — the first that anyone could have heard him make since he came back from the war, since Burle had told him about that terrible night.

At the foot of one of the cypresses was a block of blackened sandstone that had been the carved capital of a church column. Some ancestor of Séraphin's had no doubt brought it there to sit on of a summer evening. Séraphin slumped down on to it, his hands hanging limply between his legs.

"Come here!" he said, his voice subdued.

She came over and sat down beside him

quietly and deliberately, as if he had been a bird ready to slip away under the brambles at the first alarm.

"I can't get used to it . . ." Séraphin said. "It's always there before my eyes. I thought it would be the war. But no . . . This is much worse. You see, everyone was involved in the war; this is happening only to me. That's why I'm burning everything. If all that disappears, perhaps my mother . . . perhaps she will disappear too . . .

"My poor mother died in there, aged thirty, as she was crawling towards my cradle. That cradle!" he said, pointing to Marie's delivery bike. "You see, I . . . my mother . . . after that it was the orphanage. The sisters knew more about me than I did. They kept me apart from the other orphans as a precaution, as though I was contagious. When they couldn't keep me any longer, after I got my school certificate, I was sent over Turriers way, where they were working on reafforrestation. We had to plant pines in the midst of stones as sharp as daggers. It was all bits of rock no bigger than that . . . and so to plant the trees, you had to move the stones away with your fingers, because picks were no use there. All the valleys and all the hills were made of them. The only things you could use were your hands . . .

"What's more, the others were all men. Of an evening in the huts, they talked quietly amongst themselves, but stopped when I came near them. Oh! I understood that there was something very unusual about me . . . They were nearly all from Piedmont. Sometimes they got letters from their mothers. Then they cried. Sometimes they learned that their mothers had died. Then there was wailing in the huts all night long. They would all sob away together. One day a young man came up — he said to me, 'And you, don't you get anything from your mother?' I didn't have time to reply. One of them gave him a kick in the backside that sent him sprawling in the hay. Seven years . . . That's how long I was up there. I was there when the war caught up with me. I'd learnt nothing. I knew nothing. It was like I was asleep."

He drew the makings of a cigarette from his pocket and took his time rolling one. From the moment he began to speak, Marie scarcely breathed. But once launched into his story, he was no longer really talking to her. It was to the house, to the smoke that came from the chimney, to the air that his forebears had breathed around that *bas-*

93

tide[9], its emptiness echoing through the high lofts where the hay had long since returned to dust.

"There were twenty-five of us in the company. Sometimes after an attack, only six, seven, sometimes three were left. They always brought new men in. Every time I said to myself, 'You'll be next.' But no. Never. The only one who wouldn't be missed; the only one nobody would miss. But no! It never happened, no matter what!"

He threw away his cigarette and crushed it under his thick shoe.

"And then, there was one other man. He stayed alive too. He watched me all the time. He'd taken a dislike to me. A fellow from Rosans, in the Hautes-Alpes. He knew me better than I did. He'd understood the thing about me that I'd tried hardest to hide: that I didn't have a mother. He had one and she wrote to him every week. He read me her letters, nice and slowly so that I could savour them, lingering over the affectionate bits. And every time we got ready to attack, he'd say to me, 'It's your turn today, Monge!' He said it again the day he died. A shell went off near him. He took the

9 *bastide:* a typical Provençal country house made of stone.

94

full force of it and was thrown on top of me. I could feel that his body was shattered under his greatcoat. He was still moving because of his nerves. He covered me with his body. You've no idea what good protection a body can be. He took enough extra bullets and shrapnel to kill him ten times over. I felt him slowly empty out like a sack. I can still smell his warm intestines."

"That's enough!" Marie said quietly.

He stopped for a few seconds, then went on again.

"That day was the lowest point of the war for me. After that, death kept his distance, as though he was disheartened by me."

He stopped speaking then turned towards Marie, looking deep into her eyes. But he quickly looked away, like someone who is lying and can't bear to look the person in the face. In his case, however, it was not a lie, but the truth of what he was about to say, that made him feel ashamed.

"I'm going to tell you a secret," he said quickly, "because someone must understand this about me and you seem to be interested . . . Well, since I was sure I wasn't coming back, as soon as the fellow from Rosans was dead, I took his wallet from his greatcoat and stole something from him . . ."

He reached for his own wallet in the inner

pocket of his jacket and took out a piece of buff-coloured paper which he held out to Marie.

"There," he said, "that's what I stole from him. It's a letter from his mother, to the fellow from Rosans. Perhaps she's still alive, but if she loved him as much as she says, his death must have killed her. That's all I had. The others had letters from their real mothers, their girlfriends or their fiancées. I had that, nothing but that . . ."

Marie looked at him. His face was in profile as he gazed at the house, the sheds, the smoke coming out of the chimney — a false sign of life that no longer existed.

"So," he said, his voice hoarse, "at the time I could have believed that she was dead like everybody else. But no! I had to come through the war and come back here to learn that! To find that!"

He waved his hand in the direction of the open door and the fire in the hearth beyond it.

"You see, I'm alone! Completely alone! I can't even take my revenge! It's already been done!"

He hammered his thighs with his closed fists as he spoke.

Marie moved closer up the rough stone towards Séraphin. She raised his arm and leaned against him under his wing. She took his limp hand and moulded it over her breast. The hand just stayed there, lifeless and cold. He took it away absent-mindedly after a while, as though he could just as well have left it there. Then he stood up. His eyes travelled from the bottom to the top of the cypress under which they were sitting.

"It doesn't seem possible," he said. "It doesn't seem possible that you never hear anyone's voice here any more. I . . ."

He stopped short. His eyes instantly regained the sharpness that they had acquired during so many years at war. He had the impression that the grove of bay trees that separated La Burlière's courtyard from the main road was rustling as if game were moving through it. It was an imperceptible wave in the branches like an evening wind, but you had to have been both hunter and hunted to know the difference.

Séraphin immediately went towards the trees, crossing the courtyard diagonally by the longest route, as if on patrol. He didn't disturb a single blade of grass, a single stone. He was beneath the branches of the trees before Marie, still under the cypress, could do a thing. He pushed the foliage aside. Mixed with the smell of crushed, stiff leaves, the smell of a man had almost faded away. He saw a hollow. It was large and comfortable. Someone had been hiding in the grass; someone had been there for quite some time; someone had been listening to him.

He raced down the slope to the road. It was empty in both directions, except for a lorry that was entering the canal turn with its chains rattling. In the distance, the bell that announced the arrival of a train was ringing at Lurs station, but there was no trace of a man anywhere.

Séraphin walked slowly back to La Burlière. Both Marie and her tricycle had disappeared from beneath the cypress. Séraphin stood there looking at the place where she had been sitting.

"Love . . ." he murmured at last.

He slowly shrugged his woodcutter's shoulders and went back into the house to throw more furniture on the fire.

V

"Rose! I hear you've been seen talking to the road mender."

"He's got a name," Rose said.

"I don't want to know his name."

"He's been here as long as we have," said Rose. "If his parents hadn't been killed, he'd be as well-off as we are."

She put the dessert dishes on to the large earthenware plate with such force that the sound echoed. She looked out of the small window. The midday sun beat down on the dry bed of the Lauzon, on the waterfall that stuck out a tongue of chalk-coloured foam over more than a metre, and the truffle-oaks on the Lurs hillside soughing in the hot wind.

She came back to the meal table where her father was peeling an apple. Térésa Sépulcre was gathering the crumbs on the oilcloth one by one. Her sister Marcelle was counting the sugar lumps she was taking from the cardboard box and tipping them into the tin. Flies were buzzing around the cheese strainers where the curds were draining.

"Rose," Didon Sépulcre went on. "Do you understand me? I don't want him hanging around you . . ."

"It's not him, it's me!" Rose said. "I wonder why you don't want me to talk to Séraphin? Do you think it's immoral of me to marry a handsome man?"

"Huh!" Marcelle exclaimed sharply. "There's not much chance of Séraphin wanting to marry you!"

Marcelle was a tall, thin girl like her father, bony and angular, with a domed forehead, a long face and ankles like a mule. Above the line of her stick-thin thighs, you could just make out two buttocks as small as your fist, which she arrogantly but vainly tried to sway. She was green with envy as she watched her elder sister, for at eighteen, Rose had everything that Marcelle didn't, and had it in abundance.

"What would you know about it?" Rose asked.

"I've seen him talking to Marie Dormeur."

"Well, if he married her, poor man, his children would look like Clorinde! How

100

would that be, eh? No," Rose continued irritably, "you must have seen Marie Dormeur talking to him. It's not the same . . ."

"No, I tell you. He was talking to her. He went on and on! I was cutting the grass in the olive grove, under the trees. I saw them as clearly as I see you now. He was the one who was speaking. Although there was someone else who was listening to them! He thought no one could see him! You should've seen him! He was almost crawling, right up to the bay trees at La Burlière. He disappeared into them like a wild boar and stayed there listening to the very end! He was less than ten metres away."

Didon pushed the piece of apple he had in his mouth and was about to chew into his cheek.

"Who?" he asked.

"That I don't know," Marcelle said.

"Do you take me for a bloody idiot? You saw Marie, you saw . . . the road mender and you didn't see who was listening to them?"

"No!" Marcelle said, giving him an insolent look.

Didon nodded his head. A deep anxiety began to worry him.

"Marie! You've been seen talking to the road

101

mender. You shouldn't do that."

"Why?"

"Because . . ."

"That's it," Clorinde said in her bass voice, "there are just so many men left in Lurs with this wretched war. Now you're going to forbid her to see the ones that are still here!"

"A road worker!" Célestat sneered.

"What of it? What have you got against Séraphin Monge? He's a good lad, and a hard worker! And good-looking with it!"

"No, it's not true! He's not good-looking!" Marie cried suddenly. "I forbid you to say that he's good-looking. What would you know, you two, about what's good-looking and what's not?"

"Well, my goodness, she's raising her voice!" Clorinde exclaimed.

"Yes, I am. Certainly! Séraphin Monge isn't good-looking. He's desperately un-happy!"

"Right!" Célestat said. "Don't go looking for misfortune. Misfortune's catching, like the itch . . ."

He put his spoon into his plate of soup, but he wasn't hungry any more. A vague feeling of anxiety ruined his appetite.

On Sunday mornings Séraphin went to La

Burlière. He locked himself in, then the chimney began to smoke. When the kitchen was empty and only the bare walls, the ceiling and the floor were left — not forgetting the old black bloodstains that made strange patterns almost everywhere — he attacked the bedrooms, the small rooms and the corridors. He burned the wardrobes, his father's writing desk, the cupboard doors. Sometimes he emptied the cold ashes on to the flagstones of the carters' yard, and the wind blew them away during the week.

He stayed for hours, crouched in front of the fire till his face was glazed, poking the hearth with the tongs, turning over bundles of his family's perishable goods, that sometimes burned with flames of a strange rainbow hue.

He started on the varnished chairs in the alcoves with their expensive green straw that had never seen the sun. He burned piles of sheets whose folds had split because they had never been used; the blue shirts with white flowers worn by his father and grandfather; Girarde's petticoats (which he held at arm's length away from him); the smocks of his two elder brothers who died as children. These souvenirs still smelled of the lavender stalks woven in the shape of a bottle, which he found on the shelves and

103

which he threw in the fire.

One day the smoke disappeared over La Burlière. One day Séraphin was able to walk slowly around the house, making the rooms echo, since nothing remained inside but the walls, the stone floor and the ceilings.

Having found out that the chimney was no longer smoking, Marie Dormeur went down to see what was happening. She was stopped by the closed door, where she knocked to no avail. She put her ear to the panel and then she distinctly heard someone walking with those slow, heavy, solemn steps that rang out in the empty, soulless house. Those footsteps caused a chill to run up her spine. The more intently she listened to them, the more she felt that they couldn't belong to the man they called Séraphin Monge — the man whose life she wanted to share.

Séraphin brought out a double ladder that he propped against the front of the house. He got up on to the roof. He pulled off a tile and threw it down. It shattered on the stones of the carters' yard with a sound like a plate breaking. He did it once, ten times, a hundred times. By the end of that day, there was a gaping wound on the roof at La Burlière. The evening sun shining through the bare beams lit up a piece of mud wall below, under the southern loft.

The darkness was rent. Spiders terrified by the light scattered in all directions towards holes in the walls. The screenings of ancient hay raised up by the air that now streamed in from the gap in the roof sparkled high into the sky.

On that evening, an eagle owl rose up out of the rafters, with his wings outstretched, white as a ghost. He struggled with the sunlight for a few seconds, fluttering about blinded by the light, then, with a cry of surprise, he drifted on the air as if he were foundering in the direction of the holly-oak woods near Augès.

The day came when the framework of La Burlière, solidly buttressed into the stone walls, was laid bare. All its pale beams that had been drying out there for centuries were now revealed to the full light of day.

Séraphin went at it with a cross-cut saw. The 300-year-old wood, cut beneath an auspicious moon, resisted. It gave out a sound like iron when the blades scratched its surface. Sometimes, when the blade overheated, it broke in the beam. In the course of this struggle, Séraphin wore out half a dozen of them, but he wouldn't give up. He would work till midnight, even in the darkness of moonless nights, with only the murmuring of the Durance among the Iscles for company. People passing on foot heard the noise of the saw filing rather than biting into the framework of La Burlière.

The day came when the last rafter finished burning in the carters' yard, giving off a smell of larch wood. That smell seemed to bring the whole atmosphere of the mountain down there to the valley.

La Burlière became even more impressive without roofing. Bereft of its framework, it revealed the hollow space of its decapitated lofts standing between its four tall, flame-shaped cypresses, gleaming in the wind. It looked like an empty coffin, waiting for a huge body to be placed in it, before being closed up.

Then Séraphin attacked the cornice tiles. At La Burlière, the cornice tiles under the overhang of the roof were laid out in four elegant festoons forming a garland of little holes like cells in a hive, for the ventilation of the forage lofts. A swallow's nest was hidden in nearly every cavity. As the first blow of his sledge-hammer shook the wall, the whole population of swallows shrieked in horror. They darted out and flew around his ears, with a swishing sound like a scythe. One even pecked him on the forehead. He

106

just brushed it away without any sign of fear or anger. The sledge-hammer came down a second time. A terrified mother bird circled around him, blinding him and deafening him with her piercing cries. Without even shifting position, he dismantled the masonry that supported the plaster niches with regular strokes of his hammer.

"You idiot! You should be ashamed! You should be ashamed of attacking those nests!"

Séraphin looked up. Rose Sépulcre was up on the wall, standing firmly planted on the sloping hip of the roof with her arms akimbo. Her dress was stained with plaster. Her face, her eyes and the apricot skin on her cheeks all shone with anger. The swallows were also attacking her, tangling her hair and pecking at her ankles.

"What the hell are you doing there?" Séraphin shouted. "Get down! You'll fall!"

"I won't fall! I'll jump if you don't stop!"

Séraphin shrugged his shoulders.

"All right then, jump . . ."

"Murderer!" Rose screamed. "You're as much a murderer as those men who killed your father and mother, do you understand!? Just the same!"

"No . . ." Séraphin said.

"Yes you are!" Rose shouted, stamping her foot.

Her eighteen-year-old forehead was creased with indignation.

"Yes, the same! Even worse! At least they spared you. But oh no, not you! You attack little birds! Baby birds that can't fly yet, that haven't even got wings yet! You're the worst of the lot!"

"Séraphin! Séraphin!"

They turned round. Marie Dormeur was crossing the courtyard, trying to weave her way among the piles of debris.

"Oh, not her . . ." Rose groaned.

Turning her back on Séraphin, she ran lightly along the sloping wall beam till she reached the ladder. She slid down it and stood in front of Marie who already had her hands on the first rungs.

"You're not wanted here!"

"Get out of my way."

"I said, you're not wanted here."

Marie shot out her hand, gripped Rose's belt and tried to pull her aside by the waist. Rose grabbed Marie's hair with both hands. They both fell to the ground and rolled around on the bumpy stones of the court-yard. They wrestled with each other without saying a word, awkwardly and ineffectively, panting and short of breath with anger. As they rolled on the ground, their skirts flew in all directions, revealing strong grappling thighs. Their knees were grazed all over from hitting the hard paving stones.

Séraphin got down and tried to separate them, but he had scarcely reached the ground when he heard a strange creaking up above in the wall ties he had been dislodging with his sledge-hammer. He threw himself at the two girls, pushing them roughly in front of him. Still huddled together, they heard a piece of the cornice that must have weighed fifty kilos come crashing down on the place where they had been standing a moment earlier. The swallows flew out in hordes, shrieking with terror. The three young people gazed transfixed at the sight of the heap of rubble that had nearly crushed them. The two girls said nothing.

"Go away!" Séraphin said. "I'm the only one who can stay here."

He guided them gently; one towards her bicycle, the other towards her tricycle.

"Listen to me, both of you," he said. "I'll never marry. I'll never have children. I'll never love anyone."

Rose stifled a sob and rushed off. Marie hung her head and slowly walked away.

"About the swallows . . ." she said quietly.

"All right," Séraphin said. "I'll wait till they fly away."

VI

He did wait. But as soon as the nests were empty, he went up his ladder again and began pounding twice as hard with his sledge-hammer. First came the cornices and then the huge Durance pebbles, set in lime, that formed the outer walls of La Burlière.

The word got around. Now after lunch on Sundays, every idler from Lurs and Peyruis came for the fun of adding their comments on the folly of the man who had burnt his furniture and was now demolishing his house. Till then, Célestat Dormeur and Didon Sépulcre had done nothing more than gently admonish their daughters. After that, it was, "If I ever see you talking to that misery-guts, I'll knock your block off!"

One man came, and came back often, but never said a word. He sat on the piece of carved stone pillar at the foot of one of the cypresses, and stayed there with his chin in his hand, deep in thought. This stranger came from another world. He was dressed like a gentleman and smoked cigarettes that he took from a gold case. He arrived in a red sports car, resplendent with gleaming chrome pipes that were almost like a wreath around it. When he got out, he slammed the car door with a blasé sweep of his arm.

Séraphin took no more notice of him than of the idle gossipers. He just kept tossing stones and rubble down on to the flagstones in the courtyard. When there was too much, he came down. Using both a shovel and his hands, he filled up the wheelbarrow which he trundled back and forth to the Durance, tipping the contents among the Iscles.

The season was advancing. There were days when it rained, days when a cold wind blew. Then came the day when the sheep from the Hautes-Alpes began to crowd down the road. They were the *scabots*[10], about ten thousand head of them. The smell of the fallen rocks and earth at Le Queyras and the bilberry bushes under the larches still lingered on the folds of the rams' fleece. Broad-cheeked donkeys caught in their midst were slowed down and moored fore

10 *scabots:* flocks of sheep that spend the summer in the Alps with their shepherds. (Provençal dialect)

and aft by the nonchalant pace of the sheep around them. At their head, the chief shepherd, the *baïle*[11], matched the pace to his old man's gait.

However, there were always half-a-dozen scarcely pubescent shepherds who brought up the rear behind the masses of sheep they watched over. They were short-tempered and impatient. Storms, rain and fatigue had worn them down, and they were filthy under their old smelly leathers, which did little to protect them against the elements. They were louts, just spoiling for a quarrel or a fight.

Like everyone else, they had heard that there was a man in Lurs who was knocking his house down. It was just what they were after for a bit of fun. They were gathered at the foot of the wall that the giant of a man was demolishing, their whips at the ready. They were laughing and spitting through the gaps in their uneven teeth as they picked up stones to throw.

On one occasion, irritated by Séraphin's indifference, they went as far as taking away his ladder. It didn't take much of an effort on their part to take down the ladder and lean it horizontally against the wall.

11 *baïle:* chief or head. (Provençal dialect)

"All right then, coward! Since you like it so much up there, you can stay there!"

They laughed loud and long, with their hands on their hips, all the more arrogant and insulting because they knew they were safe from retaliation. They were already bending down to pick up stones when the biggest of them got a huge kick in the backside that sent him flying into a pile of debris. His whip was snatched from him. He groaned, thinking it was the *baïle.* The four of them turned round together. The leather thong of the whip curled just above their heads with a hiss and at a distance that earned the expert whip handlers' respect. At the same time they saw their attacker face to face, and this discovery stopped the bravados in their tracks.

"Put the ladder back up again," the stranger said, "or I'll take your eye out with this whip."

They meekly complied. It wasn't easy. They sweated blood over it, trembling in case they couldn't do it properly and would incur the wrath of this furious man. When it was done, they made their escape as quickly as they could, in the direction of the *scabots* tinkling in the distance.

Séraphin hadn't missed a detail of the scene. As soon as the ladder was up against the wall again he hurried down, for it seemed unlikely that a single man could control four yokels full of gratuitous aggression, who a moment ago had seemed so menacing.

Then, as soon as Séraphin put his foot to the ground, the stranger who had been following the shepherds' retreat suddenly turned round, and Séraphin realized immediately why they had fled in disarray. He was a *gueule cassée:* one of those men who had survived the war, but with a dreadfully disfigured face; one of those faces no one would dare raise a hand to, for fear that all those who had died in the war would rise in a body at such sacrilege.

"Yes," the man said, "there's a painter who does this now . . . called Juan Gris. I could be a model for him."

When he laughed — and he laughed often — it was an unbearable sight.

"You see," he continued, "luckily I had fleshy buttocks. With a piece of one of them . . ."

He laughed loud and long.

"With a piece of one, they made me a new chin. And a cheek! And you understand, I can also see . . . Well . . . To see it properly, I have to turn my head to the side a little . . . Well, it'll do . . . The most annoying bloody thing is the hair. It . . . To style it: one third goes on one side, one third on the other and the rest stays in a tuft. Oh! I was forgetting. I still have a name: I'm Patrice. Patrice Dupin."

"You're Dupin's son?" said Séraphin, addressing him formally as *vous.*

"Alas, yes," Patrice sighed. "I do have a father."

Séraphin gave a slightly embarrassed smile.

"But for you, I'd have spent the night up there . . ."

"But for *you,*" Patrice corrected him, using the familiar *tu.* "More importantly, but for me, they might have made you look ridiculous. And *I* won't have you looking ridiculous."

They looked at each other. One had a broken face and the other an angel face, but they saw beyond that to the fact that they were the same age and had carried the same cross.

"Apparently," Patrice said, "you came out of it all right."

"Apparently," Séraphin said.

They went and sat under the cypress, on the shaft of the column that served as a seat. Patrice offered him a cigarette from his gold case.

"No, thank you," Séraphin said, "I roll my own."

He got out his tobacco pouch and rice papers.

"Do you think about it much?" the man asked.

"About what?" Séraphin said.

"About the war."

"Not any more," Séraphin said.

"Ah, yes, that's true . . . You have something else to think about."

"Do you know my story?"

"Like everyone else around here."

"You're the first person who hasn't asked me why I'm doing this."

"How do you mean, this?"

"This."

Séraphin turned around and waved his arm to include the whole of the site behind him. Patrice shrugged his shoulders.

"Everyone has his own broken face," he said. "In your case, you were shattered on the inside. But . . . Why won't you use *tu* when you speak to me? We come from the same place . . ."

"I can't," Séraphin said. "You're Dupin's son."

"Ah yes! That's true! I'm Dupin's son. Who knows? One day perhaps the son of Councillor Dupin. The blacksmith at Les

117

Mées from father to son since time immemorial. But then something happened: in 1914 he got the army contract to supply horseshoes, mess tins, and other things. And after that, shells too! They gave him one order, then two! In the end, he turned out as many shells as rained down on us . . . He made more millions than I have pieces instead of a head! When he saw me he wanted to give them back! I mean it! Only he didn't know who to give the money back to!"

He gave a sudden laugh that made a black sun with the jigsaw of his features.

"In the long run, he got used to it, of course. And then, to make it up to me he bought me that!"

He pointed to the red car parked at the foot of the bay trees. The insolent gleam of its chrome dazzled everything around it.

"I have to get back up again," Séraphin said. "I only have Sundays. Thank you."

"Ah, yes. That's right. You must get up there again."

Patrice took another cigarette from his case and lit it.

"Come and see me," he said. "I have no friends . . . It's over there."

He made a vague gesture towards the other side of the Durance.

118

"Near Les Pourcelles," he said. "My father bought that house. It's called Pontradieu. He thinks it's a château and he plays the aristocrat there. It's a laugh."

He suddenly put out his hand. Séraphin gave him his. That huge hand, made for twisting and crushing, was as limp as a dead pigeon's wing.

"He'll never really like me," Patrice said to himself sadly. "To him, I'll always be Dupin's son."

He got into his car. Standing beneath the cypresses, Séraphin watched him leave, then in his usual quiet, deliberate way, he went up the ladder again.

One evening he received a visit from someone else. It was an evening an artist would love to paint. A recent storm had turned the sky black, and the shadow of the Luberon mountains was like a raven's wing that covered the Manosque valley, casting it into darkness.

Séraphin was sitting on the main wall, and had just pulled a round Durance stone out of the clay and straw cement. As he stood up, about to throw down this huge stone egg which must have weighed forty kilos, he noticed he was being observed by a monk standing beneath the cypresses with his hands on his hips. Séraphin let go of his enormous stone, which the monk watched as it crashed down on to a pile of debris, then raised his eyes again.

"Séraphin!" he called out. "Hey Séraphin. Come down off your damned perch for a moment! I've got something to tell you."

"Tell me?" Séraphin shouted back.

"Yes, you!"

"Is it urgent? Because . . ."

He made a gesture towards the sky, indicating that what was left of the daylight would soon be disappearing.

"Yes!" the monk shouted. "Terribly urgent."

Séraphin hesitated for a second. He saw the worn material of the cassock, the thin face with the skin stretched over the bones and the sunken eyes. He came down out of pity. When he was standing in front of the friar, he noticed that he seemed somewhat brighter, less to be pitied. Seen on the same level, he even appeared plump and rather jovial.

"You don't know me," the monk said. "I'm Brother Calixte. I'm from up there."

He pointed his chin in the direction of the top of the plateau behind La Burlière, where the priory was a faintly discernible white spot.

"I was there . . . well before you were born."

"You want to speak to me?" Séraphin said.

"Not me. It's our prior, Brother Toine, who's leaving us. And before he goes, he has something he wants to say to you."

"To me?"

Brother Calixte looked at him for a moment in silence.

"Your name is Séraphin Monge?" he asked.

"Yes."

"Well then, it's you all right. Come on! We'd better get going. It'll take us a good two hours . . . It'll be dark by the time we get there."

He walked with a long, steady stride as though he were mowing. Séraphin followed at his own calm pace, head down, wondering what it was all about. He really wanted to complain, to say no and go back to his work. This monk, whose flapping cassock gave off a smell of wet box wood, didn't fill him with confidence. He had seen too much of the Sisters of Charity not to be disturbed by any sort of religious habit.

"So," he said, "is your prior going far?"

"To Jesus," Brother Calixte said.

He paused for a moment before stepping over an irrigation channel.

121

"At least, we all hope so . . ." he concluded.

He grasped a tuft of reeds to pull himself up the other side. The words reached Séraphin, who was following him, in short bursts.

"Ninety-five years old!" the monk exclaimed. "He said to me, 'Calixte, go and get Séraphin Monge. I must clear my conscience . . .' "

"Is that what he said?"

"Yes. At that time his head was still quite clear . . ."

They crossed the copse of bay trees at Le Païgran — a whole alley of trees on the left of the road, that belonged to no one. The spear-shaped bay leaves rustled in the evening breeze. From there, they cut across the Pont Bernard osier plantation where the groves of shimmering aspens enticed the last skylarks into their branches.

The Ganagobie path rose up from there, just past the Roman bridge, in the hollow of the canal channel. It continued under the network of pines where the smell of resin was slowly fading as the September heat subsided.

Then the path went up straight as an arrow, marking a line on the hill without a bend where you could rest for a moment. It crossed meadows and valleys of earth and stone, always narrow and badly defined, with a surface of crumbling conglomerate that rolled under the monk's sandals. It was a path for penitents. You felt it had been created to make the person climbing it aware of his self-inflicted punishment.

Brother Calixte, who was in the lead and setting the pace, found this path of redemption hard going. It was the time of day when the fortress of cliffs rising up to the anvil-shaped plateau is clothed in raven's-wing colours — steel-blue and smoky-black — splashed across the last rays of the sun. The murmur in the sparse pines had ceased. The two men were entering the silence under the holly-oaks as night was falling. From there the path wound around wide uneven steps, deformed by exposed tree roots.

He groped his way through a tunnel of foliage and rocks, preceded by the monk who advanced blindly, finding his way by feeling the sides, in spite of knowing the route. The chalky deposits crunched under the calluses of his workman's hand.

They emerged into the moonlight, squeezing sideways through the narrow opening left by a rock fall. The trick of the moon in these parts was to play around the groves of holly-oak trees, outlining them as compact blocks among the fields of rye grass. Within this sterile amphitheatre, the moon conjured up gardens with fountains, shimmering views with glistening, non-existent pools. As Séraphin trod the soil of the plateau for the first time, the mystery of this enigmatic place crept into his memory gently and imperceptibly, as did all the significant details that he needed to register and re-member.

At the turning in a long wall, the church suddenly loomed up in front of him. There it was, sitting on the short grass, waiting for its people to come, as if it had just been born. Séraphin bent back a little. He eyed the line of apostles on the tympanum, hold-ing open books for shields.

He passed on quickly, following the friar hurrying along in front of him. Brother Calixte stopped at a low door and took an intricate key from the folds of his cassock. Séraphin heard its regular rotation in the lock.

The enclosure they entered smelled of freshly turned earth and rock.

"Watch out, lad! Don't go head first into that grave! Because . . . with no prejudice to Our Heavenly Father's plans . . . as Brother Laurent had to go on a mission, we dug it a bit prematurely . . ."

Here, the moonlight limited its illusions to making a cypress shimmer at the end of an empty ruined nave. Anonymous wooden crosses lay on mounds that had collapsed. Woven wreathes of oak and box twigs hung rotting away on crucifixes. They sat lopsidedly like hats on burlesque heads, all the more sinister for being vaguely comic.

Séraphin may well have perceived all these details in an unreal light that he was the only one to see, but because of all that was going to follow, he would never forget them. He took the vision of that sparsely populated cemetery with its wretched tombs as a warning. He was on the point of retreating and shamefully making his escape, leaving Brother Calixte standing, but the monk, who was watching him like a sly altar boy, must have had a premonition that his charge meant to run off. At the end of a path lined with sparse box bushes, he was about to walk under the a stone arch truncated by the moonlight at the level of the vault, when he suddenly turned around. He gripped Séraphin by the arm and roughly pushed and prodded him on. The words the monk whispered rose up into the softly echoing darkness of the gothic vaults.

"And if you think our prior looks in a rather sorry state, just tell yourself that —

good servant of God that he is — he's still just a man, a poor man, who is dying . . ."

He raised his finger.

"And who regrets . . ." he whispered.

It was very dark and dusty, but at the end a red reflection trembled on the carved twists of a column. Séraphin thought that he heard a vague bleating sound like a goat tied to a stake coming from that direction.

"Keep going!" Brother Calixte said.

He pushed Séraphin on in front of him, guiding him with a firm hand into a corridor with doors on each side. You could see moonlight again at the end of it, shining down in a shaft from a broken arch.

"Turn right!" said Brother Calixte. "And watch your head!"

Séraphin bent his back just in time. His hair skimmed the bottom of a pediment overhead. When he stood up again he found himself in a windowless room. The light of a candle scarcely held back the darkness that closed around it again and rose up to the pointed arches of the ceiling. The laboured, rhythmic wheeze, like a blacksmith's bellows, gave you a suffocating feeling as soon as you entered the room. It came from an old man stretched out on a board clamped between two stone supports that held it a metre from the floor.

The board was old, roughly shaped and full of knotholes. But so many of the old man's predecessors had slept there, exhausted and worn out with mortifications of the flesh till they were laid on it for the last time, that their throes had polished it, as erosion does a stone.

"Is that you, Calixte? Have you brought him, Séraphin Monge?"

"He's standing in front of you."

"Come closer because I'm almost at my last gasp."

When he spoke, the words were superimposed on the sound of the forge bellows that continued as before.

"He's still breathing," murmured Calixte. "But his mind? Is he still in his right mind? Who knows? So, whatever he says to you, you can take it or leave it."

"Come closer!" the dying man repeated. "Stand in front of me, so that I can see you properly."

Séraphin moved forward until he was touching the board that served as a bed.

Then his eyes met those of the invalid. It seemed to Séraphin that they expressed a wild terror. He also thought that the old man was trying to get up, perhaps to flee . . . A strangled cry came from the wheezing bellows of his lungs. Calixte rushed forward to support him and make him lie down again.

"I can see wings!" the prior moaned.

"Come now, Brother Toine, you can see that he's only a poor sinner . . ."

"I'm a road mender," Séraphin said.

The dying man seemed to regain his composure, his face took on a more natural expression, and he seemed to revive a little. It was as though a weight had been lifted from his hollow chest. The noise of the forge bellows now seemed fainter and more distant. Brother Toine recovered his serenity.

"Ah yes, it's true, you're a road mender . . . You're the road mender from Lurs . . . But you're also Séraphin Monge, aren't you? You're the one who's demolishing his house?"

"Yes," Séraphin replied.

"Wait a moment then . . . It's you I want to speak to."

He searched Séraphin's face, as though he were trying to find the answer to a puzzle there. His eyes were the only living things in his head. He had lost his teeth and the flesh from his nose. The only thing that had survived life's ruin was his serene brow.

"Listen," he said, "listen without interruption. I'm going to talk to you about a time when you scarcely existed. I'm going to talk to you about that night when you lost your whole family. Come close to me, come. Kneel down next to my board. You'll hear me better that way. I'm not sure whether I'll last the distance . . ."

He placed a timid hand on Séraphin's wrist, a hand that knew it would never again be of any use for anything or anyone. It had come to rest there, exhausted, perhaps in the hope of finding in Séraphin some of the strength the prior needed to fulfil the mission he had set himself. That hand already had the fineness and elegance of a skeleton's hand, but at the same time, it was still pathetic enough to inspire pity. Séraphin could not resist the entreaty that it sent out. He placed it into his open palm and pressed it gently between his own two hands. Then it seemed to him — it seemed to him — that the monk felt himself at last lying on a feather bed.

He began to speak immediately and very quickly. The words ran on, without punctuation, to the accompaniment of the wheezing bellows sound that emphasized them all.

"I was coming from Hautecombe," the prior said, "by way of the mountain. Up there we monks lived in abundance, but I wanted to live in austerity. I didn't want to die in comfort. I wanted draughts and cold, and ruins . . ."

With his free hand, he softly knocked twice on the walnut board.

"I wanted to be on this," he said. "However . . . I scarcely knew the route. I was guided by the stars — when there were any, for I was rained on for thirteen days! One evening I heard the Durance flowing and I knew that I'd arrived. That evening . . . I was soaked to the skin . . . My cassock weighed at least ten kilos . . . I had just passed the turn at Les Combes, below Giropée. The rain . . . It had stopped raining a while ago. Night was falling. There's . . . a spring of water there. You know that spring . . . You know . . . That spring at ground level . . . that flows without any sound, and if you don't know it's there, it's easy to step in it, and it's cold . . ."

"I know," Séraphin said.

"I drank at that spring and took a few steps under the willows a bit higher up . . . I thought that I'd rest for five minutes and that, after that, I would walk the last part of the journey here. Only, of course . . . Twenty-three years ago, I was already seventy-two . . . And then . . . I fell asleep . . . I don't know what woke me up . . . Was it the moonlight or the voices?

In any case, someone was saying, 'If anyone catches us . . .' and someone else replied, 'No one will catch us. The three of us will cover up.' And there was another one, but I couldn't understand him very well . . . He was talking about papers . . . He said, 'We've got to find them. If we don't, there's no hope for us!' They shilly-shallied. They argued, 'Couldn't we find another way?' 'No! We've talked for long enough . . .' That's what I heard . . . and it was too late then to show myself. I couldn't move . . . And I was in the dark under the willows and a clump of dead ash trees, while they were by the spring in full moonlight . . ."

"They?" Séraphin asked.

"Yes. Three men. And then . . . and then . . . One of them said, 'I brought you here because if you want to sharpen something quickly, there's nothing like the stone of this trough below the spring, and what's more, no one will hear us doing it. Look how worn it is. My grandfather used to sharpen his knife here.' 'Do you think we'll need to use them?' asked another. And the first replied, 'We don't know . . . but if we do, it's better for them to be nice and sharp . . .' And then the three of them bent over the rim of the trough . . . And all I could see after that was the movement of their arms, and now and again I could see the flash of a blade . . . and sparks . . . And I could hear a sound . . . Like the shrill sound of a cricket. It was the blades rubbing against the stone."

He stopped talking. His gaze slid towards the corner of his eyelids. He was still on the watch for that sound.

"And then," he continued, "when they'd finished sharpening — and it lasted quite a time — all three of them straightened up . . . They were wearing hats that shaded half their heads, and over them they had a kind of veil that they had raised. They were men . . . Like you and me . . ."

"From here or somewhere else?" Séraphin asked.

Brother Toine remained silent for a few seconds.

"From here . . ." he replied at last. "And then . . . One of them said, 'We mustn't get there before midnight. Before that, a carter or two might still turn up . . . We'll go along the lower path of the canal. We'll take off our shoes . . . We can hang them round our necks . . .' And then . . . They left. Not by the road. They nearly walked over me . . . I heard them making their way through the brambles, scattering pebbles as they went . . . I was . . . petrified . . ."

Séraphin felt the old man's hand move in his.

"I know what you're going to ask me," he said. "You're wondering why I didn't get up straight away . . . Why I didn't set out for Peyruis to give the alert . . . But you must take into account the state I was in: I'd just walked 400 kilometres through the hills, carrying my beggars' bag. I was ragged and dirty. No one would have thought I was in my right mind, especially the gendarmes . . . And then . . . Did I really understand what was going on? Were those three really planning a crime? And then . . . Oh! I tried to follow them! But . . . they were young men . . . They jumped . . . They ran . . . And me, I was seventy-two years old and my legs had already carried me for 400 kilometres. And then . . . Did I know where they were going?"

"But . . ." Séraphin said. "What about the next day?"

Brother Toine shook his head repeatedly, which made the bones in his neck crack.

"There was no next day . . . I caught a fever coming up here. My teeth were chattering. I didn't have the strength to knock, to make anyone hear. They found me collapsed against the door when they opened it to do their daily chore of fetching water . . ."

133

"And that's the truth," said Brother Calixte, who up till then had not opened his mouth.

"I was forty days . . ."

"Hovering between life and death," Calixte said. "More often closer to death than to life. But we still had to hold him down on his board. He wanted to get up. He kept talking about knives being sharpened . . . killers . . . and other things. He said the word 'gendarme' more than a hundred times."

"Forty days!" whispered Brother Toine.

"But you?" Séraphin asked. "When you heard what happened?"

"We heard nothing. Well . . . Nothing right away. Our door is closed to the world, as our minds are."

"There's no door," the prior said in definite tones, "that the notoriety of a crime can't penetrate eventually. Those who were responsible for collecting wood, those who went out to grow our vegetables, who came across hunters . . . they knew! But they hid it all from me."

"You were so weak," Brother Calixte said. "It took you two years to recover. And then . . . Brother Laurent who had watched over you with such devotion while you were delirious finally told you. In all conscience . . . Because — basically — out of respect for you, he dared not think that you hadn't been in control of your delirium."

"From the moment I found out," the prior groaned, "how your family died . . . how they had guillotined those innocent men . . . I thought of that night at the spring and I realized . . . I realized that they'd made a mistake with the murderers and that I, and only I, knew the truth. Then . . . Poor sinner that I am! I was tainted with the most glaring stain of all: injustice."

"Come now . . ." Calixte said, also sighing. "You were not the only one who was marked by it."

"But," the prior continued, "God gave me too much time. I came to understand that keeping quiet was a sin of pride. I had to say what I knew, and say it to you! One of those three had . . . had . . ."

"What?" asked Séraphin, burning to know. "Tell me what."

"Black wing . . ." the prior uttered with his last breath.

At that moment, Calixte's head was leaning over the prior's and his hands, with fingers slightly bent, were hovering just above the old mouth, perhaps to gag it.

Within the urgent pressure of his own two hands, Séraphin felt the life leave the old man's hand, like a bird whose head suddenly sinks down into the feathers of its chest. He put it down gently.

"Our Lord," Brother Calixte said, "has closed his mouth just in time."

"Do you think he was delirious?" asked Séraphin.

Occupied as he was with closing his prior's eyelids, Calixte did not immediately turn towards Séraphin.

"Even if Our Lord came to visit us," he said, "we couldn't recognize him . . . So . . . Forget everything he told you. Take no notice of it. We must leave the task of settling scores with the wicked to the angels. They'll come, have no doubt of that."

With those words, he closed the door of the monastery behind Séraphin. The night had scarcely grown darker. The slanting moon reflected the gold of the fallow land on to the dark tops of the holly-oak groves.

Séraphin stood there with his arms dangling at his sides, still hearing the sound of the door that had just banged shut.

"Perhaps they're still alive . . ." he said aloud. "And so the other three, the three from Herzegovina, were guillotined for nothing . . . Burle was right. It can't have happened like that."

He kicked a pebble into space and made

his way into the arch of holly-oaks. Down at the end of that black path a wide vista of the mountains beckoned him and he hoped for some sign from them.

"They could still be alive . . ." he repeated to himself softly. "But who are they? How can I find out? I'll never be strong enough, clever enough . . ."

At the end of the path, he dropped down on to the base of the calvary cross that dominated the horizon and put his head in his hands. It seemed as though the prior was still whispering to him from beyond the grave, "You'll do as you wish. For my part, I've told you everything I could . . . As for you, you should search . . . You should make every effort . . . You should know no rest . . . What use would your strength be? You're accountable for an injustice . . . You're accountable for an injustice."

He repeated these words two or three times, amazed that he had thought of them on his own. "You're accountable for an injustice . . . You're accountable for an injustice . . ."

"Séraphin!"

Séraphin started, jumped to his feet. The echo of his name was still rolling through the Lurs woods, when the voice that had called it out so clearly repeated it with the same commanding, reprimanding tone.

"Séraphin!"

Although it was vibrant with energy, the voice was low and desolate. Séraphin realized that it was coming from the woods below him, but he couldn't make out whether he'd heard it before.

He made no reply as he quietly moved forward to the very edge of the cliff. Holding on to a low branch, he leaned over the precipice, but saw nothing but the waves of treetops.

"Séraphin!" the voice shouted. "Forget everything he told you! Do you hear, Séraphin? Forget everything! If you believe him, you're lost! Do you hear, Séraphin? Lost! Lost! You'll never be happy!"

Séraphin rushed down the path under the holly-oaks, looking for a track that would allow him to catch up with the prophet of doom. But he had to go round the cliff as far as the church: there was no fault in the rock.

When he reached the base of the calvary, beside the monks' washing-place, all he found was a circle of flattened grass, where a faint aroma of herbs and shag tobacco still lingered. There were no traces left either in the tunnel of branches, the path was too dry.

Séraphin then went down towards the valley, through briars and viburnum, tramping a path through fields of foxgloves and nettles, scratching himself on dog rose twigs that caught hold of him as he passed. He rushed down from briar patch to briar patch and from tree to tree. He went down the slope, jumping over the fallen earth and landing in the broom, crushing it with his weight. In that way he took the shortest route to reach the spring, level with the ground, by the side of the road, where the prior had fallen asleep. Having mistaken the exact spot, he narrowly missed putting his foot in it, as it was so close to the grass. He looked for the outlet through which it poured into the washing trough below. The rim was made out of one of those special ripe-olive-coloured stones used for mortars to crush garlic. On one side of the rim, there was a long concave notch in the shape of a crescent moon. It shone like a sickle blade.

It was there, in times gone by, that so many harvesters had come to sharpen their blades. Because of that stone, they didn't need to hammer them before they set out. It was there . . .

Where his large silhouette was reflected upside-down in the limpid water, Séraphin's imagination placed three shadows leaning towards each other, until he could almost see them. Their hands trembled in the ripples of the water, as they slowly drew their knives back and forth over the notch in the ripe-olive-coloured stone.

He heard the sound quite distinctly — that shrill sound of a cricket the dying prior had spoken about.

He stayed there for a long time. He even kneeled down to look at the notch more closely, to convince himself that the monk hadn't invented it when he was delirious. He ran his open hand over the polished stone.

When he got back to Peyruis, the moon was setting. He was not at all tired. He was taut as a bow aimed at a target that he could not yet see clearly.

VII

Come rain or snow, Séraphin kept on removing the stones one by one, throwing the rubble into the courtyard, wheeling the earth and straw cement down to the Durance in his barrow, where it now formed a dyke between the Iscles. In spite of the bad weather, Patrice, the man with the disfigured face, still came to encourage him with his silent presence. Sometimes, when he had been observing Séraphin, he would say to him,

"You must come and have dinner with me at home. Watching me eat is also quite a show. You'll see. One thing though . . . You'll have to choose a day when my father's not there."

He watched Séraphin thoughtfully, as he passed in front of him, his barrow overflowing with debris, making its iron wheel grate at every turn.

"Aren't you going to ask me why?"

Séraphin put down the handles of the wheelbarrow.

"Well . . ." he said.

"Why do you think he asked me if your hands were blackened?"

Séraphin opened his arms, indicating that he had no idea.

"Anyway," Patrice said, "he's frightened of you. That's for sure."

Séraphin continued his work even on Christmas Day, in spite of the entreaties of the priest who came specially to see him.

It was a fine day and Marie Dormeur and Rose Sépulcre took advantage of the fact that their parents were making merry to steal away and bring their offerings to Séraphin. Marie had got a new bicycle. They arrived at La Burlière at the same time, both dressed up in woollen dresses and coats with fox-fur collars.

They arrived wheel to wheel, as one had caught up with the other. The moment they put a foot to the ground, they began hurling violent abuse at each other. However, anxious about their nicely set hair, this time they refrained from actually fighting.

Patrice was sitting on the seat smoking his cigarette as usual. When he heard their footsteps and then their voices, he suddenly turned around. Marie Dormeur stopped in her tracks, stiff with fear, clapping her hand to her mouth to stifle a cry. Rose didn't bat an eyelid, didn't look away, but walked past him, smiled and politely said hello.

Patrice got up, said hello and stood there transfixed.

While this was happening, the emotional Marie had been outdistanced by her rival, and it was Rose who climbed the steps of the ladder first. They shouted together:

"Séraphin! Hey, Séraphin!"

He looked like a Titan up there with his great hands wielding the sledge-hammer. Stone and rubble flew into the air as he kicked them down to the courtyard. The dormice darted wildly out of the cracks where they had been hiding and fled in all directions like black streaks. The dust that had lain forever on walls and floors now hovered like a cloud of smoke around La Burlière.

The girls scarcely gave it a thought. At the risk of losing their balance, they jostled each other on the ladder, raising their offerings to Séraphin. One offered a bag of olives, and the other cream puffs in a paper tied with a green bow.

Séraphin sent them packing, shouting angrily:

"Go away! You'll get hurt! I don't need you! Get out of here! Go on! Get out of here!"

He kept on shouting a string of other insults at them, his sledge-hammer rising and falling with the same relentless rhythm. Suddenly, the piece of wall that he was attacking at the base collapsed without warning, right in front of the terrified girls. They staggered back, covering their eyes with their handkerchiefs, groping their way in a heavy cloud of lime that smelled terribly of rat-killer.

They didn't see Patrice who was still standing there stock still, as though struck by lightning. They could only summon enough strength to shout insults at each other again as they got back on their bicycles.

That was the day, that Christmas Day at nightfall, that Séraphin could at last see La Burlière reduced to its ground floor. The blind wall that gave it such a forbidding look was now no more than a modest heap three metres high, the same colour as the earth.

Séraphin rolled a cigarette as he gazed at his handiwork. A tall holly-oak that had always grown in the shadow of the walls which had now been knocked down, breathed deeply in the evening dew, its joyful foliage ruffled gently by the breeze. Like the tree, Séraphin also breathed in the air slowly and deeply. He had the feeling that his nightmare was beginning to fade. He went down the ladder. He picked up the two prettily tied packets left by the girls. He looked at them without a smile, just nodding his head. He made his way with a heavy tread to his bicycle resting against the embankment.

Then he saw Patrice standing in front of him, still as a statue. Strangely enough, he wasn't smoking. As the darkness fell, it smoothed over the seams, the hollows and the displacements of his features, giving him a man's face again.

"You're still here?" Séraphin asked, surprised to see him.

"Ssh!" Patrice said. "I'm still dreaming . . . Don't wake me up! She looked me full in the face! She didn't look away. She . . . Oh! How can I explain it? She smiled . . . at me . . ."

"Who?"

"The Persian. Well . . . The one that looks like a Persian."

"A Persian?" Séraphin asked in amazement. "Basically, what's a Persian?"

"Ah!" Patrice said, "basically, I don't really know! But . . . It must be that . . ."

He nodded in the direction of the invisible trace of the girl far off down the road, that he alone was able to make out.

He had said the last words in a whisper. Séraphin heard a strange sound.

"Are you . . . crying?" he asked.

"Yes. That's one thing I can do: cry."

"Here!" Séraphin said. "She brought me some olives. Take them!"

Patrice sniffed and tried to smile ironically.

"I'll put them under a glass dome!"

"And this too! Take the cream puffs the other one gave me!"

"But what about you?"

"Me? What would I do with cream puffs?"

Then in a gentler voice:

"All that's meant to be eaten when you're happy . . ."

He got on his bicycle.

Patrice stood there for some time savouring the moment, while dormice skittered around him wildly in all directions, looking for another home. But he shouldn't have stayed so long in the shadow of La Burlière, for life was ebbing away from the building with every stone that hit the ground and every piece of lime that quietly disintegrated. Its lamentation could be heard in the voice of the tall holly-oaks moaning in

146

the wind.

The whispering ruins invited him to consider their dismal example, the fragments to which they had been reduced. Patrice was listening to them now, as though they were telling his own story.

That night, Christmas night, Séraphin dreamed of his mother.

His mother came towards him from a white balustrade surmounted by a black iron arbour that he didn't recognize. She was walking bare-footed on the grass, as young as he was. She was naked — well, not entirely. She was wearing some of those sexy frills and flounces he'd seen in the men's magazines that were handed around at the Front during the war, to keep up morale.

She advanced towards him to cover him with her body. The terrible thing about it was that she had a face — a face that Séraphin had never seen — and he said to himself as he dreamed that perhaps it wasn't the one she had when she was alive.

Her mouth opened, speaking words of confession. Was she talking about her life? Was she talking about her death? Séraphin was horror-struck, paralysed by an unbearable dread: the idea that in a moment, when she was close enough, he would catch those words that once said, could never be erased from his memory.

She came closer . . . and closer. Whispering . . . whispering. She had the same slow walk as Séraphin himself.

She came and lay on him, but she was weightless, as though she were filled with air. With a graceful gesture she began to remove her bodice. He distinctly heard the press-studs open. Suddenly her breasts spilled out, but there was no body behind them. Just as in Burle's account, the drop of milk frozen by death gleamed at the tip of each nipple. A smell of very old, cold soot hung around her weightless body. But at the same time she floated past, without looking at her son. That's why he hadn't felt her weight. She no longer made that slow, voluptuous movement of coming to him and fitting her body to his. Besides, it seemed to Séraphin that there was something in her unusually wide-open eyes that forbade him to look for it.

He had never before thought it possible to smell things in dreams. Yet when he woke up, bathed in sweat and with a violent erection, the musty smell of cold soot still lingered in his nostrils. With clenched fists, he struggled against sleep till morning, terrified of falling back into his dream.

One fine day, spring arrived.

La Burlière, with its sharp angles, still gave the impression of an open coffin, but a coffin sinking into the ground as its height was being reduced to nothing. The cypresses that kept watch around her like candles seemed twice as tall as she was slowly engulfed.

The Durance had one of its sudden floods that eat into the banks here, there and everywhere, like a snake when you tread on its tail. For a fortnight, diluvian rains swept over the lower snow line and all the slopes that overlook the tributaries.

When the flood waters retreated, Séraphin noticed with some satisfaction that they had washed away the dyke made by his debris between the willow groves. A smooth, clean sand bank spread over what was left of it.

What remained of the building had become soft as a wet sugar lump, crumbling easily as he struck it with his pick.

On Easter morning, Séraphin opened La Burlière's kitchen to the sun. Through the open sky of the demolished ceiling, its rays chased the shadows from the farthest corner. They searched the finely worked fireback in the hearth, the cupboard recess, the olive-oil–coloured flagstones.

Around eleven o'clock, there had been a shower of rain: a fine cleansing rain that was soon dried up by a sudden wind and the sun coming out again.

It was then that Séraphin, leaning on his pick, noticed that the spots of blood splashed on the walls, that up till then had been the colour of dirty grease, were suddenly glistening. The alternating darkness and light were reviving them.

Séraphin shivered. His whole reason for destroying everything was to banish those indelible marks from the walls and floor. Every night, and each in its precise place, they invariably sullied his memory. Now a trick of the light brought them back to life again, like lichens that are regenerated by rain after centuries of drought. He thought they were making a sign to him.

Under threat of finding them even brighter the following night, he had to get rid of them before the day's end, especially the most telling of them: those that Moungé l'Uillaou had left around the salt box under the support on the right-hand side of the chimney piece, a little more than a metre above the floor of the hearth.

Séraphin attacked the chimney piece with his sledge-hammer and immediately his nostrils were full of the smell of cold soot. Soon he was breathing the soot that came away from the hood of the hearth as it disappeared. Soon he was covered in it. When he wiped his forehead with the back of his hand, he spread it over his face. However, it wasn't the usual smell of soot; it was that strange stagnant odour that hung about his mother's body the night he had had the dream.

Now all that was left was a piece of the truncated flue, about two square metres. Above it you could see the holly-oaks shining in the sun. Séraphin carefully got rid of all the stone and sooty plaster, barrow-load after barrow-load. Only about ten centimetres more and he would finally reach the spot where his father's fingers had left their imprints in red, and he would destroy them and he would reduce them to dust and he would throw them in the Durance.

He spat into his hands, as he did so many times a day, to give himself strength. Perched on the wall, he lifted his pick and brought it down straight in front of him. It met an empty space and went into it up to the handle. Séraphin nearly lost his balance and would have followed the path of his pick head first. He was so startled anyway that he let it go. He jumped into the room from the wall. He felt the iron head of the pick stuck between two stones. He dislodged the first one. After having knocked the damp clay and straw cement off the first one, he delicately removed the other. An almost new layer of plaster was revealed, or at least it was different from the straw cement and lime that joined the walls of La Burlière. He seized a small hammer and began to dig into the plaster. At the third hammer blow, the iron head also disappeared into an empty space. The falling plaster made a dull sound as it fell against something metallic. With his bare hands, Séraphin uncovered the top of an edgewise brick, then another. These two bricks just covered the place where his father had left his bloody finger marks, and Séraphin had to push on this exact spot to get rid of them. When he moved away to throw them on the heap of rubble, the sinking sun lit up the back of a carefully constructed hiding place forty centimetres in depth and height. Under the debris that had piled up during the demolition, you could make out the edges of a tin box.

Séraphin seized it. It was heavier than the bricks he had just removed. The box was oblong in shape and was originally meant to contain a kilo of lump sugar. Judging from the colour, it must have been used for that purpose for a long time and exposed to the smoke in the hearth. You could still make out the Breton scene on the lid. There was a calvary with a Bigouden[12] woman sitting on the steps, gazing at a bay dotted with reefs.

Séraphin had no difficulty opening the lid. The box was full to the brim with twenty-franc gold pieces.

Neither the slowness of his gait, nor the time he took to reply to someone, nor his voluntary isolation, nor his determination in destroying his house, could better reveal his true nature and his great difference from other men than the way Séraphin treated this gold mine.

Just as he had pushed Rose aside, just as he had pushed Marie aside, he pushed the gold out of his way. If the people of Peyruis and Lurs had been able to see this road mender seize the box, open it and look at the warm colour of so many glittering gold louis — for no more than five seconds and without the slightest thrill of joy — they

12 *Bigouden:* A woman from Pont-l'Abbé (Finistère). The word *bigouden* comes from the name of the headdresses worn by the women of that region.

would have felt shivers down their spines. He simply closed the sugar box without touching the coins, and put it down on the wall beside him.

There were two hours of daylight left and he didn't want to waste them. There were two metres of chimney flue left to be demolished, and he would have to breathe the cold smell of soot that had clung to his mother's voluptuous ghost. He had to get rid of it as quickly as possible, to banish the piece of black wall in front of him from sight. Working twice as hard with sledgehammer and pick, he finally knocked it down. But by the time he finished — when for the first time he got down to ground level at that spot — night had fallen, a dark, moonless night.

An exhausted Séraphin wiped his face with the back of his hand for the last time. The hood over the hearth had gone, but he himself was almost disappearing under the soot: he was black and sticky, with a face like a chimney sweep and greasy particles through his matted fair hair. It was as though the chimney had made him responsible for keeping that funereal smell alive. It began in a nightmare, but was now a reality.

Wearily, he picked up the tin, which he stuffed into his haversack, got on his bicycle

154

and made his way back to Peyruis in darkness.

Then, when the sound of the pedals and the badly oiled chain faded in the distance, there was a furtive movement among the bay trees by the side of the road. Someone crept out, as warily as a cat, listened to the small stones and bits of plaster that dropped from the ruins, then began to move forward. He walked around the parts of the walls still standing and went into the kitchen through the gap where the fireplace once stood. He grumbled as he tripped over the debris. He struck a light that lit up the rest of the walls, then stopped on a level with the hiding place that Séraphin had not yet been able to demolish. The light went out. Still cursing, the man made the stones ring under his feet as he went off up the hill path into the night.

Séraphin put his bicycle away in the shed. He took off all his clothes and threw them in the wood box. He went up to the kitchen through the inside door that opened on to the stairs, turned on the tap in the trough and washed himself vigorously from top to toe with lots of cold water and soft soap. When he had finished, he washed himself a second time with a cake of perfumed

'Mikado' soap that he kept for special occasions. He shaved and then went upstairs to put on clean clothes. When he came down, he noticed the box he had handled. He washed it too, top and bottom, with a sponge that he threw into the rubbish bin. He blew his nose hard three or four times, and the handkerchief went the same way as the sponge. He smelled his hands and his armpits suspiciously. He breathed deeply. The smell of soot had left him at last.

Only then did he realize he was hungry and thirsty. He heated up the soup that he had been preparing for three or four days. He opened a tin of sardines and cooked two eggs. It was only after he had eaten, drunk his quarter-litre of red wine and cleared the table, that he pulled the tin towards him and sat there looking at it for some time.

The Breton calvary, the Bigouden woman and the ocean reminded him of his mother. She must have chosen that box at the Manosque or Forcalquier fair. *She had actually held it in her hands,* and since he had annihilated all the objects she had ever touched, he should destroy that one too. However, the sweetness of the time of day that she evoked stopped him from throwing the box out with the rubbish. He said to himself that his mother must have taken her breakfast sugar out of it every day as she sat with her coffee steaming on the table in front of her — until his father took it from her to make it into a cheap little safe and hide it away in the secret hole in the fireplace.

Séraphin stroked it for some time before tipping the coins out on to the oilcloth.

Then, when he lifted off the box, some folded pages, which must have lined the bottom, fell out and covered the pile of louis.

There were three sheets of stamped paper as official as a banknote, with its black number, its wire marks and watermark of the noble profile of Justice crowned with a laurel wreath. These sheets were covered with small writing in black ink that was clumsy but sharp, with lines so clear that they seemed to have been formed the day before.

These documents had roughly the same text, and this is what they said:

I, the undersigned, Célestat Dormeur, baker's apprentice at Peyruis, acknowledge having received forthwith and in cash, the sum of one thousand, two hundred francs (1200 francs) from the hand of Félicien Monge, master carter at Lurs. In return for this loan agreed by both parties in good faith, the said Célestat Dormeur will annually on Saint Michael's Day pay the said Félicien Monge the agreed interest of 23%, that is to say two hundred and seventy-six francs. This sum will be wholly reimbursed on Saint Michael's Day 1896, under pain of legal proceedings.

Drawn up at Lurs, Saint Michael's Day 1891.

Two signatures followed and were repeated on the duty stamp in the lower left-hand corner. Apart from the names and sums of money, the two other bills were identical. In return for 23 per cent interest over five years, Félicien Monge was lending the sum of 1000 francs to Didon Sépulcre, oil miller at Lurs, and on the same conditions, he was lending 1500 francs to Gaspard Dupin, blacksmith at Les Mées.

One thousand francs, 1200 francs, 1500 francs . . . What did that represent at the time?

Séraphin remembered Maître Bellaffaire's accounts of the sale of arable land priced at one hundred francs per hectare. One hundred francs in '97 or '98 . . . That is to say, five of the gold pieces scattered over the oilcloth. That is to say, 1000 francs in those days could buy ten hectares of fertile land in the valley . . . It was quite a sum, 1000 francs, especially with the burden of that exorbitant 23 per cent annual interest. That was enough — yes, quite enough — to wish a man dead . . . A man and his family . . . Three unidentified men . . . Three men from these parts . . . Those three men that the prior had come across sharpening their knives on the edge of the Sioubert spring were from these parts.

Séraphin picked up again the promissory notes that he had pushed away on the pile of louis to verify the dates: *"to be wholly reimbursed on Saint Michael's Day 1896".*

On Saint Michael's Day 1896, I was eighteen days old . . . And it was during that night, on the evening of that day that . . .

A memory came to him in a flash. He remembered Patrice Dupin sitting at the foot of the cypress, saying to him:

"Why do you think my father asked me if you had blackened hands?"

Séraphin struck the table with his fist slowly and deliberately. It all became clear to him. The reason why Marie Dormeur, Rose Sépulcre and Patrice Dupin came to keep him company so often — ostensibly out of friendship — it was because their fathers sent them off to La Burlière to spy on him. All these weighty suppositions

159

pointed to the three men.

"It's them for sure!" Séraphin said aloud.

Without thinking and without counting them, he put the gold pieces in the sugar tin fistful by fistful. Just by feeling the weight of them in his hand, he realized that it represented a great deal of money, the whole box . . . How had his father earned all that? It's true that lending at 23 per cent . . . But you have to have the money before you can lend.

Séraphin took out one of the coins and examined it. The face on it was framed with sideburns and a high quiff of hair above the forehead. Jowls gave it a heavy pear shape. In a ring around the edge was this inscription:

LOUIS-PHILLIPE 1ER — ROI DES
FRANÇAIS

When this king was on the throne, Mongé l'Uillaou, who died at thirty-three in 1896, wasn't even born. Where did they come from, these golden louis that slipped so easily between the fingers, sparkling as though they were new, as though they had been protected from the sullying contact of so many dirty hands, as if no one, really, had ever touched them?

When he had poured all the coins back into the box, Séraphin read the documents time and time again, as though he were afraid he might forget the names: Gaspard Dupin, Didon Sépulcre, Célestat Dormeur.

Long into the calm village night — the bell tolled the hours, the fountain flowed, sometimes ruffled by a gust of wind — Séraphin fingered the spotless sheets of paper with their beautiful blue stamp. He finally folded them up again, put them over the louis in the order in which he had found them, and closed the box again. He got up and put the box on the shelf above the sink, next to the frying pan. Whereupon, he got himself a glass of water from the tap and sat down again heavily at the table. With his forearms resting on the oilcloth, he opened and shut his enormous fists as if he were squeezing an imaginary throat. Hurt, disgust and anger gave his face the fearsome look of one of the ancient Furies.

VIII

When Séraphin went out into the street next
morning he was as calm in his mind and
deliberate in his movements as he always
was. He went about the day's work without
haste or tension. He hit the stones with his
sledge-hammer with the usual amount of
force. And on Sunday when he arrived at
La Burlière and saw Patrice Dupin there,
his face wore its usual expression. He gave
him a friendly smile. He had always had a
limp handshake, so that when Patrice put
out his hand, Séraphin didn't have to
pretend to show any more feeling than he
normally did.

He knocked down all trace of the hiding
place on the left of the hole where the
chimney used to be. He dislodged the
flagstones that still showed the streaks of
blood left by his mother as she crawled
towards the cradle. He carried them outside
and reduced them to dust with his sledge-

hammer.

It was the time of year when the swallows came back to their nests. They darted about the ruined farm with piercing cries. Sometimes several of them stopped in mid-flight and hovered with beating wings at a particular spot in the sky, as if they were clinging to their invisible holes under the eaves. In the flurry of their activity as they swooped or hung in the air, they seemed to follow the outline of the house that no longer existed. On warm evenings they carried on for a long time like this, obstinately flying around their phantom nests. Most of them went and nested elsewhere, under the eaves of churches, against the beams of crumbling châteaux or under the tiles in the cloister of the monastery at Ganagobie. But some of them wouldn't give up. The whole summer long, their cries rang out between the Durance and the holly-oak wood, as they flew around the empty space where La Burlière used to be.

There was now a ten-metre gap where the farm of La Burlière had been knocked down to its foundations. Séraphin no longer needed to take the debris to the Durance. He had pulled off the trap-door in the kitchen, which had been forgotten when he had burned all the furniture and the doors, and through this opening he tipped every-thing that remained of the old carters' inn to the bottom of the stables cut out of the rock.

The day came when he stood before an immense empty space that still had the outline of an empty coffin. It was the only time that the gold louis he found in the wall were of any use to him. He had had deliv-ered thirty cartloads of road metal, which he carefully spread with a fork over the entire surface of La Burlière.

When he had scattered the last shovelful, he straightened his back. A late summer wind swept across the new space and some-thing like a murmur of surprise went through the tall trees, looking all the taller now that they stood alone. The foliage of the four cypresses seemed to undulate like green flames as they calmly waited for a new catafalque to be placed between their cande-labras.

Patrice of the disfigured face arrived that evening in his red car and witnessed the sight of Séraphin leaning on his fork, con-templating his handiwork. The fact that his aim had been accomplished did not make the expression on his face any less sombre.

"So?" Patrice asked. "What now? How far has that got you?"

"Well . . ." Séraphin grumbled.

While rolling his cigarette, he took stock of the empty space and realized that it only existed for people who passed by and perhaps for the man who watched him from below; that elegant man who bore his face like a flag; a face that the surgeons had made eternally mocking.

But for him, Séraphin, La Burlière was an indestructible monument. Knocking it down completely would not obliterate it. Whatever he did, it was still there in front of him. He walked towards it, opened the door, stepped through the picture frame, and there was the massacre and the smell of damp soot that hung about his mother's ghost, that time he had dreamt about her.

Knocking down the scene of the crime had not obliterated it. He now had to exterminate the culprits to find peace of mind once more and banish everything: both memories and ghosts.

Séraphin knew Didon Sépulcre and Célestat Dormeur well, but he had never seen Gaspard Dupin. He had to meet that man whose son had been spying on him so assiduously. He had to meet him, find out his habits, work out how he could be attacked, without his attacker running the risk of being caught.

As it happened, Patrice was just saying, "All right then. Now that you've finished, there's nothing to stop you from coming to Pontradieu. You'll find," he added in a rather strange tone of voice, "that there are some charming things at Pontradieu . . ."

"Oh!" Séraphin replied, "You can be sure of that. Now, I'll go there for sure."

"Really?" Patrice said. "What if I take you at your word? What if I invite you for Sunday fortnight?"

"Well then," Séraphin said, "why not Sunday fortnight?"

He watched Patrice get into his car, and stood there for a long time after he left, listening to the sound of the engine fade away in the distance.

It was after that day that he began prowling around the site of La Burlière like a dog sniffing the scent of a stray bird.

Had he really got rid of everything? A brick made him feel ill as though he had eaten something poisonous. The fact that the killers were still alive was not enough to explain his agitation.

He was doubly vigilant, his eyes always on the look-out, subconsciously straining towards something he couldn't identify. He walked up and down the same places ten

166

times over. He walked with that same heavy tread over the empty space between the four candle-shaped cypresses, that now seemed to be suffering from some secret loss.

At last, one morning, the sun rising at a particular angle revealed to him the trace of a strange rut in the middle of the bare area paved with round stones. It was a path over the pebbles worn down by fifty generations of Monges, pointing in a straight line to a dome of thick green in front of the slope planted with holly-oaks. It was a tangle of viburnum, of self-sown bramble, of straight alder trees growing as close together as wheat around a long dead ash tree. A vigorous aristolochia with tentacles as thick as jungle vines wound about everything, strangled everything, climbing to the highest branches of the dead tree and cascading down in endless arabesques, like a fountain of leaves. The path worn in the stone disappeared under it, but did not reappear on the other side.

Séraphin attacked this copse, which both disturbed and attracted him. He had taken off his shirt as the sun was still beating down, and his chest and arms were torn by thorns like fish hooks that gashed his skin. He worked all day cutting down the tangle of vegetation and burning it in the open area.

At sunset he at last uncovered a well with an opening of almost four metres in circumference. The well was as white as snow. It was crowned with an arch formed by three ribbons of very worn, rusty iron joined, then bent back at the top, like bishops' croziers. At the spot where the three stems came together hung a pulley, also rusty, with a chain wound around it that disappeared into a wash trough filled with leaves next to the well.

On the stone of the wash trough, Séraphin noticed a washerwoman's paddle bleached with soda, lying there as though it had just been left the day before. He didn't dare pick it up by the handle. He didn't put his fingers where his mother had placed hers, perhaps on the very day before her death. He lifted it up by the blade and apprehensively let it go again.

A vague disquiet made him view this discovery as something alarming. He began to feel around among the dead leaves that filled the trough. He pulled out the remains of a galvanized iron bucket attached to the end of the chain. The bucket completed the image that he had in his mind, for Séraphin had already seen them somewhere in the course of his life — that paddle, that chain and that well.

He stepped back a few paces to look at that whole picture that worried him so much. The rut cut into the flagstones of the open area came right up to the well: it was the shortest route from La Burlière, and you could easily see that it stopped short at the door that was no longer there. As for the well, it made you think of something brand-new, just taken out of a box. It seemed as white as snow because of its marble coping. Far from conjuring up the graceful statuary of a bishop's garden — from which it must have come — in the dying light this marble spoke only of tombs and graves. Its whiteness was sinister. Washed by rain, bleached by the sun and still new after so many centuries, as there was no sign of erosion on its edges, it was white as a shroud. It shone out like a signal in front of the dark green of the holly-oaks. That well was a witness, perhaps as eloquent as the blood-stains . . .

Séraphin didn't hesitate for a moment. He raised his sledge-hammer and brought it down with all his strength. The handle snapped off where it joined the iron head that had done so much work. Séraphin fell forward against the rim, which he had to grasp to stop himself falling headlong into the well. He straightened up, stunned. The sound of the blow was still echoing below in the depths.

Séraphin looked at the handle, which he was still holding. The muscles in his arms were aching from the full force of the blow he had received. The only result was a piece of marble scarcely as big as a mussel shell that had flown out of the solid block.

Séraphin ran his finger over the damage. He concentrated all his passionate attention on the wash trough where the dead holly-oak leaves, with their spiky edges, were starting to rise up in the evening wind. His eyes slowly made the circuit of the expensive marble coping around the well. He observed and touched the very elegant wrought-iron crown. He knew he had already seen this bulbous, sickly white well, far too luxurious for a humble place like La Burlière — but where? Séraphin had the feeling that it wanted to tell him something.

It was nightfall before he could tear himself away and go back to Peyruis and the peaceful atmosphere of his house. He took with him the remains of his sledge-hammer and the paddle, which he had not forgotten.

However, the need to destroy that last witness of his misfortune would not leave his methodical mind. The following Sunday he arrived at La Burlière armed with quarrying tools. As soon as he had parked his bike at the foot of the cypress, he turned round to find Marie Dormeur. She was leaning against the crown of the well, looking at Séraphin with her lovely smile.

It had an enormous effect on him. He forgot what he was about to do, and he even took the haversack full of iron tools from his shoulder. It gave out a metallic ring as it landed on the paving stones.

Marie was sitting on the wide coping of the well with her legs dangling, swinging her white shoes from side to side. Séraphin advanced cautiously over the thirty-odd metres that separated them, as though he were afraid of scaring her. He all but walked on tip-toe, for a powerful desire drew him to her and he feared that she might realize it.

Oh no! It wasn't the natural desire of a boy for a girl. The fact that she was young, beautiful and pathetic in the hopeless love she had for him meant nothing. Séraphin saw her only as the daughter of a murderer.

The moment he caught sight of her, the idea germinated, grew and spread that if he got rid of her, he would punish Célestat Dormeur more surely than if he killed the man himself. He wouldn't even be able to weep over his daughter's body. As soon as he had thrown her in, Séraphin would fill in that well of misery right up to the opening. With his big road worker's rammer he would carefully pack on it all the debris he could find.

"The apple of his eye . . ." he muttered between his teeth.

Only ten metres separated him from his prey and every charming detail of the young girl was revealed as he drew closer. One hand was holding on to the wrought-iron arch and, on the index finger sparked a large pale blue stone, which must have been the colour of her eyes. Now he was only a few paces away from her. He noticed her shining lips and, on the tense hand that was holding on to the arch, the stone glinting in the sunlight that seemed to beckon him, like a lark to a mirror.

He took the next step with his eyes closed, fearful of having the picture of Marie's trusting eyes engraved in his memory forever.

Then, the air around him moved in a

gentle wave, as in an earthquake. He thought he heard — he did hear — a rustling of dead leaves, as if the surface of the wash trough was splitting as something strange swelled beneath it. He saw his mother rise up on the moving air that no longer supported her. She rose out of one of those soap boxes stuffed with straw that washerwomen once used in the old days. Séraphin had found it in pieces deep in the bushes. She stood up. She faced him. She walked through Marie and she walked through Séraphin. Reeling back, Séraphin let her pass. Her face was the same as he had seen in his dream, — a face which perhaps had never been hers in real life — her features frozen in that impassive and disillusioned mask that Séraphin had so often observed on those who had died in the war. Her shoulder was bending under the weight of an invisible bucket of water, and her left hand was held out slightly from her body to give her balance in a position she must often have taken as she docilely trod that real, well-defined path worn between the well and the house. She was moving along it now towards La Burlière, and at the exact spot where the door used to be, she stepped over the threshold. As soon as she entered the non-existent kitchen, she disappeared.

This hallucination had happened in a flash; just enough time for Séraphin to move back four metres, as if Marie were a magnet with opposite poles; also just enough time for him to situate the place where his memory had registered that well for the first time. It was in the dream in which he had already seen his mother. It was there, held in thrall by the scantily clad apparition that looked like a woman in an erotic print, that he had mistaken the well for the balustrade of a terrace and the wrought-iron crown for an arbour. At that time, the place she had sprung from had scarcely been sketched in his subconscious, but now it was obvious. Yes, it was indeed the crown, the wan marble coping, the wash trough — then full of clear water — that his mother had risen from, offering him those enormous breasts where the last drop of milk she wanted to give him had solidified.

Séraphin clapped his hand to his face with such force that it sounded as though it was being slapped.

"Good Lord! What's wrong? Tell me, what's wrong?"

Marie had jumped down from the coping. She hung by both hands from Séraphin's wrists, but couldn't manage to move them.

"Go away!" was all he uttered. "Go away! Quickly! Go away!"

His two tightly closed fists kept his face in darkness, as if it could banish the vision that had just scourged him. And it had come to him in full daylight, at eleven in the morning. The bell of the Ganagobie monastery was calling the faithful to mass; a truck was travelling slowly down the road with its sound of rattling chains; the Marseille-Briançon train was whistling around the Giropée bend. None of that made it less incredible or less desperate.

Marie, who had obeyed him and moved away, couldn't bring herself to abandon him in that state. She couldn't take her eyes away from him as he continued gesticulating at her. His hand repeatedly mowed the air in a sign that meant: "Go away! Don't stand there! Get out of here!" This gesture and Séraphin's back was all she could see, as he was walking backwards with heavy, deliberate steps, as if he were keeping someone visible only to himself at a distance.

"He backed away from that well," Marie will say sixty years later, "as though it were a wild animal."

IX

The following Sunday Séraphin Monge, wheeling his bicycle, entered the avenue of sycamores that leads to Pontradieu. That Sunday was a day when the trees themselves heralded misfortune. Their leaves and branches shrieked to each other in panic as they were tangled by the mistral.

The avenue was long and curved. Stubble and vines petered out against the foot of plane trees. Further away, glimpses of water stirred up by the wind shimmered between the thick branches of spindle-trees trimmed in a perfectly straight line. A path between low box bushes split off from the avenue and seemed to invite him to follow it. Séraphin leaned his bicycle against a tree and began walking down the path. The spindle-trees were like a curtain in two serried rows before him, and when he went past them, he immediately came upon the rippling surface of a very large ornamental pool. He reckoned that it must be more than forty metres long and twenty wide. Italian poplars formed a vertical escort that further widened the perspective of glassy water.

Patrice had spoken to him about this great pool. Gaspard Dupin had taken enormous pride in patching up the cracks and refilling it. Before him, it had been full of dead leaves — a real eyesore under the poplars. He had also had the white marble coping restored. He had unearthed the partly crushed ceramic pipes over an area of more than five hundred metres. After that, the fountain flowed once more. It was a Louis XV–style ornamental façade with heavy scallops extending right across the width of the pool at the northern end. Set into it were the heads of four ancient gods with coarse features that had been dug up by the counts in earlier days. The copper pipes stuck in their mouths had spoiled their lascivious smiles as they spewed out four twisting spouts of water as thick as a pulley rope.

Séraphin stayed musing for several minutes in front of the tranquil surface of the water. He was standing on the marble coping which was as pale as the well at La Burlière and no doubt dated from the same period. It was more than fifty centimetres wide, which made it quite easy to walk on. Séraphin slowly went round it. As he looked down at his own heavy shoes, he thought he could see the furtive steps of the bishops who used to walk there, heads bowed in meditation.

As he went back for his bicycle at the foot of the plane tree, he could think of nothing but the great pool. It fascinated him as though it were giving him a sign, as though it were inviting him to make use of its power. He dreamed he was drowning Gaspard Dupin.

As he walked further on towards the house, thinking of that easy solution to his problem, he suddenly felt that the wind was blowing in different trees. He raised his head. He saw a windmill and a pergola under a mass of roses. He saw a pavilion in the form of a pagoda, buried under Virginia creeper. And there was Pontradieu, rising up in front of him behind some tall transparent aspens that softened its outline against a watercolour background.

The house, long and high with many cheerful shutters in tones of faded green, was bleached by the sun like ink on an old letter. Behind one of these closed shutters, someone was playing a piano. The notes rippled on the midday air.

At first Séraphin thought it was Patrice, but he was standing at the top of an elegant flight of stairs, looking down from the front of the house, anxiously scanning the horizon.

"What the hell are you doing?" he shouted from afar.

He quickly came down the steps. He advanced towards Séraphin, his arms wide open as though he wanted to embrace him, bravely armed with his hideous smile.

"What the hell were you doing?" he repeated. "I thought you weren't going to turn up!"

He was still inwardly quivering from the anxiety he'd felt, and it vibrated in his fingers. For the first time in his life, Séraphin was tempted to press someone's fingers, instead of giving the hand as limp as a wet rag that he usually offered everyone. But no . . . Patrice Dupin was Gaspard's son . . . Being a disfigured veteran didn't count now. The world had lasted longer than four years. The war was only an episode; it had no power to bury the past. On the contrary: the past had risen out of it. No. He wasn't here to get side-tracked by this friendship. The only response to Patrice's expression of feeling was that reluctant hand lying like a dead bird in his.

"I stopped to look at the pool," Séraphin explained.

"Ah! You saw how beautiful it is? It's my father's pride and joy. He walks round it every day! Even when he comes home late, he just has to go round his ornamental pool."

"It's a fine pool . . ." Séraphin said, as if in a dream.

"Come on! We eat at twelve here! My mother has already begun."

He led him into a well-lit hall that smelled of walnut liquor[13] and beeswax. He guided him through a glass-panelled door towards a more dimly-lit room, as the blinds had been drawn. The glow on the furniture and indoor plants was modest. In fact, the only thing that indicated opulence was a small amount of ostentatious crystal on the large table covered with a white cloth. The room led out into a long corridor with no doors. At the end of it, the last notes of a piano were just dying away.

"My mother!" Patrice said.

Séraphin saw a lady seated at the bottom end of the table. She was wearing mittens

13 Rough, home-brewed alcohol made from walnuts, also used to darken scratches etc. on furniture.

in spite of the warm autumn weather: all the better to tell the rosary that she always carried. She was smooth, neat and ageless. You concluded that she must be about fifty, but she had an air of lingering youth that life had never been able to penetrate. Fresh, baby-pink, with a complexion enhanced by the lightest of make-up, she looked at everyone with the same expression filled with eternal joys. Behind her, camouflaged under long stems of tradescantia that cascaded down from baskets hanging from hooks in the ceiling, a sort of grenadier stood on guard, tough as a tree trunk. The only way you knew she was a woman was because she was wearing a dress. This person followed Séraphin with ever watchful eyes, as she bit her lips with reserve and reprobation.

With a slight but imperious gesture the lady with the rosary held out a kind of notebook and pencil to Patrice, who rapidly wrote something in it.

"Ah? Oh! Are you Séraphin Monge? So it's you . . ."

The words formed by her thin, reedy voice skimmed her lips and flowed like a thin trickle of vinegar from a flask, toneless and expressionless. She extended the mittened hand still holding half the rosary, while she nodded her head and repeated:

"So, is that Séraphin Monge? If I'd known . . . If I'd ever thought . . ."

Patrice led Séraphin towards the window.

"Preserved in piety and deaf as a post. That's my mother."

"She's still with you . . ." Séraphin murmured.

"How do you mean, still? Why, she's only . . ."

He suddenly remembered that he was talking to the orphan of La Burlière.

"She's never heard me laugh or cry," he said. "When she was eighteen, she was looking after her father's cows under a walnut tree, up there at Chauffayer in the Champsaur.[14] Lightning struck so close to her that both her eardrums burst. My father married her, deaf as she was, because she had 'expectations'. Except, well! Those expectations took a long time in coming . . . The two uncles in question took a while to die."

He brought Séraphin back to the table laid for four people. He sat him in a chair of faded blue rep. It was a long table, meant for a large number of guests. At the upper end, facing Patrice's mother, a larger, strangely eloquent chair seemed to preside

14 *Champsaur:* a small region in Dauphiné.

over the table although there was no place set on the cloth in front of it.

"If your father's afraid of me," Séraphin said, "I shouldn't have come."

"What are you talking about? That'll be the day. Don't forget, I'm his *memento mori.* What's more, in business I'm as good as he is. And let me tell you, as far as that's concerned, being a mutilated veteran does wonders! A real guarantee of people's respect!"

Séraphin nodded and smiled, but he kept his eye on the empty chair at the end of the table, where he tried to imagine the figure of a man he didn't know and whom he had to kill.

"And don't forget: we have certain rights over them!"

At that moment Séraphin was looking at the setting opposite him, where no one as yet had come and sat down.

Suddenly a decisive step could be heard at the end of the corridor where the dying piano music had been coming from a short while ago. Someone was approaching, heels tapping the floor quickly and energetically. Someone suddenly entered from the corridor.

The person Séraphin saw was a war widow. In front of him, he saw a war widow with a supple body swathed in black silk. She was draped in black and white from head to foot. She was black and white like the chequered floor over which she moved. She had round, close-set eyes like a bird of prey, with deep green lights, the colour of the forest floor. A powerful but restrained anger seemed to find its way through every smallest chink in her reserve. This vision hit Séraphin full on. He reeled. He immediately understood — he who never understood anything — the unhappiness which inhabited that body. No one had ever taught him to stand up for a lady and he had never done so before. But in the presence of this one, he instinctively rose to his feet, almost knocking over his chair in his haste. He didn't know whether it was to pay homage to her or to put himself on his guard.

Patrice had stopped smoking and was watching the expression on Séraphin's face to gauge the effect her entrance had had on him.

"If he doesn't like her," he said to himself, "I won't be able to like him any longer."

"My sister Charmaine," he said. "Her husband was killed in October 1918. I don't know if you can imagine that?"

Charmaine's eyes were locked into those of Séraphin — who had not had time to look away. She held her hands slightly out from her body. She made a kind of quick, ironic curtsey, which failed to raise a smile from him. "Yes," she seemed to be saying, "see the state I'm reduced to . . ." The black and white of her dress was draped over the hollow of her stomach and spread up into a sheath that managed to highlight the shape of her barely covered breasts, in spite of all that severity.

Patrice was observing Séraphin. Having suddenly thrown Charmaine at the road mender, who would hardly have dared dream of someone like her, he expected that Séraphin's past, his fantasies and his infantile obsession would disintegrate with the impact. He had arranged this surprise for him because he loved them both and wanted, naively, for them to make each other happy.

Once the initial bedazzlement had passed, and he had been able to release his gaze from Charmaine's and turn it towards the tradescantias in the distance, Séraphin nonetheless noticed the young woman's hand stretched out towards him over the table. He put out his own, but all she received was that pitiful lump of flesh that was incapable of pressing the hand it received.

"Well," she said, "do sit down! I'd hate to see you grow any taller."

Her voice, which was a little nasal, lengthened the final syllables.

Séraphin slowly did as she asked, and lowered his head towards his plate.

At that moment, the female grenadier who had earlier been mounting guard near the deaf woman, stuck a boiling-hot casserole under his nose. She brushed him with it as she did so — rather awkwardly, he thought. She served him with a bad grace, and using the pretext of tipping the plate towards him, she gave a nasty snap of her jaws near his ear, as if she wanted to bite him.

"So!" Charmaine remarked. "Our dear father isn't here today?"

"Come now! You know very well," Patrice said, "he's in Marseille. It's Conchita's day."

"The chick's day!" Charmaine said mockingly. "How much do you think she'll get out of him to feather her nest this time?"

Patrice shrugged his shoulders.

"How should I know? In any case, not less than five thousand francs. I heard my father telephoning Hispano-Suiza to order a car and chauffeur. She must need it for her Spanish tour."

"Oh well . . ." Charmaine sighed. "I suppose it's all right as long as he doesn't get

186

her pregnant."

"Someone," Patrice said, "could well do it for him . . ."

"You don't mind," she said, "if we wash our dirty linen in front of you, do you?"

Séraphin didn't reply. He was looking out of the corner of his eye at the place where Gaspard Dupin usually sat and was not paying attention to anything but that empty chair.

"You'll have to get used to it," Patrice said. "He's a man who doesn't talk."

"I wouldn't mind that," Charmaine declared slowly, "if only he would look at me."

Feeling that someone was observing him, Séraphin turned round a little too quickly, for he met Charmaine's gaze again. Somewhere in the seaweed green of her eyes, he saw a gleam of surprise and alarm. He felt that the young woman's intuitive sense was circling around his secret, sniffing it out. He shrank in on himself, to give her the least possible hold on him, and forced himself to put up with his hostess's attention by bestowing his most placid smile on her.

"This chair that you seem to admire," Charmaine said gently, "I'll have you know it's a genuine Louis XV . . ."

She swallowed slowly and continued:

"There's another . . . Less faded than this

one . . . It's in my bedroom. I'll show it to you in a moment, if that would interest you . . ."

When, on emerging from the corridor, she had seen Séraphin get up, she had said to herself somewhat flippantly, "There's one I must have." But when she held that limp hand he offered everyone, she was disconcerted and the impulse died.

During the last few minutes, however, she had begun to realize that the road mender, who was so prodigiously strong and stupid — since she had no effect on him — was perhaps less straightforward than he seemed.

She noticed his hands that were never open, but closed in a fist as though always ready to strike — his hands that looked incongruous holding the silver fork and horn-handled knife.

"It would only take the smallest burst of anger," she said to herself, "for him to reduce them to pieces without knowing it, and throw them back on the table in shreds. And that silly smile he always has never shows in his eyes, never disturbs their gaze, never seems to move him. And besides, that look held no promise of anything when it met mine a moment ago. The only thing he succeeded in doing was to turn me cold, and yet . . ."

Sitting at the table opposite Séraphin, who was eating with very small, deliberate mouthfuls, Charmaine slowly, slowly took stock of the man in front of her. She had the impression that everything, right down to the label of "road mender" that he wore, combined to hide the real person, to camouflage him, like those insects whose colour automatically adapts to those of whatever surroundings they happen to be in.

The presence of this mystery, which for her was inseparable from love, filled her with a delicious excitement. But she didn't let Séraphin see the renewed interest he had inspired. On the contrary, she kept her disenchanted air and appeared to lose interest in him, treating him with the detached politeness she would use towards a friend of her brother's.

"Yes . . ." Patrice sighed. "Our father worries us a lot. You see, he's become besotted with a diva from Marseille who has delusions of grandeur. She's booked the Alcazar three times, and three times there were only fifty people there. My father paid for the lot. The worst thing is that it's become common knowledge, and now the diva finds all doors are open to her. You understand: now she has *credit*."

He dislocated the jigsaw puzzle of his face to swallow a mouthful of hare. When he had resumed his usual mocking expression, he added:

"He'll beggar us in the end . . ."

"And she's got a behind like a pear. He's making a laughing stock of our name."

"And he's neglecting the business . . ." Patrice pointed out.

"He's becoming a public danger for the family," Charmaine added.

Patrice turned towards his mother. She was explaining something by gesturing to the grenadier, who kept her eyes on Séraphin.

"It's true," he muttered, "that with her, his nights can't have been very jolly . . . Well! He got his sack of gold . . . But at what cost . . ."

"Did he have to wait . . . very long?" Séraphin asked.

"Yes he did. Well, at least five years. The two uncles died around 1900. I was four . . ."

"And I was one," Charmaine said.

"That's a long time . . ." Séraphin said.

Patrice suddenly stood up.

"Come with me. We'll have a cigarette in my studio."

He took Séraphin off towards a highly-

190

polished wooden staircase. He opened a door to a stuffy room that smelled of turpentine.

"Take a seat wherever you can," he said.

The only furniture in there was two sagging divans and a bulbous chest of drawers supporting an enormous marble head, with a fine nose, delicate chin and a dreamer's forehead accentuated by a laurel wreath. His eyes were white like someone blind from birth. Séraphin ran his hand over the marble. A profusion of canvases were scattered all around him, some turned to the wall, others hanging askew. All those that were visible were heads of beautiful men and women.

There was also a canvas on the easel, but back to front. One word was written on the stretcher in aniline, a single word: *Waiting.*

Patrice swiftly turned the picture around, while Séraphin sat concentrating on rolling a cigarette. When he raised his eyes he saw a three-quarter-face painting of a woman who seemed to be asleep, lying languidly with her head bent. It was cut diagonally into two triangles by an imaginary line. Half of her white body was framed in black, and half of her black body was against a white background. The painting was in black and white, with a highlight of sulphurous pink containing a shadowy sketch of an unbridled peasant festival.

"Don't you think?" Patrice said quietly, sitting down beside Séraphin. "Don't you think it's a sin, that superb body going to waste?"

"Is it your sister?" Séraphin asked.

"If you like," Patrice said. "It's an ensemble, but she's the basis of it. I intended to do a long study of war widows visiting tombs. It's been reduced to that, with the festival behind it."

As he spoke, he noticed that Séraphin was no longer listening to him. He was staring at a painting hanging crookedly on the wall next to the window. Séraphin had almost finished rolling his cigarette when his hands suddenly stopped moving. He got up, went over and stood still in front of the picture. It was the severed head of a man placed on a tray the colour of old gold. It had been painted in minute detail so that no one would find it attractive.

It was the head of a common man, with a vulgar expression and a heavy chin. His features had a look of male energy, moulded as they were by a roughly-hewn bone structure — something that would normally be considered a fault. It exuded the dogged determination of a fair-ground orator or a horse trader.

"That's my father," Patrice said. "Don't you think I look like him?"

He burst out with a loud laugh that wet his reconstructed lips.

Coming so closely face to face with one of his mother's three murderers had an extraordinary effect on Séraphin. He was riveted by that face illuminated with the lively colours of good living. He tried to imagine what the man looked like twenty-five years ago when he was young, in the kitchen at La Burlière. Perhaps then he'd been thin and scrawny.

Charmaine had come in through the open door behind them and was sizing up Séraphin's back as he stood there looking at her father's portrait. She also saw the black and white painting on the hazy pink sulphur background, which was her body as the artist imagined it, but all the more real and eloquent for the light and shade that cut it into two long triangles. To that melancholy evocation full of voluptuous ambiguity that Patrice had captured so well, this tongue-tied peasant — Oh!, he didn't have to say he was a road mender! It was written all over him! — preferred to look at the self-satisfied head of her profligate father who devoured wealth with the compulsive gluttony of someone who had known what it was like to be hungry.

Like the model in that painting, whom she despised, she thought she could despise Séraphin. But at that moment he turned around to face her, and once again their eyes met. Before he could look away from her, she saw the same gleam that had been there when he was gazing so intently at the empty chair. The placid smile immediately covered it again. But Charmaine was now on her guard, and an inexplicable uneasiness spoiled the desire she felt for the athlete.

Evening came. Séraphin said he had to leave, as he didn't have a light on his bicycle.

"I'll go with him to the gate," Charmaine said.

Patrice shook Séraphin's limp hand in both of his.

"Come back whenever you like," he said. "It does me good to see you. I have no friends. I don't want any. You understand . . . seeing them come . . . telling me they've got married . . . and saying, "We'd love to have invited you, but you understand . . ."

He gave that laugh that always sounded unnatural.

"I understand all right! My face! In those

days when joy is unconfined . . . ! Definitely not! No friends! With you at least, I don't have to worry about that!"

"No," Séraphin said, "with me, you don't have to worry."

As they went downstairs together with Charmaine preceding them, Patrice held him back by the arm.

"By the way . . . That girl, you know, the one I saw . . . One Sunday at La Burlière . . ."

"Which girl?"

"You know!" Patrice hung his head as though confessing a misdemeanour. "The one who said hello to me . . . The one who smiled at me. The one I call the Persian."

"Oh! Yes," Séraphin said. "That's Rose Sépulcre."

"Do you still see her?"

"I bump into her sometimes . . ." Séraphin said, not forgetting that she was the daughter of another murderer.

"If you happen to see her, tell her . . ."

Patrice stopped short. They had reached the bottom of the staircase. They could see both their reflections in a pier glass. Patrice gave one of his harsh laughs.

"Tell her nothing at all!" he exclaimed, "Nothing at all! What on earth could you say to her?"

Séraphin turned away from him and went to fetch his bike at the foot of the tree. Charmaine was waiting for him and began walking beside him. Patrice watched them move away. He would like to have painted the two of them receding in the perspective of the avenue: one in his velvet cast-offs and the blue floral shirt, and the other in her black and white domino costume, both in step, timidly but so eloquently silent. And yet, at the end of the avenue they would separate. Séraphin would extend his limp hand to Charmaine, and Charmaine would come back crestfallen. And they would each have taken another step towards old age.

The evening took a long time to fall, to settle over the earth. There must have been heavy storms over the high valleys between the Ubaye and the Clarée, for the pink-tipped clouds quickly spread out from the mountains like a bouquet that had been held together for too long. You could hear the sound of the Durance in the mistral, the sound the river makes when it starts to rise.

"So there's a Rose Sépulcre in your life?" asked Charmaine.

"No," said Séraphin, "there's no one in my life."

When they reached the spindle-trees that hid the ornamental pool, she went ahead of him towards the fountain wall with the grinning masks. She leaned over to drink from the spout and he looked away, as he found it difficult to look at her in that position. She stood up and wiped her mouth with the back of her hand.

"How much longer," she said, "are you going to avoid paying any attention to me?"

"But . . ." Séraphin said, taken aback, "I'm a road mender . . ."

"What of it? What does that mean? An excuse to have no life? You seem to look for excuses."

She quickly put her hand into the front of her low-cut dress and brought out a lace handkerchief, which she then unfolded. A shining key lay in it, as if in a casket.

"Take it!" Charmaine ordered. "At the end of the pergola, between the garage and the winter garden, there are some stone steps and a narrow door. Open it with this key. It gives on to the main corridor. My bedroom . . . is the first door on the right. I'll leave it ajar and the night-light on. I'll wait for you," she said, "for as long as it takes."

Séraphin stared at the key and the soft flesh rising from the top of her dress.

"Well!" Charmaine exclaimed impatiently. "What are you waiting for?"

She turned around and bent over the edge of the pool in the same submissive yet provocative pose as when she was drinking from the grotesque mask in the fountain. She studied the couple they made in the mirror-like surface of the water. But, although he was there, with his thick hair, his wide ears, his high cheekbones and his flute-player's cheeks, she had the distinct impression that she was alone in the reflection.

"Come now," she said, "who's to stop us indulging in a little nostalgia? Let's look at ourselves in the water . . . Don't you know that if we can still see ourselves in it thirty years from now, we'll have all the regrets in the world?"

"I know," said Séraphin in a whisper.

He put out his limp hand towards the key hanging from Charmaine's fingers, which she was no longer holding out to him. He gently took it, turned around and left.

It was night when he got back to Peyruis. The bass voice of a dance-band trombone and the feminine voice of a shrill accordion could be heard in the distance. Lights were travelling quickly down all the roads — people rushing to enjoy themselves.

Séraphin went down the deserted street where goats bleated behind dilapidated barn doors. He dragged his feet as though he

198

were carrying a heavy burden. The misery of not being able to live like everyone else overwhelmed him.

He pushed open his door. Like everyone here, he left it open when he went out. As soon as he entered the kitchen, he realized that someone had been there.

Every evening when he came home, he opened the sugar box, as if he feared he might forget. He would take out the three sheets of stamped paper and avidly reread the three names: Gaspard Dupin, Didon Sépulcre, Célestat Dormeur. He then folded them up again, always in the same order: the order in which he had found them; the order in which he had decided to do away with them.

Now that night, he noticed that they were in a different order. Gaspard Dupin was on the bottom, Didon Sépulcre on top and Célestat Dormeur in the middle . . . Someone had come there. Someone had found out about those papers . . . Séraphin gave the louis in the tin a gentle shake. They made their usual full, rich sound. No. Judging by their weight and volume, they were apparently all there. Besides, if someone had come to take them, he would have taken them all.

Séraphin stood up, holding the tin tightly in both hands. He sensed the presence of someone else who was not interested in the louis; someone who had walked slowly and confidently around the kitchen, the scullery and the adjoining bedroom. He sensed it and yet no trace of a smell remained. What's more, that presence remained there all night. The memory of it hung, immaterial, but thick and heavy, over the bedroom and kitchen.

Séraphin had forgotten Charmaine and happiness. He was on the watch for the frightful dream that would come and punish him for wanting to leave the strait and narrow. But he watched in vain. This time he was not visited. His conscience remained as silent as the Peyruis streets below the ring of the fountain.

All night long he had the impression that someone was at his bedside, watching over him as he slept.

X

When Gaspard Dupin came home that night, well after Séraphin's departure, a dilapidated pick-up truck on four worn tyres was following slowly in the wake of his Hudson Terraplane, which moved as silently as a ship on the ocean. Four enormous red-eyed dogs, their long tongues hanging out, ceaselessly scanned their surroundings from behind its rattling rails.

Gaspard stopped the car with its lights still on in front of the paddock. He had bought Pontradieu for three reasons: firstly, the ornamental pool that gave him the feeling of wearing lace cuffs like an aristocrat; the little pavilion, for its wind rose showing all the points and degrees of the compass; and the paddock. This fabulous word "paddock" had grown to such proportions in his mind that it had grown to represent a complete ideal image of England. Throughout his childhood he'd heard his father say it when he came to shoe the "Messieurs' " horses.

These "Messieurs", who hadn't been addressed as "Count" for a long time now, in the end had only one son, after ten prolific centuries, and he got killed in '14 — just out of Saint-Cyr military college — in plumed hat and white gloves. His relatives, left empty-handed, died off of grief or uselessness during that interminable war when Gaspard's family made so much money.

Gaspard had got the property for a song after four auctions without a bidder.

That evening he had some difficulty getting out of his car. It had been a long time since he'd been thin. Through the high iron grille gate, the copper mangers of four empty stalls at the bottom of the paddock shone in the headlights. Gaspard was pleased to see that his instructions to spread straw in the boxes had been carried out.

"It'll be perfect," he said rubbing his hands.

He got out with that certain formality which he had acquired along with corpulence and political ambition. Moreover, ever since he'd become the master of it, he never came back to Pontradieu without the feeling of trampling a beaten animal underfoot.

He turned away and signalled. The pick-up truck came and parked in front of him. A young man got out — all fat torso and waddling short legs. He bowed his large soft belly to the ground before Gaspard.

"Put them in there," Gaspard said pointing to the paddock.

"Is it solid?" the little man asked.

"They used to keep stallions there."

"Right."

Taking four leather leads from his belt, he climbed on the platform of the vehicle and disappeared among the tangled bodies of the four impatient animals. He let down the railing and jumped to the ground, holding the four leads in one hand.

Gaspard had undone the bolt on the outside of the paddock gate and was pushing back the leaf of the door. The rusty hinges made a loud, harsh, grating noise that excited the animals who growled in the most nervous, threatening way. They moved forward sniffing the ground, pulling on their taut leads. The little man went into the enclosure with them, to let them off their leads. He came out and firmly bolted the gate.

"And remember, most important of all!" he said. "Feed them yourself every evening. Because . . . If you don't . . . they won't recognize you, *not even you!*"

He deferentially whipped off his cap and put out his hand.

Gaspard counted the notes as he took them from his wallet and slapped them into the man's palm. He didn't bother saying good evening, but simply nodded in his direction. The man climbed back on to his seat and started up the engine again. Gaspard was left alone in front of his car. He turned off the headlights.

The light over the flight of steps was on and Patrice, who had come to see what the noise was about, was waiting for his father at the top.

Gaspard was walking with his head down, preoccupied, giving the odd sidelong glance at the dark corners of the pergola. Patrice had never known him to move in any other way than in this watchful, circumspect manner, always on the alert like a hunter or a hunted animal.

He watched him approach with a critical eye, without the least indulgence. His father wore a monocle, leggings, leather hat and trousers, but to no avail: the blacksmith's voice, which has to shout to make itself heard over the din in the forge, always betrayed his origins. And his hands had ugly raised calluses that he didn't bother to trim back.

"You're asking for trouble . . ." Patrice told him when his father was in earshot. "Those animals are as dangerous as loaded guns. They can go off at anyone . . ."

"That's just it! I want them to be dangerous and I want people to know it!"

He took a cigar from its case and lit it.

"I've been thinking about it for a long time. I've wanted them for a long time. Conchita's father breeds them. I've known them since they were pups. A simple look or a gesture, and they obey me straight away!"

He was in raptures.

"Can you hear them? They're dobermanns from America. They don't bark, they growl. Those dogs can kill a man in complete silence."

"Kill!" Patrice said scornfully. "Have you any idea what it means to kill someone?"

Gaspard took his cigar out of his mouth and turned around as though he'd been stung. At that moment he saw Patrice's disfigured face in the full light of the lamp, and said nothing. The nightmare that this face so perfectly represented always had the power to silence him.

His thoughts, however, were rapidly taking another turn. He looked down at the steps he had just climbed. He peered into the dimly-lit hall behind him through the door that Patrice had left ajar. He raised his eyes to the tops of the trees from which the moon would soon emerge. His attention then centred on the weather vane that creaked as it turned this way and that, like a warning.

"Did he come . . ." he whispered.

"Who?" Patrice asked.

"The road mender."

"Yes. If it's Séraphin Monge you mean, yes. That's right. He came. I invited him to lunch. I introduced him to Charmaine."

"I can sense him . . ." Gaspard said.

"But . . . You've never seen him, have you?"

Gaspard looked at his son suspiciously.

"I don't need to see him," he said, "I can feel where he's been . . ."

"How can you have such a deep dislike for someone you don't know?"

Gaspard removed his fancy monocle, which made his eye tired, and slipped it into his fob pocket.

"He gives . . . a bad example."

"Oh! Because you think you give a good one?"

"Ah! Is that what you resent so much?"

206

Patrice shrugged his shoulders.

"I don't resent anyone any more. No. I like to observe you. You amuse me!"

"I wonder what it is you hold against me?"

"You don't suffer."

"What would you know about it? Everyone suffers what and how he can."

He leaned on the balustrade with his back to his son.

"People think that men always stay the same," he said quietly. "We're judged on what we've been. And yet, we change so much."

He suddenly turned to face Patrice.

"Has your road mender finished demolishing his house?"

"From top to bottom. All he needs to do now is to spread salt over it, and I think he'll do it. He's a very unhappy man. You should pity him."

"Unhappy people," Gaspard said with deep conviction, "the Good Lord hasn't made them all . . ."

He looked anxiously in the direction of the paddock, where the dobermanns were growling plaintively.

"I don't think I'll take my walk around the pool this evening . . ." he said. "But," he added, as though someone had defied him to do it, "I'll start again tomorrow!"

He heard a kind of whistling sound behind him. It was the grenadier, who had asthma and made her presence known in that way. Standing flat against the wall in the hall like a grandfather clock, the poor woman was waiting for her master so that she could give him her report on the eventful day.

"You'd better hurry up and go to her, or she'll choke on her own spleen."

"She loves me," Gaspard said, very pleased with himself. "She'd throw herself into the fire for me."

"Yes," Patrice said, "and more than that — she'd throw others in it."

Turning his back on his father, he went down the stone staircase and walked towards the paddock. The moment they heard him, the four beasts stood up side by side against the grille without making a sound. Standing on their hind legs they were a head taller than Patrice. Their lolling tongues and red eyes made you think of flames. Under the indirect light of the lamp on the staircase, their smooth short coats took on the aubergine colour of a lamprey. A chill went down Patrice's spine as he looked at them, ever-watchful and panting. He said later that he didn't know what had stopped him from getting his gun and shooting them that night. But the fact is that he went away to escape the eager, greedy look in their eyes.

From the next day onwards, Gaspard kept his word. He began walking in the park again. Only now he left the house armed, his gun across his shoulder. Under the cartridge-pouch, he was strapped into a back belt made of Cordovan leather as wide as a saddle with a large snap hook riveted into it. He would walk to the paddock, always with some treat in his hands. He attached a couple of dogs firmly to his waist by clipping the hooks on the leads into the hook on his belt. In this manner, bristling with defences like a tank, he went on patrol in the sombre park.

He walked under the pergola, through the labyrinth, the Chinese pavilion, and the formal rose garden that had disappeared under the three-metre high briar rose bushes. He came out into the night under the dense cedar grove that surrounded the ballerina-shaped box bushes set out formally in alternate rows. In front of their round moon-shaped heads, the dobermanns always made a stop, excited at the idea of possible prey. Gaspard finished his walk with two circuits around the coping of the ornamental pool. It was there that he felt most expansive, strutting along, imagining himself dressed in a satin waistcoat with blue braid.

His itinerary followed a set route like a king's promenade. He never departed from it by a single step.

He had previously done it without a care in the world, his hands in his pockets, and his head full of ways to make the place more beautiful and more splendid. That's the way it had been until that autumn day when he had learned that over there in Lurs, on the other side of the Durance, at a place called La Burlière, a man called Séraphin Monge was knocking his house down. From that moment on, fear took hold of him and wouldn't let him go. Now his shoulders were hunched and he was scared stiff, expecting something, but he didn't know exactly what. He would wake up at night with a start as he lay beside his deaf wife (who immediately reached for her rosary), and grab the gun which he kept within reach.

This anxiety reached its peak when his son became so obsessed with Séraphin Monge, as though demolishing one's house was a heroic exploit. From that moment, he thought the danger was coming closer, and he got the idea of adding the savage dogs to the reassurance already afforded by his gun. Besides, Conchita's father had been begging him to take them off his hands for six months now.

However, from the second night, the added protection of the dogs ceased to be of any use.

From that night on, the weather vane that had turned this way and that for so many weeks suddenly stopped creaking. The wind immobilized it on the north–south axis, where it stayed, as stiff and straight as an arrow.

The *montagnière* began to blow. It's the wind that people mistake for the mistral, except that it comes from the north-east and doesn't drop during the night. During the whole time it rages over the countryside, it's difficult to think of anything else. It doesn't blow in gusts, but in a steady stream, like a river.

The people who live on the plain are the only ones who can really tell you about it. If they have three plane trees in front of their farm, they have to resign themselves to letting them take over, to hearing no other sound but them and to putting off all serious conversation. All the doors have slammed already.

If you are forced to walk into it, your eyes water and the tears are whipped from your cheeks. After that, the only way you can see is by blinking constantly. You see double: two postmen arriving on their bicycles, their clothes inflated like balloons, and with as many arms as an Asian goddess.

The shepherds — who only believe in the force of nature when it suits them — keep on working. Then you see flocks in the stubble, forming a spiral with the sheep head to tail, refusing to eat, refusing to drink, refusing to go forward or backward. The dogs take it more philosophically: they give up and lie down. They look up at the shepherd, asking him what to do. He doesn't know what to do, and shakes his fist at the wind, blames God Almighty, kicks the dogs unmercifully, and finally just stands there alone with his eyes streaming, a perfect picture of futility in front of a flock that will obey no one or nothing but the elements.

And what's more, when that wind blows in autumn, it creeps through the loose joins in old dry doors and right down into the black depths of the cellars. Then the wine itself, at the bottom of any vessels that haven't been topped up, seems to complain about it like a sour old man.

By the end of the third day, it beats good and bad alike into submission. It casts down the proud, but doesn't raise the humble.

Without that wind, perhaps nothing would

have happened.

Pontradieu had become the hub of all this tumult. Seven hundred and fifty trees grew in the grounds, without taking into account the cedars that grew in wild profusion at its boundaries. Most of them were more than thirty metres high, as their roots went down deep into the subterranean river that is a counterpart of the Durance. The *montagnière* roared through the trees as though they were an organ case, crashing its thundering chords, growing louder and louder. All nature's fury was unleashed in this continuous noise, which flooded the ears and locked everyone within themselves.

When Gaspard went on his rounds at dusk, the wind leapt at his face, wrapping around it close and clinging like a wet shroud. It wouldn't let him go, dancing around him with the snapping sound of a sail in a storm. It was like a butterfly net that just missed him every time. It played on his nerves all the way to the paddock, where he was going to fetch the dobermanns.

As soon as the *montagnière* had risen, the dogs had begun to screech like night birds, screeching so loudly that they couldn't hear each other, and so wildly that their enormous mouths went dry. Finally, resigned to the loss of hearing and smell, and bereft of their usual vigilance and hope of prey, they lay sprawled morosely on the straw.

The only thing that got them up, and then reluctantly, was the crack of the stick Gaspard was wielding. Their useless ears drooped like floppy pieces of felt. They no longer pricked up at the slightest warning sound, for there weren't any. The wind was the only sound to be heard.

Gaspard pulled two of them out — never the same two — and attached them securely to the snap hook on his belt. He peered at the trees in the moonlight. He said, "Son of a bitch!" very distinctly, and set out on his way.

He quickly realized that the gardens were out of his control and could defy him. He was no longer happy to carry his gun over his shoulder, so did his rounds with it by his side, with his finger on the trigger.

At the same time as he realized that he could be ambushed, someone else realized it too. It was the grenadier who decided to cover him, as she was also armed with an old blunderbuss that she had brought down from Le Champsaur as her only dowry, and which she polished like a wardrobe. From the second night onwards, when he sud-

214

denly turned round, feeling someone watching him, there was the silhouette of his trusty follower creeping from tree to tree. He shouted things to her that he couldn't hear himself. He rushed towards her with the dogs and could only finally get rid of her by kicking her out of the way. It was all right for him to be afraid, but he would not allow anyone else to be afraid for him.

It was in this wind that Séraphin began to watch his victim. He thought he had seized the key Charmaine held out to him because he felt something for her. Yet, in reality, if he had taken it — and perhaps he didn't realize this himself — it was to justify his presence at Pontradieu at any time of the day or night. He never forgot that Gaspard Dupin was *only one* of the La Burlière murderers, and that he must not be found out until he had punished all three.

He came on his bicycle, which he left in a ditch at the foot of a culvert. One day he found another lying against the grass in the same ditch. It was older than his and had a bag rack. He'd have thought it had been abandoned, had he not seen the current year's registration plaque on the bar. He didn't pay much attention to it, and hid his own bicycle further away.

From a distance, at dusk, he could see the battalion of black trees among the vines and open fields. The plain bristled with serried ranks of tree trunks standing straight like the pikes of an ancient army. Choosing well-hidden paths, he only ever took the longest routes with the thickest vegetation. He crept into the swaying thickets, and immediately he too was at the mercy of the wind. But this is where his war experience stood him in good stead. He knew that, at ground level, even the deafening noise of a barrage of fire couldn't block out the sound of the hurried steps of the opposing company mounting an attack. And so he immediately threw himself to the ground, crawling through the nettles, over grass full of sharp thistles. He made his way along the paths that led to the house, camouflaged behind the winter-loving giant saxifrages.

After three days, he knew Gaspard's set itinerary, from leaving the paddock to arriving at the pool. It was by the edge of this pool that he saw him for the first time. While he was crouching against the wind in the marsh reeds between the poplars, Gaspard suddenly emerged from between two spindle-trees into the moonlight in front of him. Séraphin saw a common-looking man, short, very heavily built, and from the way he was moving, very much on his guard. Preceded by his huge hounds, he was walking with his rolling gait along the rim of the pool. His gun was by his side, ready to fire. His moustache and the arch of his eyebrows were visible in the shadow of his wide-brimmed hat. Séraphin could see that he was pale with fear. Gaspard went around the mirror surface of the water twice before disappearing behind the spindle-trees.

Séraphin was not surprised that he felt no hatred for this man. During his sleepless nights, he had forged his soul into that of a dispenser of justice. He was the mere instrument of a poor victim. He had to obey her on pain of hearing the rustling of dead leaves on the surface of the washing trough, where perhaps the soul of that poor dead mother still remained; on pain of seeing her walk towards him, intent on putting his hands around her breasts with those last drops of milk she meant for him twenty-five years ago.

Nor did he wonder how he was going to get rid of a man who was armed and protected by two enormous dogs. That evening, he crawled up to the edge of the pool on the side that was in the deep shade of the poplars. He ran his hand back and forth over the white marble to make sure that it was smooth and without any rough patches. He became convinced that it should all take place there.

On the fourth day, the *montagnière* reached its height. Its harsh moaning filled your mind with dismal memories. The trees cracked like masts on a ship. On the splintered branches that hung limply like broken wings, the empty bird's nests broke up bit by bit and blew away.

That evening, Séraphin was scouring the dark areas, either on his stomach or bent double. He found himself in front of the Chinese pavilion, which seemed to him a good place to lie in wait. Completely hidden by creeper, this elegant caprice of some idle nineteenth-century country squire gleamed in the moonlight. It was so dark within its walls of thick green vegetation that Séraphin hesitated to venture in. He hadn't yet found out exactly where the master of Pontradieu was at this time. He could very well be there, as going through this arbour was part of his itinerary.

Very cautiously, Séraphin went through the entrance the gardener cut in the Virginia creeper every year. He blindly took several steps into the shadows. Through a similar opening opposite the one he had entered, he could see the rose bushes bending and rustling in the moonlight as the wind whipped around the pergola.

At that moment, a light hand descended on his shoulder. He had expected a blow, not a caress. The ghost that haunted him was always so quick to persecute him, that at the touch of the hand that stroked him so gently, he recoiled in panic and confusion. He stepped back so suddenly that he bumped into something, stumbled, tried to grab hold of it, and finally fell on to a bench.

The wind made the thick leaves of the creeper sound like an orchestra of castanets to Séraphin.

"Who is it?" he whispered.

"Who could it be?"

He recognized Charmaine's voice in his ear.

"Surely you haven't forgotten me completely?"

"It's very dark."

"Yes, but my perfume is the same."

"The wind blows it away."

"The wind blows everything away. Except us. Why didn't you dare come in? I've been looking for you everywhere."

"You've been looking for me everywhere?" Séraphin said to gain time.

"Yes. All around the grounds. I even

thought I saw you crossing a ray of moon-light. I even called out to you . . . But . . . No doubt it was the wind . . ."

"It wasn't me," Séraphin said.

He didn't add, "There's no way you'd have seen me."

"It must have been your father . . . or your brother," he added hurriedly.

"No . . ." Charmaine said after thinking for a moment. "Neither of them. But it's not important since you're here. And if the perfume I wear doesn't reach you, that's probably because I'm too far away."

Séraphin hadn't had the presence of mind to get up while they were speaking. He felt her sit down on his knees and put her arms tightly around his body. Then he felt two breasts pressing against his chest, which was bare under his open shirt; two breasts searching for the points of his.

He became like a stone statue, yet a surge of heat penetrated every part of him. With his fists clenched and eyes closed, he tried to prepare himself for the imminent attack by the vision lodged in a dark recess of his mind — that vision which would use this new sensation to change Charmaine's breasts into two cold ones with milky nipples. He could see them already taking their beautiful but ghostly shape in the dark.

He squirmed like a worm in Charmaine's embrace, knowing that the vision would vanish as soon as desire left him.

"To see you . . ." he finally managed to say.

Charmaine stood up again.

"Ah! That's it . . . To see me . . . You'd like to see me? And I'd like to see you . . . to look at you . . . Come with me!"

She pulled him to his feet almost by sheer force of will. She took him through the door that was opened by the key she had given him. And without letting go of his wrist, which she gripped like a vice, she brought him into her bedroom.

"Wait!" she said.

The room was dark. The wind blew here too, howling down the chimney of a cold fireplace. Charmaine put the light on. Séraphin turned towards the lamp. It was a glass statuette of a humbly kneeling figure topped with a blush pink shade, and it stood on the grand piano. Séraphin also saw a writing desk, a high country-style bed in heavy solid walnut. It looked like a wedding present, which was probably the case. He saw women's things through a half-open wardrobe. He saw books spread over a large carpet in front of the empty fireplace where the wind came down in gusts. Cushions scattered over the carpet indicated that someone often lay there on the floor. A perfume floated over the charming room, the same no doubt as the beautiful widow wore. The word "happiness" had never had such meaning for Séraphin as he stood surrounded by these lovely things. Later, much later, when he was all alone, deep in the mountain forests, determined to remain silent at all costs, he would remember these details — all the time — and they would break his heart.

He was alone with this woman in a room like none he had ever known, he, Séraphin Monge, the road mender. But he was also alone with a truth that had preceded it, a truth that he could not share with her. Oh! If only he could say to her, "Like you, my mother wants to make love to me. My mother, who has been dead for twenty-five years! Your father cut her throat! That's why she stops me from coming near you! That's why she takes your place. You wanted the truth? Well, there it is!"

For that was what he sincerely believed to be the truth.

Charmaine followed the hunted, trapped look Séraphin gave everything and everybody, except her. The enigma that she had sensed in him from the first day she met him excited her curiosity.

"I'll give it whatever time it takes," she thought, "I'm not counting on it happening tonight . . ."

"Well," she said gently, "you wanted to see me . . . Look at me then . . ."

On this occasion, she was wearing a dress in a black and white diamond pattern that can only be worn by women who know they have the right figure and eye-colour to carry it off. But had he even noticed the colour of her eyes?

Surrounded by so many sensual vibrations that emanated from the objects she touched every day, Séraphin stood there awkwardly, avoiding contact with her eyes. The panic at finding himself being haunted by his visions again terrified him. Until then he had managed to control them just in time, but here he was caught. His presence in the grounds at ten o'clock at night could only be explained if he was there for Charmaine. As she had been looking for him, there was no further obstacle between them.

"Would you prefer . . ."

She took a step towards him where he was still standing between the fireplace and the piano, a few paces away from the door that she had closed behind him. She repeated:

"Would you prefer . . . to watch me

undress? To do it yourself? Or should I go over there and do it?"

She had the feeling that she was striking the wrong note and saying the wrong words. She had never before found herself faced with a man who just stood there and did nothing — a man she had taken up to her own bedroom. She nodded in the direction of the bathroom door that had been left half open.

"Over there," Séraphin said.

She obeyed him, but just before leaving the room she turned to him.

"You won't make your escape while I'm out of the room," she said, "will you?"

"No . . . Why would I do that? No, of course not . . ."

He blushed at the idea that she had read his mind so well, for that was exactly what his instinct urged him to do: rush outside as soon as she disappeared, run to get his bicycle, and then pedal like fury to Peyruis four kilometres away. And then get into bed, pull the bedclothes around him, wait for the panic to subside and try to forget . . .

But, no matter how far she was from suspecting the truth, he mustn't give her any cause to think, "So he wasn't in the pavilion because of me. Well, what was he doing there? Why was he prowling round our grounds so far from home, and on a work day?"

When he killed Gaspard, a thought like that could be fatal to him. No. If he wanted to see full justice done, he would have to bear anything: make love to Charmaine until she became the go-between for Girarde. And find in that embrace the strength to bear what that ghost was intent on telling him through another's mouth. Still, he was tense with apprehension as he prepared himself for that confrontation.

He didn't hear Charmaine slip out of the bathroom. She just seemed to appear before him. Her body, which had been confined by the lines of her dress, however delightful it was, now seemed to occupy more space in the room, as if it had been a bud that had suddenly burst open.

He stood where he was, his arms hanging by his sides, his fists clenched. At the sight of Charmaine materializing in front of him naked, his cock had suddenly come to life and was hurting him because of his tight clothes.

Charmaine observed this result with a secret smile. She sat down on the bed, then stretched out languidly on the red counterpane, which outlined all the curves of her body. She whispered to him, but from where he was standing, he could scarcely hear her because of the wind in the open fireplace.

"Look," she said, "look what your timidity makes me tell you . . . I like making love to myself . . . yes, nearly as much as I like being made love to. There! Are you satisfied? Did you want to know the mysteries of woman? Well, see . . . Look at me . . . Take a good look . . . Without turning your eyes away . . . Without turning your eyes away . . ."

Her long pianist's fingers lightly brushed over the black triangle, like a fleece with tight curls as regular as though they had been knitted, which set off the softly rounded shield of her belly.

Silently, his eyes fixed on her hand, Séraphin took a step on to the carpet, then two, then three. He towered over Charmaine, standing there in his faded shirt, solid and heavy as a tree trunk. She watched him through almost closed eyelids, filled with the powerful desire that sharpened all her senses. Suddenly, as if she could wait no longer, she placed her free hand on his cock standing erect as a column. But the difference between this flagrant proof of desire and the detached, gentle expression on the uncertain features of that face so far above her, disconcerted her and slowly chilled the pleasure of her anticipation. She felt more and more uneasy, as though she was on the edge of a mystery still deeper than the one she thought she had detected in him.

However, she could see that the man's knees were giving way, and he may even have begun to lean over the body that was so obviously hungry for him.

At that moment, the sharp whine of two shots, one immediately after the other, pierced the noise of the wind, pierced the walls, pierced the cocoon of perverse delight that enclosed the prospective lovers.

"Patrice!" Charmaine screamed.

She sat up, then ran over to Séraphin who had taken a few steps back. She stood there panting with her two hands over her bare breasts.

"Patrice!" she said again.

The sound of the gunshots had rung out in his spinning head like the syllables of that name. She had screamed when she heard it, as she had expected the worst with Patrice for some time. He spent too much time looking in all the mirrors within reach. She was sure that one day he would no longer be able to bear that harlequin's face drawn by a cubist painter, and that he would blow his head off.

"Patrice!" she whispered.

Séraphin found her at his side dressed again in a flash before he had even moved. All temptation between them had disappeared like smoke.

"It came from outside," Séraphin whispered.

That very moment two more shots rang out. Charmaine rushed into the corridor, out the door and down the flight of narrow stone steps. Lights could be seen far off in the direction of the farm, darting about, crossing, flashing in the moonlight and in the dark. Charmaine sped off towards them like a startled animal. She had forgotten Séraphin. The anguish she felt took her over completely. Patrice . . . Patrice and she — isolated by their mother's deafness — had been close, devoted accomplices since childhood. Patrice . . . His face was so handsome . . . He looked like a romantic adolescent, gazing with his chin in his hands into the distance at the clouds on the hills, the villages that always seemed new and inviting in the sunlight, the pale gash of the Durance cutting through the valley. Patrice, who used to nod his handsome head in that direction and say to her, "That's everything I love. I have absolutely no curiosity about the rest of the world. I love only that and

228

you, when you are playing your piano."
Gentle, peace-loving Patrice, whose soul
was killed in the war.

She ran and ran towards the lights in the
distance that were now converging, coming
from the farm. The dogs were growling furiously behind the paddock fence.

Séraphin should have made his escape and
not shown himself, but Patrice's name that
she kept repeating so breathlessly made him
follow after Charmaine.

The lights were now concentrated around
the pool. Straight away they saw Patrice in
silhouette, standing on the rim. He was
holding a gun in his right hand.

"Oh God!" Charmaine whispered. She
sank exhausted against Séraphin, trembling
violently, like a dying bird. She said over
and over again like a chant. "Thank you,
God . . . Thank you, God . . ."

The wind had miraculously fallen. It was
spending the last of its strength so high up
in the trees that it now only sounded like a
sigh of regret.

XI

At nine o'clock on the same evening, when the squall was at its height, Gaspard Dupin went out of the paddock with his gun lowered and two dogs attached to his belt. He cursed the wind, jammed his hat on his head and strode, head down, along the paths in the grounds. His stomach was tight with fear, but he was also furiously angry.

"Bloody wind!" he said to himself. "These are *my* gardens, for God's sake! And the first person I find there, I'll let my dogs have a go at him!"

But for all his blustering vulgarity, he couldn't fool himself that he was on the right side of justice. Actually, it was a rather pathetic means of dispelling the dreadful images that been haunting his mind recently — images that he thought were buried deep within him forever. The sudden intrusion of the road mender into his life had resurrected them from their pit, as new and fresh as ever, and richly embellished with frightening detail.

He was well aware that fear had never left him since the distant event that caused those bad memories, even when he wore the gown of a judge in the business tribunal, even in the midst of all his prosperity, even during the wild nights he spent with Conchita. Scared all the time . . . Scared as a rabbit.

Oh! If only there hadn't been that wind that took away the dogs' hearing and sense of smell. The army of trees and bushes on each side of the paths thrashed about in the air, imitating every fearful thing that his mind might conjure up.

He reached the pool, relieved to be in the moonlight, in a space open enough to avoid being taken by surprise.

"I'll have to get the overflow outlet raised," he said to himself. He had just noticed once again that when they had restored the marble coping, pillaged through the centuries, they had set the outlet holes too low, and because of that the water level was down forty centimetres from the top.

Thinking about this practical building problem settled him down. He could see himself pointing to everything that had to be done, standing in front of the contractor, who was listening cap in hand. He gave his masterpiece a self-satisfied look. The sight of that ornamental pool always had the power to buck him up.

He pulled on the dogs' leads. He had forgotten his fear, basking in the warm glow of pride. A movement in the bushes, different from the general direction of the wind, revived it immediately. He turned, with his gun aimed and the dogs facing the suspicious waving of the leaves. But no, it was nothing but the wind, playing at blowing foliage in different directions deep in the tangled thickets.

Gaspard ventured on to the wide rim of the pool, his dogs close to his legs. Yes, he would definitely have to raise the overflow outlet to get a mirror-like surface in all weathers.

The wind beat like surf against the coping, blowing the water the wrong way and pushing the continuous jets that flowed from the spouts back into the grotesque masks. This made the gods shed tears down every stone wrinkle, and these tears oozing over their frozen smiles seemed sinister in the moonlight.

Gaspard walked on with blasé nonchalance. Now that he was in the wide space that separated him from the trees, the fear in his belly was only a small knot, just enough to keep him on his guard. He had even allowed himself the luxury of lighting a cigar (with great difficulty), which he smoked with an arrogant air. He felt at last like a man who has richly deserved his rest.

That was the mood he was in as he walked half-way round the pool: uneasily self-important, with his haughty dogs panting by his side in the vain hope of prey, and his gun ready for anything.

He had just taken a voluptuous puff of his cigar when his foot slipped. Did his foot slip? Did the ground give way under his feet? Who knows? The fact is that he plunged into the water with the full weight of his ninety kilos, his arms uselessly flailing the air. The gun fell from his hand and sank to the bottom. As he fell he pulled the two dogs with him. Besides, their feet had also slipped and they were off-balance. They all hit the water with an enormous splash that was doubtless only heard by the wind.

Although he knew very well that the homing of the wind in the trees would cover his cries for help, he instinctively called out nonetheless. In spite of the height of the coping in relation to the water level, he tried to get a hold on the edge and just missed, because with one jerk the dogs pulled him away from it. They could swim, but as nature had not endowed them with the instincts of a Newfoundland, they each pulled in different directions trying to reach dry land. Gaspard couldn't swim, and what is more he knew that the bottom was two metres fifty below him from one side of the pool to the other, and that the pool itself, of which he was so proud, was forty metres long and twenty wide.

The water came from a hollow in the mountains, distilled high up in a flint deposit and filtered through layers of clay shaped by the movement of the tectonic plates. It then went deep down under the bed of the Durance, re-emerging 600 metres away from here in an osier bed, where it had been harnessed, having lost none of its original coldness.

Now Gaspard realized, once he was in it, that this water he'd taken such pains to redirect into his pool, this water with its charming mirror surface, had a life of its own that was not meant for man's pleasure. It was elastic, viscous and icy. It got into his skin; its icy cold permeated through his tissues to his blood, which it began to freeze.

And while he clung to the leads as the dogs dragged him this way and that, he thought that for dinner he had eaten trotters and tripe, carefully prepared for him by the grenadier; trotters and tripe that had put his mind at ease a little and given him a sense of well-being.

Now, while he thrashed about, breathing at the wrong time and swallowing that water which hit his teeth pure and sharp as liquid diamonds, he thought of those trotters and tripe with horror. He felt that the icy water was starting to solidify them in the pit of his stomach, where they would form a hard lump stuck in the centre of his body, stopping his breathing and paralysing him. It was then that he cried out a second time.

At that moment, the dogs were dragging him towards the side where the poplars grew. Gaspard was still clinging to their leads and kicking furiously to keep a little warmth in his body. The dogs reached the coping, pulled themselves half-way up, braced themselves on it, desperately trying to push with their back legs, but their claws slipped on the marble and Gaspard's ninety kilos pulled them backwards, especially as they were not working together. They fell back into the water. They began to swim again, making straight for the fountain jets that combined to pour a single sheet of water into the pool.

As Gaspard, only semi-conscious,

struggled between the streaming, laughing faces of the gods on the fountain, he noticed a man standing on the coping in the moonlight watching him struggling to stay alive, just standing there without a smile and without hatred, as if he were simply curious. Although he hadn't seen him for a very long time, Gaspard recognized him immediately. He knew that if he was here, showing himself clearly in full moonlight, standing there calmly with his hands in his pockets, it was because he was certain that he, Gaspard, was going to die.

It was at that moment, no doubt, when he was paralysed with fear and vainly feeling about for his gun, that the solidified trotters and tripe blocked his breathing.

He opened his mouth for the last time, giving a long deaf-mute's gargle, before turning face down into the glassy water, drowning his fear forever.

As they had dragged him along when he was alive, the dogs now dragged him dead. They kept trying to cling to the coping and haul themselves up. Gaspard's weight pulled them back again. They tried again. Sometimes they managed to get out of the pool as far as their chests. They were in that position, mouths open, tongues hanging out, panting with impotent rage, when the grenadier found them.

The poor woman. Gaspard's threats had forced her to give up following her master step by step. Nevertheless, she still prowled around with her blunderbuss in her hand as soon as he went out into the grounds, but too far away to be able to help him.

When she reached the pool, she was faced with the two hellish mouths and panting red tongues. She understood what had happened in a flash, and she knew that those dogs would never let her near. She took aim and fired. Once, twice. She hit the first dog in the head but missed the second. It started to swim, this time struggling to drag two bodies behind it. Then it began to tire and rather than try to reach the other side tried desperately to get up on the near side again.

While this was happening, Patrice was coming home in his red car. He had been playing his mandolin under Rose Sépulcre's window in the mill by the Lauzon. The skinny sister had glanced out of the little window in the attic and Patrice was sure that Rose had sent her to see if it was him, for she had discreetly half-opened the shutter of her window straight away.

When Patrice drove into the avenue of wind-tossed trees leading to Pontradieu, he felt on top of the world, despite the elements. The servant's two gunshots startled him as though he had been jumped on by fierce cats. He braked suddenly. He always kept an army revolver in the car, which he sometimes took out of the glove box and stroked. He took it and got out.

He thought it was his father who had fired the shots. It must have been round about the time he took his evening walk twice around the pool. He raced in that direction. Once he had passed the spindle-trees he saw the dobermann's head over the coping, its mouth open and straining on its front legs. He saw the servant with the blunderbuss in her hand. With a quick look he gauged the situation and fired twice at the dog, which fell backwards. He rushed forward and threw himself flat on to the rim of the coping. The bodies of his father and the two dogs were drifting slowly, pushed by the wind. Patrice plunged his hands into the icy water. He just managed to grab the collar of one of the huge animals.

"Help me!" he cried.

The grenadier had also laid herself flat on the coping and was pulling one of the leads that was floating in the water. In that way they pulled Gaspard's body to the edge. Patrice groped for the snap lock on the belt and released the bodies of the dogs. Gaspard's body then turned over on its back and his face could be seen in the moonlight. Congestion had frozen an expression of terrified surprise on his face, with his mouth wide open and his eyes staring.

Patrice and the grenadier tried to haul the body out of the cold water. Behind them they could hear people shouting. Lights swept across the surface of the pool. It was the farmer with his son and daughter who were hurrying to the rescue.

"We were just going to bed!" they shouted. "We knew from the gunshots that something was happening. Luckily we're down wind. Otherwise there's no way we'd even have heard gunshots!"

They all lay flat over the edge of the coping, plunging their hands in and grabbing Gaspard's clothing wherever they could. They brought a certain excitement and morbid curiosity to the task.

"Close his eyes!" the farmer shouted. "Close his eyes right now! Cold as he is already, you won't be able to do it later!"

There were six of them clinging to the dead man's clothes, but even working in unison, they couldn't manage to get him out of the pool.

Patrice looked up and saw Charmaine

running towards them out of the spindle-trees.

"Move aside!" said someone behind him. "Leave it to me."

Patrice turned round and saw Séraphin who was pushing the farmer and his daughter aside. He lay down beside him, put his arms in the water and turned Gaspard's body over to bring him in on his back. He grasped the collar of the shirt and jacket with both hands and began to pull slowly, straightening up as he did so, while the others did their best to help him. Finally, when he was almost upright, he held the full weight of the body against him. He gently laid it down flat on the marble paving.

They were all shivering with cold, although the wind had miraculously stopped blowing. They all looked at the dead man who had weighed so heavily on all their lives in one way or another, and who had come to such a simple end.

"You'll have to move him from there!" the farmer said, always practical.

"Séraphin . . ." Patrice said, "you take his feet and we'll each take an arm . . ."

Séraphin bent down.

"Not him!" the grenadier barked, cocking her rifle. "It's your fault!" she said turning to Patrice, "if you hadn't brought him here, nothing would have happened! Didn't you know he brings bad luck? Look at him!"

She made a dramatic gesture in Séraphin's direction with a hand like a battledore. She had gone up to him and the weapon she was aiming at him almost touched his chest. She barked in his face:

"Just look at him! You don't see it, all of you! You can't see it. You don't come from Le Champsaur! But I'm used to it. I can see it. Oh, he can try to hide behind that holy-picture face of his, but I know who he is! I know who he is!"

"Be quiet, you poor silly woman!" Charmaine muttered. "For heaven's sake, be quiet!"

Patrice gently took the gun from her hands.

"She's had a dreadful shock," he said. "It's not her fault . . ."

They all bent down to pick up the heavy, soaking thing that was already stiff as a tree trunk and not so easy to handle.

The farmer and Patrice took the left arm while his son and sturdy daughter took the right. Séraphin gently pushed Charmaine back as she bent over to help. He harnessed himself to the body with one leg in each hand, as he had so often done at the front and sometimes under fire. The grenadier

241

tenderly cushioned the dead man's head in her hands the whole way to the house.

The cortège progressed up the avenue to Pontradieu with heavy steps. The deaf woman must have felt some fibre in her heart vibrate from the depths of her silent world, for she was standing under the light at the top of the stone staircase. Charmaine ran to her as she began to come down the steps.

Gaspard Dupin had come home for the last time. His body left behind a long trail of cold water that he had drawn from the bottom of that beautiful pool, his pride and joy.

Throughout the night, Séraphin watched over the body of his slain enemy with Patrice. The furniture in the drawing room, shapeless and unrecognizable under their dust covers, had been pushed aside to make room for a makeshift bed. Gaspard had been laid out on it, his feet inflexible in his gentleman farmer's boots. They hadn't been able to pull them off: the icy water had stiffened his body faster than usual.

The farmer stood there awkwardly moving from one foot to the other, asking permission for himself and his family to leave. They were due to harvest their grapes next morning. Patrice nodded.

Charmaine was biting the skin round her nails with impatience. Now and again she chanced a sideways glance at Séraphin. That idiot! He wouldn't be thinking by any chance that she was going to sit there moping all night over the body of a father she'd never loved? Desire, so suddenly interrupted and stifled by the gunshots, now returned, stabbing like sharp needles at her body, which had been so receptive only a short time before. The deaf woman, who had cried a lot, but whose face was serene, was now saying her rosary more fervently than ever. You could see from the peaceful expression on her face that she was sure her dead husband was already standing with clasped hands before the face of the Almighty. However, now and then her face crumpled. She lost her rosary in the folds of her skirt. She threw herself in a ball against the grenadier's rugged body. She buried her face in the coarse material of her dress. In a thin, quavering voice, she called her to witness.

"My poor Eudoxie! My poor Gaspard!"

She ventured over on tiptoe to look at him again.

What Patrice felt at the death of his father was the pained indulgence he had always

243

shown him, and he also regretted the fact that he would never see him alive again. Yet these thoughts, which had arisen while he had been experiencing such intense happiness, were not strong enough to break that spell. He was still up there in the mill at Saint-Sépulcre. He was certain that it was Rose who had told her sister to look out of the window and make sure he was the one serenading her with his mandolin out there in the wind on the highest rock of the waterfall. He could still see the acceptance in that half-open shutter and the silhouette of Rose standing behind it.

Séraphin was the only one who had any really deep feeling about the dead man. He had gone once or twice to look at Gaspard Dupin's hands, now joined by force around the beads of a rosary. So they were the same ones that had sharpened the knife on the edge of the Sioubert spring and later plunged it into Girarde's neck. Now his life had also come to an end, but it was an ordinary, quite untroubled death, escaping remorse, escaping justice.

Séraphin considered the effects of this stupid accident that had cut the ground from under his feet. Gaspard Dupin had died, granted, but in the ordinary way, not in the presence of someone who would have told him first why he was dying.

He'd waited too long. He'd allowed himself to be lulled by the widow on the other side of the deathbed, who couldn't take her eyes off him. He felt that Charmaine's desire for him was as strong as ever, that it hadn't even been curbed by the smell of stale water that came from the body and wouldn't dry. He moved on his chair, then half stood up.

"Where are you going?" Charmaine asked.

"I'm going home. Tomorrow morning I have to . . ."

"Tomorrow's Sunday," Charmaine said, "and besides, you must stay. The doctor and the police will soon be here. Patrice telephoned them. They'll want to know . . . You were on the spot . . ."

She thought he was about to make a gesture of denial.

"Don't worry . . . I won't say why you were here."

Séraphin's serious nature reacted angrily, rashly. Who did she take him for?

"I'm not afraid! Not for myself!" he muttered, and sat down again.

But straight away he thought that he couldn't allow himself to be touchy. He mustn't give anything away. He mustn't give the least cause for surprise. He must always be the humble, submissive road mender. This one was dead, granted. But there were another two. He said nothing more. He kept his eyes riveted on the body, trying to get his fill of it, but he felt that even though he was dead, Gaspard Dupin had escaped him.

The doctor arrived at five o'clock in a pre-1914 Voisin with metal struts. He started when he saw Gaspard's body. They'd had a good time together only three days earlier at the Touring Club dinner at Sauvecanne's restaurant. Even doctors can still be surprised by the death of a mortal.

"How did it happen?" he inquired. "How long ago?"

He was told and seemed surprised, but said nothing.

"What had he eaten?"

"Trotters and tripe," the grenadier sniffed.

"Trotters and tripe!" the doctor repeated, raising his eyes to the ceiling. "And then fell into ice-cold water . . . I ask you!"

With his chin in his hand he looked all around the room at the living, dutifully sitting around the bed. He was more than familiar with families faced with a sudden death. This same Gaspard, who had earned so much money for them, had been in the process of squandering it, and a lot of it, because of a mistress everyone knew about . . . This doctor, by the name of Roman, was well aware of inheritors' sensibilities in these parts when it comes to money, as he himself was from Dauphin. Drowned in a pool while walking in the moonlight — that was easily said, but . . .

He walked around the dead man with an expression full of misgivings. He examined it thoroughly, palpated it, inspected its clothing. He hoped to find some trace of a blow, a suspicious bruise, or an unexplained scratch which would justify him refusing a death certificate, so that a more thorough examination could be made. But no . . . The body was in perfect condition. He had died from an immersion syncope, full stop . . . He couldn't find a thing, and finding nothing made him more puzzled than ever, for despite all evidence to the contrary, he was convinced there had been foul play. Only you can't refuse to issue a death certificate because of a personal conviction. Yet once the body has been put in a coffin and buried, it would be the devil's own job to get it exhumed if necessary, and that's when the doctor's responsibility would be damn well called into question . . . He sighed.

"You over there! the strong one, and *a priori* not one of the family — he's not one of the family, is he?"

He pointed to Séraphin, who stood up.

"Help me undress the victim," Dr Roman ordered.

But the body refused to be undressed. It was as rigid as a tree trunk from head to toe. They would have had to cut the clothes off with scissors or a razor, which the doctor decided against.

He was going to ask a most important question when he was silenced by low, bassoon-like growls coming from outside. It was the two surviving dobermanns announcing the arrival of the police.

"Well now," the sergeant asked, "what's happened here?"

He was still unnerved. He'd never seen wild animals jump so desperately to get out of their enclosure and devour him. He mopped his brow.

"They're dangerous animals you've got there," he said.

"They don't even know *us*," Patrice said. "They were my father's. I'll have them put down."

When he heard that the victim had fallen into the pool and had been pulled out and brought into the drawing room, a doubtful look came over his face and stayed there.

"He should have been left where he was."

"We didn't know if he was dead or not,"

Charmaine said. "We were hoping he wasn't."

Day was dawning. While all the witnesses were giving their particulars, Dr Roman made up his mind. Stirring up the troubled waters of this drowning would only bring repercussions and unpleasantness to him and others, and after all, the most likely explanation was that the deceased could well have slipped and the trotters and tripe had done the rest . . .

"Well?" the sergeant asked. "You've examined the body, Doctor. What happened?"

The doctor replied as if he were giving evidence.

"He slipped. He fell into the icy water, pulling the dogs in with him. Only a short time before he had eaten a meal of trotters and tripe. He died of congestion. It's as clear as day!"

The sergeant took down the details as he spoke.

"Naturally, you found no suspicious marks on the body: bruises, blows, scratches etc?"

Dr Roman took a deep breath before answering.

"Not to my knowledge."

Knowing how important it was to choose one's words carefully, he wondered whether perhaps the gendarme did not.

"No other questions?" he asked.

"None, for the moment," the sergeant replied, writing diligently.

Dr Roman opened his briefcase and took out a form which he slapped down on the table.

"We, the undersigned, doctor of medicine, declare that we have examined the body of . . ." etc.

Everything would have returned to normal and Gaspard Dupin would have been buried entire instead of being opened up like an animal in a butcher's shop, if gendarme Simon hadn't been conscientious and gone sniffing around the pool to get the feel of the place.

The suspicious gendarme had therefore decided to walk slowly around the pool, his thumbs tucked into his belt, trying to put himself in the victim's shoes. His foot slipped at exactly the same spot as Gaspard Dupin.

"He died of natural causes!" Dr Roman declared.

At that moment the dripping-wet gendarme burst into the room, leaving a trail of water on parquet in the corridor.

"Well, Simon?" the sergeant asked. "Good God! What happened to you?"

"Natural causes, no doubt, Chief," mumbled gendarme Simon, "but someone at least gave him a helping hand down the slippery slope . . ."

"What the hell are you talking about?"

With an astonishingly fast reflex, the doctor had already whisked away the death certificate and put it in the bottom of his briefcase.

"You'll catch your death of cold!" he exclaimed. "Get undressed. Get out of your uniform straight away! Someone find him some dry clothes. This man could die of cold!"

When he'd been revived by two snifters, and weirdly got up like a peasant in the farmer's clothes, the gendarme was able to relate what he'd found out. Everyone then proceeded to the pool. Everyone leaned over the part of the coping that he was pointing to.

"Lean over, Chief! Run your hand over this!"

The chief crouched down and did as he was asked. He ran his fingers along the marble. The surface was as slippery as ice. It was scuffed in two places by different boots: the victim's without hobnails, and the gendarme's.

"It's slippery like that for more than three

metres!" Simon exclaimed. "Anyone walking on it was sure to go head first into the water!"

Dr Roman ran his nose along the coping, just above the rim.

"It smells of soda . . ." he said. "Of freshly polished floor . . . I'd say a mixture of soap, soft soap probably, and beeswax. It's like an ice rink," he said thoughtfully, "a real ice rink . . ."

"When I told you, Chief, that someone gave him a helping hand down the slippery slope . . . !" the gendarme said triumphantly.

Human life only ever hangs by a thread. There's absolutely no need for dynamite, a gun or a knife to destroy it. The person who had thought up this clever trap, using cheap materials that any good housewife would own, must have known that. Unless he didn't want to soil his hands by touching his victim . . .

Séraphin looked with disbelief at the coping, which a bit of soap and wax in the right proportions had transformed into a death trap. The person who did it must have known, as he, Séraphin did, that the master of Pontradieu went out every evening to take a walk in the fresh air around his pool, with the dogs attached to his belt hampering his movements . . .

And so, Gaspard Dupin had indeed been murdered, but it wasn't he, Séraphin Monge, who had killed him.

XII

"Find the person who stands to benefit from the crime . . ."

Within three days it had been established that the victim had a mistress, that she was fleecing him, that his children had complained about that state of affairs, and in the presence of others.

In the course of their thorough search, the gendarmes found a stock of soft soap and wax in the outbuildings. They discovered that three jars of each had been opened. Why had three jars been opened? Why not use one after the other? This question was put to everyone. The replies they received satisfied no one and certainly not the magistrate.

They respected the grieving deaf wife. They did not bother the war widow. Just meeting the perverse boldness of her gaze was enough to frighten the magistrate. Dealing with her was like trying to hold a live coal. He ruled her out. And the grenadier vainly pointed an accusing finger at Séraphin, saying: "He's the one! Don't you know him? He's the one who demolished his own house. He's quite mad. He's the sole survivor of a crime. Some time ago his whole family was murdered. Do *you* think it's quite normal that he was the only one to escape? Crime follows him wherever he goes! It sticks to him! Wherever he goes, he brings it with him! It's him! I can feel it here!"

She pointed to her heart.

They discounted Séraphin Monge. For one thing, he didn't stand to inherit anything from the victim; for another, he didn't look smart enough to have thought of a trap like that; and thirdly, he was under the protection of M. Anglès, the Highways Department engineer. M. Anglès signified two things: authority and influence. If M. Anglès didn't get his road worker back, he could bring his influence to bear as far as Paris.

On the other hand, the magistrate disliked Patrice's mocking look, not realizing that he owed it to the surgeon's art. Forty-eight hours after the crime, he had him sitting there in his office. Several objects were lined up on the desk: a jar of soft soap, a tin of wax, a regulation revolver and a mandolin. The magistrate pointed an accusing finger at the pot of soft soap and the tin of wax.

"What were these two ill-assorted objects doing in your car? Can you explain it?"

"Of course," Patrice said. "The engine breaks down — quite often. I know a bit about it, so I do the repairs myself . . . And when I've finished the repairs, my hands are dirty with grease, and more often than not in the places I go to, I can't turn up with dirty hands. That explains the soft soap . . ."

"Right! And the wax?"

"The gendarmes must have noticed that my car has a lot of mahogany accessories: the dashboard, the backs of the seats, the inside of the doors. They have to be polished from time to time."

"Very well!" the magistrate exclaimed. "And what about that?"

He gave a sharp rap to the mandolin, which was right under the nose of the accused. It twanged softly.

"I was unaware," Patrice muttered, "that my father was killed with a blunt instrument. What's more, this is much too fragile."

"No doubt!" the magistrate exclaimed. "But there's a gap of two and a half hours in your account of your movements. Now follow what I have to say closely. At nine o'clock on the morning of the crime, the farmer's son comes as usual to rake the dead leaves from the pool. He walks right around it and he doesn't slip. So at that time the trap hasn't been laid yet. From that moment, we can follow the comings and goings of all those close to the victim, and your own in particular. The movements of all the others tally perfectly. As for you, you leave at ten past nine. The farmer's son sees you pass by. You go to Manosque, where you have arranged to meet the engineers from the electricity station. You have lunch with them. You leave them at three o'clock. You go to a site where you have a work meeting. At five-thirty you are seen at the news-agent's in Manosque. At six, you have a game of bridge in the back room of the Café Glacier with a dentist, a notary and a clerk of the court. You leave this company at eight, having drunk two glasses of mint mineral water and from that moment on you disappear from view until ten, when you pop up in front of the pool where your father is struggling in the water!"

"Where he's already dead."

"I concede that. Nonetheless, you fire two shots from this revolver . . ."

The magistrate lifted up the firearm and let it fall back on to the desk.

"At the dog! My compliments, by the way. You hit it between the eyes . . . But that's not the problem: between eight and ten in the evening, we lose track of you. You had time then to come back and soap the rim of the pool. So, I want to know where you were. And there's one thing in particular that I want to know: why were you carrying a mandolin around in your car?"

"You won't find that out in a hurry . . ." Patrice muttered.

"Are you refusing to answer me?"

"Not at all! I went up on the Ganagobie slopes to practise playing this instrument . . ."

"Where no one saw you, no doubt?"

"The wind was blowing. I wasn't keen to let anyone hear my wrong notes."

"That's not a good enough answer," said the magistrate. "I'm obliged to keep you here. But let's be quite clear about this! I'm not charging you directly with your father's murder. I'm charging you with being in possession of a prohibited weapon. War souvenirs are all very fine, but it's illegal to take them out of the house. And don't forget this: it's an offence that can end up in the court of assizes."

"It's not a war souvenir," Patrice said quietly.

He restrained himself from showing his face with the comment: "The only war souvenir I've kept is the one I wear." He disliked crushing others with sledge-hammer arguments. He merely explained:

"I had a buddy with roughly the same face as mine, perhaps a bit worse. One day he got tired of fighting — as you might say — and he blew it off . . . With that . . . He left me the weapon as a legacy and as a mockery."

"You have the right to a lawyer," the magistrate said. "We'll see about the possibility of bail in forty-eight hours. But in the meantime, I'm sorry!"

When he left the magistrate's office — they had spared him handcuffs, for the gendarmes at least knew the respect owed to a disfigured war veteran — the greatest happiness in the world awaited Patrice in the foyer of the court house. There in front of the tall glass door, standing timidly to one side, he saw Rose Sépulcre looking at him with her eyes full of tears.

She must have come from Lurs on her bicycle, and there she was, standing there with her legs slightly dusty, her hat slightly askew and her eyes . . . her eyes from the *Thousand and One Nights* — each one the size of a large almond — her eyes full of tears he saw dropping from the ends of her lashes.

When he drew level with her, Patrice put a finger to his lips. He went into prison wild with joy.

Rose's decision to go to Digne on her bicycle had been made as the family were having their meal, when Marcelle, who always knew what was going on, had announced that Patrice had been led away by two gendarmes and that he was the one who murdered his father.

"It hasn't been proved!" Rose exclaimed. "You're making it up!"

"It's not certain . . ." Térésa said.

"Yes it is!" Didon shouted.

He struck his fist on the table, making the cutlery jump.

"He's the only one it can be, do you hear? He's the only one!"

There were beads of sweat on his forehead. Luckily he had just swallowed his hot soup, which could explain it, but there was cold fear in the pit of his stomach.

"He's right," Marcelle said, "who else could it be?"

"Shut your mouth!" Didon barked. "No one asked you!"

From the moment he had learnt of Gaspard Dupin's strange death, he had been on tenterhooks.

"Anyway," Rose said, "I'm going."

"Where to?" Térésa asked.

"To Digne, to help Patrice. He mustn't think that everyone has abandoned him. I don't know how I'll get to see him, but I will . . ."

"You stay where you are!" Didon shouted. "Or I'll . . ."

"You'll do nothing at all!" Térésa shouted over him.

She continued very quietly:

"Even if he is unfairly accused, he's still Dupin's son . . ."

Flat-chested Marcelle was looking at her sister with a spiteful gleam in her eye.

"You fall in love with every man you meet!" she whispered.

Rose, who was on her way out, turned around as though she had been stung.

"Do you want your face slapped?"

"I'm right! You're fickle-hearted, that's what you are! Hardly two months ago, all you could think and talk about was Séraphin. You can't deny it!"

"That's true," Rose admitted. "But with Séraphin, what could I do . . . ?"

She shook her head dispiritedly several times.

"He's not a man . . ." she said softly, finishing her sentence.

It was old Tricanote bringing her goats home as usual who had told Clorinde Dormeur about Patrice's arrest. The village of Lurs was always a bit late hearing what was going on, especially in autumn when there is so much to do.

Célestat had just taken the mortar of yeast for the night batch from the scales where his wife had weighed it.

"Those magistrates," he complained, "always want to get things over and done with as fast as possible."

"What did you say?" Clorinde asked.

"Oh! Nothing . . . I was talking to myself."

He didn't for one moment believe Patrice was guilty. He glanced longingly at the gun hanging on the canopy over the fireplace in the room behind the shop. If all those standing on their doorsteps taking the cool of the evening saw him pass by carrying the gun, they'd never stop talking about it . . . And yet . . . There was a distance of 200 metres between the bakehouse and the shop. Two hundred metres full of dark nooks and crannies, stables as damp as cellar doors, staircases leading down from archways, carriage entrances with no doors, as dark as tunnels;

houses in ruins huddled behind nettles, elder trees and Spanish lilacs, as though they were lying in wait for him, all with gaping windows opening on to empty space and memories of the dead. Having lived with a strong whiff of fear for the last twenty-five years, Célestat never felt at ease walking past these dark recesses. He even took care not to turn his head towards them, for if he did so without thinking, he would see them studded with dark red, as if a whole rostrum of prosecutors had been waiting there, somnolent but quite ready, for a quarter of a century.

Now every night between 4 and 5 a.m., Célestat went back home for a little nap while the first batch of bread was cooking and a thin streak of emerald green light was only just dawning towards the top of Estrop. He was all alone in that street in Lurs, where there was only a dim electric light on the end of a pole every 200 metres. What help could he expect? Every morning Célestat heard his customers snoring behind their shutters. What's more, he never failed to call them lazy good-for-nothings as he passed. But none of that made him feel any less alone. If he were attacked, providing he could call out, the people sleeping in their houses would take a full quarter of an hour to come to his aid. And when they did arrive, who knows what he would have done to him, the man who had already killed Gaspard? Putting soap on the rim of a pool is hardly the way a real man would act. A gun, a knife, a *courregeon* (those leather laces, as long as a day without bread, used on hunting boots), you could understand all those . . . They're men's weapons. But soap and wax! Who knows what he would come up with next time, that son of a bitch? From time to time Célestat would catch himself staring strangely at the trough, which looked so much like a coffin, the oven always alight and burning, the sacks of flour piled up twice as high as himself. A single one of them could break his neck, with only a dull thud! Gaspard had been a man of some importance and filthy rich. He would steal away when their paths crossed by chance or hold out a few limp fingers when he couldn't avoid him. Now if Gaspard had got caught in such a stupid way, all the more reason why he, Célestat, could be too, and by any means at all.

Besides, although he had never breathed a word of it to anyone — especially not to Clorinde, who would have split her sides laughing — for more than a month now, every time he left the bakehouse at about 4 o'clock, someone had been following close behind him. Oh, it was someone very clever, very agile, who was so close to him that when he turned around to surprise him, the other person turned with him, as if he were part of his own body, as if he had been attached to his back. In that bumpy street in Lurs, through the gaps on top of the crumbling walls, he thought he saw — he had seen — a swift shadow dash behind a tall clump of elders growing up out of the ruins.

"They make you laugh," Célestat said to himself, "those people who talk about forgetting the past. People who say to you: 'That's all a long time ago.' Now and again without realizing it, you find you're dragging the past along behind you. You turn around and say to yourself: 'Well! There he is!' At other times . . . what happened twenty-five years ago is more of a threat than the war that's hanging over everybody's head or the little lump like a juniper berry that rolls around under your fingers when you're shaving and will probably turn out be a cancer, but in twenty years time! And to prove it . . . Who would have thought that with so many dying in the war, Séraphin Monge would come back home, and above all that he'd take it into his head to knock down La Burlière? Who would have imagined that Gaspard Dupin, with all the precautions they say he took, could have slipped on some soft soap? That not so long ago they were ready to believe his death was due to natural causes?

"If you think about all that, it's all well and good not to take down the gun from over the fireplace for fear of being laughed at, but when he, Célestat was found dead between the bakehouse and the shop — and God knows how — those who laughed at him would stand around his body and perhaps wonder: 'He should have taken his gun after all.' If that did happen, it wouldn't seem ridiculous at all."

Once these thoughts had come to an end, Célestat took down the firearm without hesitation, put it over his shoulder, the packet of leaven under his arm and went up the two steps to the shop. Clorinde was just lifting up the bead curtain to come in again.

"What on earth are you doing?" she said.

"Can't you see? I'm going to knead the dough."

"Have you taken to kneading the dough with a gun now? Aren't you being a bit silly?"

"Gaspard Dupin is dead," Célestat said.

"What of it?"

"Well, you can say what you like, but from

now on I'm taking the gun."

She shrugged her shoulders, yawned, took the weights off the scales and raised her eyes towards the chiming clock. It was about to strike eight o'clock. She would be able to do the takings. But another idea suddenly struck her.

"Good Lord! Eight o'clock, and Marie isn't back yet!"

In the course of the long conversation with her neighbour about the murder at Pontradieu, which injected a little excitement into the daily routine, she had forgotten about her daughter. Tricanote, who had already seen Célestat go by with his gun, now saw Clorinde dash out, scurrying along as fast as her flat feet and short legs would carry her.

"Clorinde! What's the matter?"

"Heavens above!" Clorinde shouted to her without turning round. "The girl's not back yet."

Tricanote, who loved a bit of drama, rushed after Clorinde. Both of them leaned over the rampart, and straight away they saw Marie riding her delivery tricycle up the Lurs hill in the dusk.

"She'll have been to see her Séraphin, for sure."

"For sure!" Clorinde sighed. "That road

mender will be the death of me!"

No. Marie had not been to see Séraphin, or
at least if she had hoped to see him, she
had been disappointed, as Séraphin was not
working on the section of road that Marie
was taking. Marie had to deliver bread as
far as Pont-Bernard, because Coquillat, the
baker at Peyruis, had a whitlow and couldn't
knead the dough. For the last week, half the
people of Peyruis had been going to Lurs,
and the other half to Les Mées. For Célestat,
that meant doing a double batch.

As she was coming back from Pont-
Bernard, a tyre on the tricycle got a puncture. It wasn't the first time. Marie was used
to it. Her saddlebag contained everything
she needed to repair it. But you had to have
water to find the hole, so she had to push
the bike for more than 500 metres to Sioubert spring. She didn't like that concealed
spring, which was at ground level and made
no noise. Its wash trough was deep under
the branches, which made it dark all year
round. But she had no choice.

She rolled up her sleeves and set to work.
It was only when she got the wheel off that
she noticed she was still wearing her ring
and that she might scratch the aquamarine.
She took it off and was about to put it down

where she could see it on the driest part on the rim of the rinsing trough, when she noticed the big sickle-shaped notch cut in a curve out of the olive-oil–coloured stone. She didn't know what it had been used for, but she instinctively reached over to put her ring further away on a flagstone in the light at the overflow outlet, where she could see it quite easily.

The puncture took a long time to fix. It was a tiny hole from which the air escaped one bubble at a time. Marie got more and more annoyed as she tried to find it, and then roughen the surface of the inner tube. What's more, she had to tighten the wheel with an adjustable spanner that slipped . . . She grumbled, then she fumed. She hated getting her hands dirty and she would have to wait until she got home to wash them properly.

She was in a foul temper, especially as her hair was blown about and she couldn't touch it with her hands, when she got on her bike again and began pedalling furiously. She had gone no more than two hundred metres when she let out a cry of horror. She had forgotten her aquamarine! She turned her bike around with one powerful movement as though it were a horse. A chain truck, which appeared in the turn of the road frantically cranked its horn and just managed to miss her. Marie didn't even see it. Her beloved aquamarine that her parents had presented to her in her bedroom on the morning of her eighteenth birthday! How could she have forgotten it!

She leapt off and rushed towards the spring. It was already very dark under the overhanging foliage. Sure of where she was going, Marie went towards the pillar at the overflow outlet and reached out her hand. The ring wasn't there. She panicked. She thought all sorts of ridiculous things: that she had mistaken the spot, that a rat had made the ring fall into the trough. She felt right around the wash trough on all fours, moaning with distress. She reached her arm down to the bottom, but the mud rose and it was useless to feel around in the black water. Nevertheless she kept looking until the darkness under the branches made it impossible to continue. Dreadfully upset and in tears, soaked by the cold water that had splashed all over her, she made her way back to Lurs.

Three days after Gaspard Dupin's death, Séraphin was still only going through the motions of everyday life. The astonishment he felt at the sight of the body had not disappeared. Who could have frustrated his revenge? Who had cut the ground from under him? He was no more convinced of Patrice's guilt than Didon Sépulcre or Célestat Dormeur were. Didon wanted to believe it, but Célestat had no illusions on that score. More than a dozen times, Séraphin was on the point of throwing down his sledge-hammer on the pile of stones he was breaking, getting on his bike, racing down to Digne to tell all he knew. But every night he had to protect himself from the dream that pursued him and which more or less dictated the road he had to follow. His nights were peaceful provided he didn't stray from his goal, but as soon as he forgot it, the threatening nightmare roamed through his sleep, trying to pass on to him the secret that he definitely did not want to know.

The days were short now. It was dark soon after six. Séraphin tried to cling as best he could to that life, so ordinary but so very appealing, that he felt existed parallel to his own.

It was the time of year when Peyruis was filled with the smell of crushed vines and wine bubbling behind the small cellar windows. Two stills had been set up in the little square, and Séraphin often wandered around them, breathing the smell of the pine-wood fire beneath the boilers and watching the spirit trickle like a glass thread into the vats where the thermometer bobbed about on its cork.

So many generations of Monges before him must have ensconced themselves on these benches under the canvas awnings to discuss the quality of the brandy, pewter pots in hand. That could have continued for generations to come, were it not for those three murderers.

Sometimes the men working the still would invite him to sit on the bench reserved for the growers. They offered him the brandy from the bottom of the barrel in which the marc cooled down. He moistened his lips without swallowing it, for he remembered only too well the smell of the trenches in the morning before going over the top, when the grog was handed out.

He could be seen wending his way through the shafts of sunlight and the steam and smoke, then melting into the night, pushing aside the dead leaves and, like a child, kicking the horse chestnuts so that their husks split open on the road. He went home. He opened the sugar tin and spread out the acknowledgements of debt. He reread them. He had drawn a thick pencil line across

Gaspard's. He thought of Patrice, who had been in prison since the previous day. He thought of Didon Sépulcre, down there in his oil mill preparing for the harvest. He thought of Célestat Dormeur, all alone in the night, up there in his bakehouse which fed a whole village. These people, the ones who had done him the greatest harm in this world, were all he thought about, to the exclusion of any possible friendship. These feelings of hatred were all he had to live on. But were these men, after all, the same ones who had wiped out his family long ago? And if they weren't the same ones, what good did it do to hate them? Ever since he had seen Gaspard's body, he doubted whether reducing someone to such a sorry state could satisfy a ghost, even if it was one he carried within him. He found it a hard task and he considered his mother, wherever she might be, very demanding in asking so much of him. These moments of confusion, however, did not last long. They were wholly due to the part of his being that was affected at times by all those brief moments of happiness, by the temptation to live like everyone else.

One dark October evening, when it's not good to be alone, he was making his way slowly up the stairs. He pushed the kitchen

273

door, which stuck on the floor tiles. He turned on the light and found Charmaine sitting there in front of him on his chair, looking at him intently. At first he didn't understand what she had been doing. However, the sugar tin was wide open, revealing his honey-gold coins. It took a while for Séraphin to come to terms with the idea that she had spread out the three debt documents on the oilcloth, with the one he had crossed out in red pencil in the centre. Both of them remained glued to the spot for more than a minute, staring at each other.

Here in this room with its low ceiling, he had never seemed more handsome to her. She saw him like a sword in the shape of a crucifix. She felt that before she had known him, she had never met a real man. Even though he might kill her for having found out his secret, she was still not afraid. The perverse sensuality, which she accepted as part of her nature, was her form of armour. She lived the present moment with a voluptuous physicality. She cared little for what followed. She began to speak with her usual nonchalance.

"I won't give you away," she said. "I didn't like my father and I think I know now what he did to you."

She pointed to the papers on the table.

"So was he the murderer at La Burlière?"

"There were three of them," Séraphin replied.

His legs seemed to give way and he fell into a chair opposite her, without taking his eyes off her.

"So was that your secret?" she said. "Are you the avenger? Are you the righter of wrongs?"

She reached out her hand towards his, but he quickly hid his hands under the table.

"Do you enjoy exacting punishment?" she asked him quietly.

Séraphin clenched his jaws. Telling her the truth would be of no help to him. He could see her lips shining in the lamplight. He knew what she wanted, and he knew that she thought of nothing else. He knew where she would lead him and that on this occasion there would be no gunshot to save him in the nick of time.

She picked up the papers on the table, folded them up again, piled them on top of the gold louis and snapped the lid shut. She took the tin and put it back on the shelf, next to the frying pan. The small of her back swayed as she took those few steps. She was wearing black lace, which made her seem either naked or in tatters. She came back to the table, pointing her finger towards

Séraphin until she touched his chest through his shirt.

"From now on, I'm you and you're me, as if we were shipwrecked. And just in case you might have been feeling any remorse, I can tell you that Patrice is being released tomorrow."

"He's not the one . . ." Séraphin murmured.

"Of course he isn't."

She walked round the table. He was still sitting rigidly on his chair. She leaned over and whispered in his ear:

"You've done us a great favour. He would have ruined us . . ."

His knees were still pressed together and his fists clenched. He was thinking that he could easily kill her, but that he would never get away with it: he would be arrested immediately and the other two men who killed his mother would still be alive. But he also knew that he would never have the courage to kill Charmaine. On the contrary: he could feel soft currents of that melting sensuality humming around him, just like a bumblebee barely caressing the flower that intoxicates it. It emanated from her eyes, her voice, her perfume with its hint of bergamot, paralysing him with desire, curiosity and terror.

"Go now!" he said. "I can't . . ."

"You can't? Truly?"

Standing behind him, she put her arms around his chest, pressing her breasts against his rock-hard shoulders; her long hands made the triangular movement of a diver and slid down, feeling the band of muscles above his waist, then further down still. She undid his clothes with the gentle deliberation of a nurse removing a dressing from a wound. She took his cock firmly in her two hands.

"And now? Are you really sure you can't?"

With almost masculine strength, she pushed the table out of the way. It made a dreadful noise as it scraped across the floor. She planted herself in front of Séraphin and he heard the lace tear as she pulled it over her head. He saw her belly rounded like a shield and her triangle of unusually closely-knit curls.

By that moment, Séraphin could already hear the sound of a whip whistling through the air as Girarde shook out her shroud of dead leaves at the well of La Burlière. Her image became clearer each time she appeared. That night, the vision revealed a new detail: his mother's pale blue eyes, which were not deep-set, did not look straight in front of her. The gaze of one of them, the one on the left, was a little higher and a little wider than the other.

Was it this ghost or Charmaine who mounted him as though he were a horse. Who was it who put her legs tightly around him as if she were climbing the trunk of a tree? But beneath the lascivious thrusting of her hips, he remained as still as a block of stone. The only human response that he could not control was that member rising stiffly, almost despite him, like a petrified priapus incapable of feeling anything.

She shouted insults and obscenities at him, but he never unclenched his fists, never moved, never touched her in any other way than with that impersonal member, which her thighs held in a vice-like grip, but to absolutely no avail.

She cried with humiliation, for it was usually she who disconcerted men with her impassivity, her silence and her lucidity. But how could you disconcert a person for whom you do not exist, someone who is rigid with fear and, terrorized as he is by a ghost, is scarcely aware that it's a woman making love on top of him.

"It's not possible, not possible, not possible!"

She moaned this litany through clenched teeth. She could never know that in the back of that marble head, so like the one in Patrice's studio, Séraphin was struggling against his dead mother. He kept retreating, she advancing, with that enigmatic silence and that slightly turned eye which he now knew, but which still did not look at him squarely in the face. He turned his head from side to side to avoid the wet, red lips — his mother's? Charmaine's? — which sought another contact; he turned his mouth away to escape the resilient breasts which demanded to be clasped by a baby's little fists and which, he was certain, would feed him with dead milk.

Charmaine worked on the man for a long time to make him give in. She tried everything she knew. She surpassed herself, surprised at how much lust she was capable of, sure that she would at last overcome that uselessly stiff lingam, and that Séraphin would then wrap his arms around her. That was what she really wanted: the consolation of being rocked in his arms.

Suddenly she seemed to collapse and give up the struggle. She stayed there still astride him for several minutes, but the life had gone out of her and she no longer had the strength to hold him. She was exhausted, but unsatisfied. Furiously angry, she hit him repeatedly on the chest, the arms and the belly. She tore herself away from him. She spat on his cock.

He still sat there without moving. His eyes were still full of other visions. She slapped his face hard. Her hands hurt as though she had hit stone. He didn't even turn his head.

She got dressed again in her lace as best she could. She said:

"I'll come back every night! Do you hear me? Every night! You'll give in!"

She intended to slam the door as she left, but it stuck on the tiles and the effect was lost.

Séraphin heard the sound of an engine starting up, but unconsciously. For the drop of dead milk, which was the most vivid part of his hallucination, seemed to be moistening the inside of his mouth, spreading over and around his tongue. It tasted like damp soot.

He rushed to the sink and thrust his fingers into his mouth. What he brought up was black and the taste of soot rose into his nostrils and stayed there for the rest of the wretched night that followed.

He came back and collapsed into his chair as though he had been fighting with someone of a strength equal to his own. He could smell Charmaine's perfume on the hairs on his chest and the hollows of his hands, even though he had not really unclenched them. It dominated but did not dispel the smell of soot — a mixture full of mystery he couldn't fathom.

Suddenly the idea crossed his mind that Charmaine had read his papers and he was therefore at her mercy. He could not permit himself the luxury of seeing the desire she felt for him turn into hate. If he wanted to devote himself to what was essential — getting at the two murderers who were yet to be punished — he would have to cut through his fantasies and strange sensations, cut right through them like an arrow. Even if it meant drinking his fill of sooty milk. Even if he had to hear the secret that his mother was trying so hard to whisper to him.

If he wanted to prevent Charmaine from thwarting his plans, he would have to give in to her whims. It was the only way she would be a party to them. And if his mother punished him for the pleasure by telling him something that he already found repellent, so much the worse. After all, he had been through a war. No nightmare, no mystery could come anywhere near that horror.

He stood up, then ran out and down the stairs. He went into the shed, got on his bike and pedalled furiously towards Pontradieu.

He had to take Charmaine in his arms and ask her to forgive him.

XIII

When one is mad with jealousy, one balks at nothing. And Marie certainly was jealous. From five o'clock in the afternoon she had been going around with a knot in her throat. It was all she could do to answer with a yes or no. At five o'clock, when Marie was doing some ironing in the room behind the shop, Tricanote had put her head through the bead curtain.

"Clorinde! Have you heard the news? It seems that the merry widow . . ."

Clorinde was weighing out unrefined flour for the Sisters of the Rosary.

"Which one?" she asked.

"You know! The one who's in the paper. The daughter of old moneybags Dupin!"

"Oh!"

"Well!" exclaimed Tricanote. "Her father's death, especially in such tragic circumstances, hasn't stopped her from leading a fast life. Listen to this, my girl. It seems she's having a good time with Séraphin!"

Clorinde raised her eyes to the ceiling.
"Oh, him!"

That is when the knot stuck in Marie's throat. From then on, she was champing at the bit, her mind made up. At nine o'clock, her father usually tucked his packet of leaven under his arm, took down the gun and left for the bakehouse. Ever since he had been so affected by Gaspard Dupin's death, he no longer came back until morning. He had made a bed from sacks and took naps there between the times he had to work, his gun between his legs.

As for Clorinde, that was simple: at nine o'clock she did the till, yawning all the while. She put the money in an old shepherd's hat and went upstairs to her bedroom, stumbling over each step. Marie, who was already in her own room, could hear her moving about for two or three minutes, give a jaw-cracking yawn, wipe her face and feet with a jug of cold water, then out like a light! The performance began after about three or four minutes. She had a strong, steady snore. At each intake of air, the base of the kerosene lamp shook on the marble top of the chest of drawers.

Marie didn't wait for it to rattle more than ten times. She opened her door, went downstairs, went out through the hall into the shed, took down her new bicycle and went out into the street. She didn't get on straight away, but carried it for a while down the dark, deserted street.

Everyone in the town was bottling in the cellar or sorting fruit in the storeroom. Conversations drifted out from the small cellar windows, as if rising out of the ground. It was the best time of autumn: rich, warm days full of the smell of the newly stored harvest. The Lurs area was waiting for the rain that followed the sea wind. Peace was in everyone's heart, except Marie's.

Marie was hurrying towards Peyruis to set her mind at rest. Setting the mind at rest is the devout wish of all those who are jealous and still young. It took her barely a quarter of an hour's frantic pedalling to cover the distance from Lurs to Peyruis.

She knew the little square, with its fountain and its mixture of rich and poor houses, well. She stopped her delivery tricycle there every day to deliver bread to the Sisters' school. The square was an odd shape: its nooks and crannies hid the beginnings of dark little streets and sheds without doors, housing carts with their shafts raised. The various façades were pierced with windows

of different sizes, some dark, some lit up;
there were green louvres and black shutters
hanging off their hinges; light behind the
window panes came from electric globes;
kerosene lamps or even little oil lamps
burned in stables where a few goats were
kept and where old men shuffled about in
the straw.

Three plane trees overlooked the fountain.
The light from a single lamp, attached by
its bracket to the outside of the notary's
house, was often eclipsed by the movement
of the branches. The dead leaves from the
plane trees played at forming patterns like
an oriental carpet between the puddles of
water.

But jealousy takes away all peace and
tranquillity. Marie shivered, standing alone
and wretched in that square. She was long-
ing for the sight of the dull light that
indicated Séraphin's window. She looked
up, but there were slow-moving shadows
between the bead lampshade and the dirty
window panes. Marie could only see the
ceiling of the room, but all the rest, which
she could not see, was definitely present in
her imagination. However, that was not
enough for her: imagining is not the same
as putting one's mind at rest. She looked
around her for some means of seeing more

clearly through the window. She noticed the open entrance to a shed, in line with the house but to one side, and inside it she could see the legs of a trestle used for harvesting olives.

She was about to move towards it, when something blocking the light made her turn her head. She was no longer alone. She had been so absorbed in finding a better observation point that she had taken her eyes off Séraphin's house for a few seconds, and it was precisely over there that her watchful eyes had noticed the furtive shadow.

She could see a man from behind stealing away beneath the waving branches, between light and darkness, sometimes visible, sometimes shadowy. No doubt he had just come out of the door opening on to Séraphin's dark staircase. Marie had not seen him at the precise moment when he went out, but as her eyes covered the whole square, he could not have come from anywhere else.

The moving lattice of leaves waving in front of the street lamp cut the silhouette into four, giving the vague outline of a light and dark harlequin disappearing behind the fountain into the shadows. There was the sudden glimpse of a cyclist's swaying body and the sound of a buckled wheel fading in the distance.

Marie followed the silhouette and the noise with a feeling of blessed relief. If this man had just left Séraphin, his presence there would explain the suspicious movement of the shadows in front of the lamp a moment ago.

It was only then that she saw a parked car in the dark corner behind the fountain where the man had just disappeared. This black shiny vehicle, sitting high off the ground, with fine red outlines on the wheels, had the smart appearance of a woman's car. Marie raised her eyes towards Séraphin's window. The shadows were still moving about in there. Without a moment's hesitation, she ran to the open shed, took down the trestle and leaned it against the trunk of a plane tree. The thought never crossed her mind that someone might arrive, cross the square or come out of a house.

Jealousy is bold: nothing can restrain it. Besides, Marie thought that ten seconds would be enough to put her mind at rest. As it happens, she stayed for an hour. She stayed until Charmaine, literally hurtling out of the house, ran to the car and sped off.

But before that Marie, standing dumbfounded on her trestle, her mouth dry, her legs nearly giving way under her, had every opportunity to put her mind at rest. Although the latticework on the window cut up her view, she could feast her eyes on the sight that was still visible through the dirty panes of glass.

After Charmaine's departure she stayed clinging to the bars of the trestle for a few minutes, breathless and trembling, before she had the strength to get down, lean against the tree and wait for the strange new tingling sensation deep down in her belly to subside.

She thought it was anger that caused it. She was preparing herself to go up the stairs and scream some home truths at Séraphin, kick him and scratch his eyes out. But actually she hoped to have the courage to force him to do with her what he had done with Charmaine, and to offer him anything he wished to make him forget her.

She hadn't time to take the first step. Séraphin ran out of the shed pushing his bicycle, then leaped on it. He set off in the same direction taken by Charmaine a moment ago and the unknown man who had disappeared a while before that.

Without a moment's hesitation, Marie also got on her bike and followed Séraphin at a distance. So as to put her mind at rest, she told herself, but in reality she hardly knew now whether she was coming or going, as her mother would say.

Charmaine was still quivering, like the string of a bow which keeps vibrating after it is slackened. She was stunned, disorientated, all her senses aroused but unsatisfied. Was the exploit she had just engaged in laughable at her age? "Left stranded," she thought, "astride that accursed triangle somewhere between satisfaction, appeasement and frustration, like a rank beginner or a woman who has been in a bad marriage for too long . . ." But basically she knew that these words, said lightly, gave only a superficial idea of the sensations they described. None of them was capable of expressing the turmoil deep within her. She felt as empty as a drum and stiff, as though all her internal muscles had become petrified. Cold welled up from the muscles deep within, suddenly detached from their prey, intensified low down in her belly, then spread out in tentacles which attached themselves throughout the flesh of her body. She felt as though she had lost herself in the arms of a lover made of bronze, a statue, an image . . . "And what's more," she said to herself, "that face without any lines or expression that he set against me all the time . . . Where does it come from?" She then asked herself the same question, but more precisely: "Who does it come from? Who had dressed him up in it? Or rather, who had masked him with it?" For that is what she really felt: through sex she had encountered someone who carefully concealed his true self, as though he were wearing a mask.

"Patrice . . ." she whispered.

She had to wait through that interminable night before she could join her brother again — when he was set free — and throw herself into his arms. He at least would close them around her. She would explain everything to him. She would tell him everything. She would ask him the question that was forming in her mind as she drove full speed towards Pontradieu: "Why is Séraphin's cock the only part of him that is a real man? Why? Why the devil does he refuse to love me?"

A person can never work out alone why he or she is not loved. Patrice, her friend since childhood, her accomplice, would console her.

She braked hard at the garage door and got out to open it. The engine stalled. Charmaine found Pontradieu strangely silent.

Without thinking, she raised her eyes. The shutters at the window of her mother's room had not been closed. There was light in the room, and also further up at the small round window of the grenadier's bedroom. Both were no doubt mourning their dead man, each in her own way.

Charmaine hesitated. She was not keen to be in her room again. Her mind still glowed with the image of Séraphin's face so close to hers, and she knew she would end up calming her distress by fondling herself until she was exhausted before her dark deep mirror, ideal for reflecting Narcissus. For, never having found a partner intuitive enough to allow her to solve the riddle of her sensuality, her celebrations of the flesh always ended in dismal solitude.

That particular evening, however, nothing could release her from the grip of painful reality. All she could find, as usual, was the cold consolation of the broad valley at the bottom of the park, the wind in the trees, the rustling of nocturnal animals and birds: the apparent innocence of the night.

The moon was in its last quarter, but it was still bright enough to be able to walk by its light. Charmaine went down the side path. She took pleasure in letting herself brush against the box trees. The smell consoled her, as it usually brought clusters of happy memories to mind. She tentatively crushed a few twigs so that she could smell them.

The path turned at that spot. The quiet waters of the pool could be seen ahead of her. Charmaine was walking towards it when she heard the sound of stealthy steps running up behind her. She was about to turn around to see who was looking for her at that hour and in such a hurry. She did not have the time to complete the action. An enormous weight crushed her shoulders. Something like pincers broke the bones in her back.

Leaning over the handlebars, a tragic expression on his mask-like face, Séraphin pedalled furiously. Whatever the consequences, he now wanted wholeheartedly to take Charmaine in his arms. This impatience spurred him on. He wanted to run his hand over her hair with one movement of his great hand. He felt he must see her eyes raised towards him to thank him for that tenderness. He was ready to face his mother's secret for what he had sometimes heard people call happiness. So be it. He would suffer, but for at least once in his life he would have been of some use.

He got off as usual near the gateway, in front of the tall poplar. He hid his bike in the culvert and proceeded down the avenue of sycamores. Everything was strangely silent. The moon had almost gone. It lit the underside of the trees. A light breeze was rising, bringing with it the smell of box that Séraphin liked so much. He could see Pontradieu through the light foliage. Two windows were still lit up. Was it Charmaine's room? Would he find her playing the piano? He imagined himself quietly creeping up behind her. He would put both hands on her shoulders, whisper the truth in her ear, and the real reason why he couldn't make love . . .

Preoccupied with these thoughts, he found himself in the alternating rows of trees, at the crossing of two paths bordered with box. Further away, in the gloom dappled by the moonlight with shapes like eyes on a moth's wing, a strange undulating mass seemed to be crawling on the ground. It was like a mound shaken by shivers and convulsions, rippling sometimes as it passed from the shadows into the light. Four dull opal-coloured gleams of light shone out of it. Séraphin heard a kind of contented growling and the noise of strong jaws getting the better of a bone.

This sound froze Séraphin's heart with hurricane force, but he had no time to dwell on it. A large part of this unidentifiable mass had just detached itself and was bounding towards him with strides three metres long. It was an enormous dog.

Without a moment's thought, Séraphin rushed towards it with the speed of someone running the hundred metres. He saw the jaws opening in front of him. The beast was crouching ready to spring, but Séraphin did not wait for it. He hurled himself at it and struck it in full flight with all his weight, all his speed and all his fury. The beast's fifty kilos and the man's ninety-five kilos hit head-on with a dull thud. The dog was aiming for the larynx, but Séraphin had jumped so high that the teeth could only lacerate his torso. Stunned by the impact, the dog turned over and fell. Séraphin leaped at it, bent double like a diver. He heard the animal's rib cage crack. He had no time to draw breath. A second watchdog was coming at him and this time it was jumping right towards its target, its mouth wide open, straining towards the man's throat. Séraphin put his left hand in front of his neck and thrust his closed fist straight out in front of him. It disappeared into the dog's mouth. Séraphin felt that a life and death struggle had begun between the dog's teeth and his clenched fist which prevented them from locking on to his wrist and hampered the animal's breathing. With his free hand, he seized the top of its muzzle, put his fingers through the gap in the jaws and gripped it under the teeth. The beast tried to pull him off balance, but Séraphin's legs were solidly planted on the ground. The beast clawed at his thighs with its back legs. It loosened its vice-like grip on Séraphin's fist for just one second so that it could get ready to bite again. At that moment he felt the dog's breath on his face as he was bending over it. From somewhere within the smell of mangled flesh rose a hint of bergamot perfume, which went straight to his heart. His left hand gouged the dog's eyes. His right fist closed on the lower jaw. Séraphin braced himself as the dog squeezed both of his hands like a vice. His body was now a smooth knot of muscles and bones. The animal's canine teeth went into his flesh, hooking into him like nails. That was what he wanted. With one of his hands firmly gripping the upper jaw and the other the lower jaw, he began slowly pulling them apart, with all his strength and with all his hate, his own jaw tensed and his eyes looking upward to the sky. He had managed to wedge the beast's body between his thighs and he pulled and pulled . . . Then, all at once, in the depths of that red throat, something cracked and tore. The dog gave a desperate cry and stopped struggling. It was still hanging from Séraphin's hands by its teeth, tearing the flesh. Séraphin had to take them out like hooks. Once released, the beast began to turn in circles, unable to close its gaping mouth. Séraphin filled his chest with as much air as he could. He threw himself on the animal and seized it by its hind legs. He swung this fifty-kilo mass once, twice, three times around his head. Each time he smashed it on the ground. He was reliving the fury of the war, the attacks with a head numbed by alcohol, with all man's bestial instincts, but here it was because of a hint of bergamot in the smell of fetid breath. He was covered in blood, blinded by blood, both his own and the animal's. He did not stop until he could no longer close his own mouth for lack of breath.

He fell to his knees. It was on his knees, almost on all fours that he dragged himself over the 150 metres that the dogs had covered to get to him.

"Charmaine . . ." he whispered.

It was the first time he had ever said a

woman's name in that tone of voice. He managed to take off his shirt, which was in tatters. He spread it over the remains of the war widow. The perfume of the superb body she once had been still came through the smell of torn entrails, and wafted like a memory into Séraphin's heart.

He joined his hands, which had been pierced by the animals' teeth and were bleeding profusely.

"Our Father who art in heaven . . ."

In all the time that had elapsed since the Sisters of Charity had drummed it into him every evening, this prayer had never crossed his lips, not even during the war. He now paid back their efforts with a flood of tears. He understood word for word what it meant.

He suddenly heard a familiar sound. It was a gun being cocked. Through the mist of his tears, he could see the grenadier standing in a ray of moonlight, aiming her gun at him. He said to himself that this would be the end of him. But then he saw a shape rushing through the box trees. This irresistible force threw the old woman to the ground, snatched the gun from her hands, fired two shots into the air, smashed the weapon against the border of the path and threw the pieces far away into the trees.

It was Marie. She turned to face Séraphin and came up to the other side of Charmaine's body. She too fell on her knees.

"Good Lord!" she exclaimed. "Your hands!"

She pulled the scarf she was wearing from around her neck. She held it out in front of her.

"No," Séraphin said.

"If you'd seen him!" Marie will say sixty years later. "He would have made the Devil himself recoil in horror! It looked as though he was under a fountain of blood. Even the tears that fell from his eyes were red. Never, do you understand? Never! If I hadn't adored his very soul, I'd never have been able to go near him without fainting. And do you know what I asked him? Oh! You had to be a girl, and young, to forget that frightful mass of flesh the dogs had made a meal of, lying under the shirt. You had to have a terribly strong nature not to say to yourself that only two hours ago, that *thing* was a flower of a woman who'd made me pine with jealousy! And so, do you know, do you know what I asked him? Eh? Well, you had to be a woman! And above all," she will add, with her finger raised, "believe in God!"

■ ■ ■ ■

"Did you love her?" Marie asked.

"No," Séraphin replied.

"Dear Lord, don't say that! At least let her have something! Yes! You loved her!"

Séraphin shook his head, still weeping.

"Well then. Why are you here? Why are you crying? Why are you on your knees? Why are you clasping your hands?"

"I feel compassion for her," Séraphin murmured.

"I had to lean over to hear that word," Marie will say later. "And I was crying like a baby too and on my knees. We couldn't see each other any more. The moon had disappeared and there was the smell of that body the dogs had mauled . . .

"And then, listen to this: People arrived on the scene. First the farmers, hearing the shots I'd fired. The old woman I'd disarmed had twisted her ankle when I pushed her over. She was hobbling around and if looks could kill, I'd have been dead ten times over. 'My gun! My gun!' she was barking at me. 'You've broken my gun!'

"She couldn't have cared less about the poor woman torn to pieces by the dogs. And

then, listen to this, loads of people arrived
after that, all through the night! And they
all turned their heads away from Charmaine's body and Séraphin. And then, let
me tell you: never, do you understand,
never! They were never able to get him to
stand up, and even less, to unclasp his hands
so that they could treat them. Neither the
gendarmes — there were only two of them
— nor the farmer and his son and daughter,
nor even less the doctor, who kept saying to
him: 'You'll get hydrophobia! You'll get
tetanus! You'll die of gangrene!' He said the
same thing to all of them: 'I don't care!'
And he kept his hands clasped, and you
should have seen what they looked like!
Three bottles it took! Three bottles of arnica
that the doctor had in his bag and managed
somehow to pour on to him. And I could
see that the teeth had made holes the size
of carpenters' nails and tears like but-
tonholes. The arnica ran into them like
water in a mole hole! And do you know
what arnica's like? As for me, when they
put on just a drop because I had jammed
my finger, you could hear me yelling all the
way from Peyruis! And they put three
bottles on him! Not even a sigh . . . And I
was looking at his face. Nothing. He was
crying. Silently. And his face — Oh! His

301

beautiful face — it never changed. It was covered in blood and weeping, but not a sign. He never cried out once; he never winced. Nothing! He felt nothing . . .

"And then, listen to this: ten times over the doctor ordered him to open his hands. Ten times over he said no! Even the gendarmes, let me tell you, couldn't force him to get up. There he was, in front of that body, or what was left of it. You'd have thought he was honouring it by staying with it to its last resting place. You'd have thought . . . But I'm going on too much! And he stayed there on his knees, even when they took the body away. Without saying a word! Just weeping! And there was I, on the other side of that empty space, crying too: for his sake!"

. . . Marie will say sixty years later.

XIV

The padlock on the paddock gate had been cut with pliers. One side of the gate had been pushed back and then attached to the hook holding it wide open, as if inviting the dogs to go out and throw themselves on the first prey they came across.

The magistrate, who had reluctantly freed Patrice for the time being, came hurrying down again from Digne during the morning. This mystery exasperated him. He had familiarized himself with the interviews carried out by the gendarmes. He had read the doctor's report. He had gone to the laundry where Charmaine's remains had been laid on a rack. With his own hands he had lifted the sheet that hid them from sight. He had crossed himself without thinking.

When he went into the living room at Pontradieu, the first thing he saw was Séraphin Monge, covered with dried blood, his chest barely covered by the bloody shirt they had given back to him. His enormous hands were black with blood and punctured by deep holes and gashes, still oozing serum.

The magistrate felt a vague uneasiness in his presence. The gendarmes had told him the story of this colossus who, when he was three weeks old, had been the sole survivor when his whole family was murdered; who had demolished the house in which he was born, stone by stone, to escape the nightmare they reminded him of, and who once again found himself at the centre of these two murders.

The magistrate had seen the path where the tragedy took place. He had seen the remains of the two dogs, which certainly gave him food for thought. One was squashed flat, as though it had been run over by a steam roller. The other was literally torn to pieces. Each one of them must have weighed fifty kilos. How could one unarmed man get the better of them? It's true that the fellow was in a sorry state . . . but nonetheless he was on his feet, breathing easily, with his reserve and his veiled expression. Was he a hero or a murder suspect? It was tempting to accuse this force of nature of the crime. Was he capable of having set up the whole thing, which it seems could have cost him his life? Let's see now: what did that blonde girl say — the one with the plaits that had come undone, the one who couldn't take her eyes off the very suspect Séraphin Monge? What was it she had said to the gendarmes, who had later put it in their report?

"I waited until my mother went to sleep. I went down to Peyruis." — "Why?" — "To keep an eye on Séraphin." — "Why?" — "Because I heard that he was seeing the merry widow." — "And did you see him with the victim?" — "Yes, I saw him." — "Was the victim alive at that time?" — "Oh yes. She was very much alive then!" — "What time was it?" — "My mother goes to sleep at nine. The time it took to come to Peyruis." — "Why did you then follow Séraphin to Pontradieu?" — "Because I love him."

So, Séraphin had been watched by Marie from nine in the evening, the time when he was with the victim, who was oh so alive! And she had only left him to go home again. "Why did she leave you?" That's the question he didn't want to answer. Not that he answered any of them. It was the blonde girl who did it for him. He had also set out for Pontradieu, with Marie close on his heels. He couldn't have arrived at Pontradieu to release the dogs before the victim, any more than jealous Marie could.

The farmers and the servant in the sackcloth dress had heard Charmaine's car arrive.

"But if you heard her car arrive, you must surely have heard her scream? Well now! She must have screamed when she was attacked?"

"No," said the doctor, interrupting. "She must have had her back to the animals. The first one that jumped on her, broke her cervical vertebrae. When that happens, there's no cry . . ."

"But you must have heard the dogs barking?"

The farmer's son, "No. Those dogs don't bark. They only howl when they're dying, but normally they never bark."

"Who had the key to the padlock?"

"I do," said the farmer's son. "But there's no way I'd use it! I fed them too, but I put the food in through the flap on the saltbox, and was very careful doing it, I can tell you! No, I like dogs — I've got three of them — but those animals, they were really like men . . . real men. They had the killer instinct. They'd been trained to kill. They recognized no one. M. Patrice had talked of putting them down, but unfortunately . . ."

The gendarmes' report had considerably

used the dot, dot, dot, although it wasn't in the regulations. "Unfortunately, you stopped him," thought the magistrate, completing the sentence.

He began to wonder, "Why not the farmer's son?"

He's a sturdy, full-blooded, taciturn lad. Why not? A fairly accommodating war widow. A fit of jealousy. She gave her favours to the road mender. He gets the dogs to dispatch her. That's it. And those ferocious dogs leave him alone after he's opened the gate for them. And then there's Gaspard? Two murders committed in the same house by different people? Even if the farmer's son is strong, he doesn't seem terribly intelligent. Now, you'd have to have a fertile imagination to think up the ingeniously simple idea of putting soap on the rim of the pool.

What's more, up to the time when they hear the gunshots fired by the blonde girl with the untidy plaits, the farmer and his son and daughter aren't alone. They've been loading grape stalks on to the home distiller's truck since dawn, and they're with him when they come to see what damage has been done.

"The mother?" the judge wonders. She was there, collapsed on the divan with her head in her hands. The farmer's wife, who must have weighed something like a hundred kilos, had taken her under her protection. The mother? She was deaf and no doubt her faculties were considerably diminished because of it. He shrugged his shoulders. Why would the mother do it?

"We had regard for her feelings when we questioned her," the gendarmes' report stated. "We had to stop her from going and throwing herself on her daughter's body."

That left the servant in the sackcloth dress who was staring at the blonde girl as though she wanted to kill her. "And you then. How did you happen to be next to the body of your young mistress with a gun in your hand just at that moment?" — "I had just heard the car drive up. I was still up, mourning my poor master. I was walking past the window. I saw the car parked in front of the garage. Charmaine had forgotten to turn out her headlights. I went down to tell her." — "With the gun?" — "I always take it with me, especially since . . ." — "And you aimed this gun at Séraphin Monge?" — "Yes." — "Would you have fired?" — "Yes. If this idiot of a girl hadn't pushed me over, I'd have killed him all right! By the way, I'm lodging a complaint against her. This girl smashed my rifle." — "Would you have shot him because you thought that Séraphin had just killed your mistress?" — "No. When I started down the path, Charmaine was already dead and he was further away, dealing with the dogs." — "It didn't occur to you, since you were armed, to go and help him?" — "Help *him?* I said to myself, 'They'll get him for sure.' No such luck! He got them! It only goes to prove what I've always said: to kill those beasts, you have to be in league with the devil! That's what I say!" — "Is that why you wanted to shoot Séraphin?" — "He's calamity's child. If Charmaine hadn't lured him here, nothing would have happened. What would you do to calamity's child? Kill him, that's all there is about it! Someone who is born in the blood of a murder is never rid of it! It's not true that he's all the more innocent! A murder is like a poisonous mushroom — it poisons everyone, murderers and victims alike. A murder is more contagious than the plague. And him! Can't you see him? Just look at him! Every time fate can catch him and cover him with blood, that's what it does. Oh, what a pity I'm the only one who can see things as they are! But don't you know that if you could see him as I do, *you*'d be the ones shooting him?" — "He killed the dogs. He kneeled down next to your mistress." — "Oh, her! They made a fine pair, the two of them, I can tell you! She'd hidden the picture of her late husband, the hero, under a pile of her frippery, as if that could prevent him from seeing what she was up to!" — "Do you persist in your declarations?" — "I certainly do! My mother always told me, 'Eudoxie, always tell the truth as you see it. With the truth as your catechism, you'll always be at the right hand of God!' "

The gendarmes had conscientiously transcribed all that, word for word, licking their pencils from time to time, writing deliberately and legibly on those wads of paper in quadruplicate.

The magistrate had to yield to the evidence. There was only one line to pursue: the same person had done away with Gaspard and then Charmaine, either because she was in the way, or because she knew the secret of her father's death, and she had to be prevented from talking. It was both crystal clear and totally incomprehensible, as the principal beneficiary of both murders — oh, the pity of it! — was in prison. At least he was there the previous night, but now he should be en route for Pontradieu in his red car. — And of course! What a pretty sight he was going to find! — As for all the others who were here with him, awaiting his decisions, if all of them had the opportunity to soap the edge around the pool, none of them could have let the dogs out without suffering the same fate as Charmaine. Who then could have done it with impunity, to the extent of feeling safe enough to open the paddock gate and hook it back? The magistrate was confronted with a real mystery, which was getting deeper and deeper. He thought of instituting letters rogatory in Marseille to establish the movements of the diva's father, the man who sold the dogs and apparently the only person who could have known them well enough to free them without harm to himself. But what motive would he have? As he had a record for minor offences, they had already thought of him in connection with Gaspard's murder, but his alibi had proved watertight. Why would he come and kill Charmaine?

"Find the motive," the magistrate said to himself, "otherwise . . ."

It was getting late and he had too many suspects. The gendarmes had already had a phone call from the squad. The blonde girl's parents had raised the alarm everywhere. All the inhabitants of Lurs were combing the thickets, for the distraught baker's wife was in no state to sell bread. Her daughter must be found. They had started to look in ponds. They had cut off the water in the canal, so that they could drag it.

"A decision has to be made," the magistrate said to himself. And he took a bad one. Since that servant insisted and had signed . . . What was her name again? Ah, yes! That's it: Eudoxie Chamechaude. Well then, since the Chamechaude woman had freely admitted having wanted to do away with the said Séraphin Monge, and would have done it if the girl Marie Dormeur hadn't intervened, so be it: all he had to do was take the Chamechaude woman into custody.

It was the only time Séraphin's quiet voice was heard.

"I'm not laying charges," he said.

"What! She wanted to kill you. She admits it. And you don't want to lay charges?"

"No. I'm not laying charges. I haven't the right."

"What? What's all this nonsense? Who gives or refuses you this right? Since justice entitles you to do it, I can't see why you're hesitating!"

The judge gave a furtive look at Séraphin, who said nothing more, and who now looked black under the dried blood and the

312

bruises. This colossus of a man was looking more and more suspect. Having already escaped a massacre at his birth, he also escaped the slaughter of the war. And the magistrate knew that he had fought in the most dangerous areas, which he envied, what is more, as one envies a man who has had a lot of mistresses. And here he is now, having just escaped death once more, thanks to a girl's love and his own suspicious strength. That added up to quite a lot. However . . . for the moment he was still the victim. And the accused was this poor woman in her sackcloth dress, who admitted her guilt with her own statements through a love of the truth. He couldn't help taking quite a liking to her. He liked devoted servants.

He beckoned the gendarmes.

"And that, my dear man, was the very moment when Patrice arrived! Oh! Just looking at him made the blood rush to my heart. You couldn't imagine it. These days there are no more of those disfigured veterans of 1914 left. Well, almost none. They all died in the end. It was especially his chin, his forehead . . . and his ears . . . Well, what was left of them. Anyway, the other girl, Rose Sépulcre, was with him. She'd understood pretty quickly which side her bread was buttered on, that one. Mind you, I've got to hand it to her. It took courage to do it! I couldn't have. Well, the two of them were there. They'd been told about it. He came out of prison only to find his sister eaten by the dogs, and if you only knew how much he loved her! We understood because he said, 'Where is she?' and then strode off towards the laundry. He went in. He made a gesture. Rose screamed. She clung on to him. He walked forward like a robot with her hanging on to him. She screamed again. He pushed her aside impatiently. If I told you the actual truth, I'd say not impatiently, but roughly. He fell on his knees, took hold of the sheet that covered his sister's body and threw it back. And then . . . the one thing that was still intact was her face. And Patrice started to stroke it very gently, then leaned over, and just as you might console a little child who is very upset, he planted little kisses on her eyelids, her forehead, her hair, which were wet with his tears . . . Oh! Seeing that mutilated face crying just broke your heart! 'Cover her up!' Rose screamed. 'Please, please, cover her up!' It was her stomach and her breasts that you couldn't bear to look at. And then I saw that Rose couldn't cope with it. She was going to faint and be no use whatsoever. I must say in passing that she could tolerate Patrice's face, and that took some courage. I always had to look away from him, but as far as Charmaine's ripped stomach was concerned, I could look at that without flinching. Don't ask me why! Nature's a strange thing. And then . . . Well, what would you have done if you were in my shoes? I caught Rose just as she was going to fall and held her tight against me. It was a very strange feeling to hold my closest enemy in my arms . . . But, what else can you do? . . . Christian charity . . .

"Then I saw Séraphin kneel down next to Patrice, and he was the one who pulled the sheet up over Charmaine's remains. Then he put his arms around Patrice and held him as I had done Rose. But he . . . how can I describe it? The way he held him wasn't like a brother or a friend. I was going to say it was like a mother! No, not even like a mother. He didn't hold him tightly, by the way. He enveloped him. And cried with him. Séraphin was like a cradle. He was . . . Oh! How could I not love him? And I could see his poor stumps of hands, all black with the tooth holes still in them. I said to myself, 'They'll have to amputate them! How does he manage to hide the pain

315

he's suffering?' My teeth were chattering as that thought went through my mind because . . . It must have been there, in that laundry open to the four winds with its big wash trough and the sound of the tap still running, and that oozing body . . . It must have been there, my dear man, that I caught my death.

"And we stayed like that until the door suddenly burst open. And then my parents came in. They saw nothing of all that. They showed no respect for anything. My mother was shouting 'Marie!' and they shoved Rose aside, though she could scarcely stand. They covered me with tears and kisses and exclamations of 'my poor little girl!' They dragged me out and took me away. My father had his rifle over his shoulder. He was shouting, 'Let's go! Let's go quickly!' They had hired the car from the garage man in Peyruis. They held me so tightly it was like a strangle-hold. My mother had never held me like that. 'The apple of their eye.' Since then, my dear man, I've never been the apple of anyone's eye . . . As for me, I was struggling and shouting too. I wanted to stay with Séraphin. And you know, at that time I weighed sixty-two kilos with a willpower to match! Now to get me to move . . . I shouted that there was something I wanted to say. It was true. Something I'd forgotten to say. It was true. When I was going down the road at night behind Séraphin, I'd passed a bicycle without a light, but with a buckled wheel . . . The whole time after that I was obsessed in my delirium by: buckled wheel, something to say . . . Something only you noticed . . . But there you are. They didn't give me enough time. They felt that I was feverish and my teeth were chattering. Their love had a brute force that was much stronger than my will. They took me away. And it was that evening . . . or maybe the following evening . . . or three days later? I can't remember any more. I must have been hanging around for a while. Oh! All of that was so long ago. Anyway, it was some time then that I went to bed, intending never to get up again. Twenty-five days, my dear man, twenty-five days! Everything else happened without me."

. . . Marie will relate sixty years later.

Two days later, Séraphin was back on the roads, his swollen hands gripping the handle of his sledge-hammer hard enough to break it, crushing stones with the same steady rhythm, trying to forget.

Panic seized the popular imagination, and the dogs he had killed were soon held to have been rabid. Children and cyclists gave him a wide berth. Everyone watched the road mender for the appearance of the first symptoms. In Peyruis itself, six burly men were practising in secret so that they could smother him between two mattresses, should the need arise.

Séraphin did not become rabid, but, on the contrary, as weak as a child from the terror that overcame him. Someone had taken it upon himself to put his plans into practice. Someone was spying on him, following him, guessing what he was about to do, and killing in his stead. "No! No! Never!" he said to himself. "I would never have killed Charmaine. Even if she'd informed against me. I could never have . . ."

He stayed for hours on end, shattered, staring into space, sitting on the bench at the table, which was still at an angle since Charmaine had pushed it away so that she could come and sink down on to him. He couldn't take his eyes off the empty chair where he would never dare to sit ever again. Charmaine was still present in the room. Even her perfume still lingered in the air.

One evening Séraphin opened the tin. He took out the papers, lifted the cover on the stove — for the cold weather had slowly settled in — and held them above the flames. But he didn't dare. To burn them seemed a sacrilege. He put them back where he had taken them.

"Never again!" he said quietly.

He thought he would never have the courage to wish anyone else dead.

For a little while, this decision seemed to bring him peace of mind once more. He stopped living entirely within himself. He slept. He slept for two nights. He let his guard down. When he slept, he relaxed his enormous fists on which new flesh was filling the wounds with an irresistible surge of growth. He let them rest defencelessly on the counterpane.

The dream hit him full on, when he was completely relaxed, just as though someone had jabbed him in the back with a fork. This time it was without the warning sound of dead leaves rustling, which usually gave him the opportunity to escape from sleep. Not this time. He found himself imprisoned by lustful flesh, smelling not of soot but of bergamot. Not knowing where he was, he found himself besieged by a body with great strength. It was already upon him when he became aware of the dream. He heard the words in his ears, and this time they were perfectly audible. And this time the embrace held him like a vice until he surrendered. She drew a great spurt of semen from him, which he was powerless to hold back. He came in absolute terror.

He found himself sitting up, the roots of his hair crawling. What had she said? What had she wanted to say to him? What was her voice like when she charged him to carry out her commands? He had never heard it in his life. She had spoken for some time, and yet he could only remember the last words, the only ones he needed to remember, "I didn't send you to feel compassion."

From that moment, something strange occurred in Séraphin's heart: just as his wounds were healing without leaving any scars, the burden of Charmaine was lifted from his mind. It forgot Gaspard, forgot Patrice and found its attention concentrated on the victims his mother was waiting for him to offer up to her.

From the evening that followed the dream, he went prowling around the hills surrounding the mill at Saint-Sépulcre, where the second murderer of his family was hidden away.

XV

The Saint-Sèpulcre mill is set under the oblong rock of a waterfall on the Lauzon river, in the narrows of a short mountain pass which opens out on to the soft curves of the Lure mountains, where they first appear. You can almost stretch out your hand to stroke them.

There is no paddle wheel, as you find in romantic picturesque mills. The current of the Lauzon never was strong enough to drive it; it's a system of locks, a series of ponds, hatches, valves, paddles, wooden tenon and mortise gears, jibs, racks and counterbalances. When it's working, it makes a clicking sound like a skeleton orchestra. If you could take the whole mechanism in at a glance, you would think you were looking at a village clock that ground olives instead of time.

At the Saint-Sépulcre mill, each successive Sépulcre found some ingenious little solution to compensate for the occasional scarcity of water. After all these generations, the system is now so complex that it has to be completely inspected and adjusted every year before it is used, starting with the millraces.

Early that day, spade on shoulder and honey bucket full of pink grease for the grooves of the sluice gate, Didon Sépulcre went out of his house into a fog so thick that he couldn't see the smoke from his cigarette. The waters of the Lauzon were beginning to make themselves heard. The river had been anaemic all summer, disappearing in places under the gravel in its bed, finally becoming green with moss, and people were no longer aware of its presence.

Didon sniffed the air before venturing on to the steps cut into the earth leading to the millrace. It was definitely the wrong day to do it. On a day like this a week earlier, he thought he had seen a man standing deep in thought leaning over the bridge above the waterfall. As if you could think with all that fog in your nostrils. As if you could admire the countryside when you can scarcely see the ends of your fingers.

In weather like that, all those places that allow wrong-doers to lie in wait looked highly suspicious. People could indulge in dirty tricks to their hearts' content. At least that's what Didon Sépulcre thought as he ventured out of the house. For if Célestat Dormeur took his gun to go and make bread, Didon took his to go and clean out the water channels. It was no protection really: what use is a gun in the fog? And how can you use it if you're leaning over in a channel up to your shoulders in water? You're forever bending over and straightening up again, with your head barely higher than the top. And if anyone crept up behind you in the fog, walking on the soft mud that you spent your life removing from the bottom, they'd be in the best position to knock you off. What about the gun? If you put it down too close, you were in danger of hitting it with the shovel and it could go off and get you in the stomach. But what of it? It was better to take it anyway. It was reassuring . . .

And so, with his honey bucket in his hand, his shovel on one shoulder, and his gun slung across the other, Didon Sépulcre was a sight to make anyone laugh, if anyone had been there. But in that fog . . . Térésa was the only one laughing, and laughing heartily. That's because she didn't know. If she had known, she would have loaded the gun herself and come as far as the sluice gate, watching over him with her finger on the trigger. But how could he tell her? How could he say to her, "Séraphin Monge has knocked down his house . . . Gaspard Dupin is dead . . . and since then, well, I've been afraid . . ." How could he say all that without her asking why he was afraid?

Didon sighed and went up the steps leading to the millrace. It was a fortnight before St Catherine's Day. The harvest had been brought in, the ploughing had been done, the grapes had been picked. Every year it was the same story: "This year I won't be caught. I'll clean the mill and get it in working order as soon as . . ." but "as soon as" never seemed to come. A mill isn't enough to live on. Every year there was all the rest to think about. The mill was the last on the list . . . So, there you are. In two weeks' time it would be St Catherine's Day . . .

As they say in these parts, "For St Catherine's Day, oil is in the olive". The normal run of pickers, and that includes the overcautious, those who think they are provident because they pick the fruit scarcely ripe, those who fear harvesting in the rain, the mistral or the snow, all of them leaped on St Catherine's Day as on a hare in its form. After that, they were already there with their sacks on the first of December at the latest. They stood there waiting for the oil to flow, staring suspiciously like discoverers of treasure. They would have drunk it as it came out of the shallow baskets, if they had been allowed. They caught it in their measuring vessels and let it flow into their wicker-covered bottles. As soon as the demijohns were full, two people rushed them to the barrows and carts. The child formed a rear-guard defending their retreat; the grandfather stayed with the bottles yet to be filled, watching with an eagle eye, as though the miller were a thief, as though all the neighbours and friends who were waiting their turn were capable of pilfering with a demijohn or two.

Then, off they went! People took cover in their houses, the doors slammed shut, sadistically watching the others suffering in the olive groves, bent double over their trestles. Not that it prevented them from going to bed with frozen feet, stiff knees and such bad chilblains on their ears that they hardly knew where to lay their heads on the pillow. Sometimes it didn't stop sciatica or flu sending you to bed and keeping you there. For, St Catherine's Day or not, the weather did as it pleased, and it sometimes happened that the 25th of November and the following days were dismal ones when the bad weather bit savagely into the flesh.

For the olive tree is the tree of pain. It brings peace only to those who see it through God's eyes. Besides, you should suspect as much, just by looking at it: it is twisted, knotty, bent right over like an old man worn out by all the sly tricks the weather has played on him. You should suspect as much, seeing it standing stoically under the frosts, still bearing its fruit. Sometimes there are only a few on each twig and sometimes there is so much that the weight nearly breaks the branches. This should make you think that if you want to go and pick them, you'll have to get in tune with the tree and be as stoical as it is. But in spite of that, every year we never tire of trying to outsmart the weather. We try to guess it and suffer as little as possible. That's what the St Catherine's Day proverb is for.

"Yes indeed," Didon Sépulcre sighed. "And if we do have bad weather like that, afterwards we get a fine, mild January when it would be a godsend to do the harvest. No rain, no mistral, one glorious day after the other, so that the violets grow and the gullible almond trees are tricked into flowering yet again like the silly fools they are!"

Didon heaved a big sigh.

"Yes indeed!" he said to himself. "But St Catherine's day is sacred. If the mill wasn't ready to receive the olives on the first of December at the latest, that miserable bunch would come and drag you out of bed by the scruff of the neck!"

These were the thoughts of Didon Sépulcre as he walked with his shovel on one shoulder, the gun over the other and the pot of grease hanging from the tips of his fingers. He was walking towards the slope of the millrace, with the sound of the river Lauzon starting to make itself heard. He was walking in a fog that weighed down the aspen leaves and made them fall like rain. It was rotten weather. The season was deteriorating fast. The oaks were three weeks early. They had already turned gold before losing their colour under their winter coat.

Didon was wandering about in this beaten egg-white of a fog, which he wasn't used to. His land was tricking him by not looking as it usually did. It made him collide with the sluice gate support, when he thought he was at least three metres away.

He went down into the slimy race. He hung the gun on the support. (It wouldn't be easy to get it down in an emergency, but what else could he do?) He spat in his hands and began working with a will. It was work well done. He put the solid sludge by the side of the channel on top of last year's, flattening it with a sharp tap of his shovel. He cleared the base of the lock. This drop lock went back perhaps as far as the first Sépulcres. It was as old and as well preserved as family furniture tucked away in a bedroom, although it had lost its colour long ago.

Behind this oak door, the Lauzon was flowing over the gravel, with a few white horses of foam already showing. This was a capricious river. At the mill, he often had to harness the horse to the millstone beam as a back-up, because the flow of water was so feeble and the level so low. He sometimes had to wait forty-eight hours for the mill-races to fill up. On the other hand, there were some years when it had to be physically held back like a stallion; when it collected enough water in the hollow of Mont-laux, the northern valleys of Ganagobie and the rock slabs of Maltortel, to roar like a wild animal and determinedly be a part of nature's malice.

Didon took handfuls of grease and sensually rubbed up and down the grooves to facilitate the movement of the hatch. At the same time he listened to the Lauzon, which sounded as though it were carrying bottles along in its current. There would be a lot of water this year. Didon was rarely wrong on that score. When he put his ear to it like an eavesdropper while he was cleaning the lock, the sound he heard then told him what would happen in that fickle stream from then until St Catherine's Day.

They would harvest the olives as though they had a ball and chain on their feet; lumps of zaffre stone weighing five kilos each clinging to the soles of their shoes every time they moved the trestle. You'd see people arriving at the mill with their knees so stiff they could hardly move. They would still be talking about it . . . Didon smiled at the thought. He liked to hear tales of the olive pickers' woes around the warm mill-stones.

Suddenly a warning shiver went down his spine. Was someone looking at him? He seized the gun, turned around anxiously peering into the misty cocoon that surrounded him. He was alone. But what did that mean, alone? If someone turned at the same time as he did, out there on the edge of the fog, hiding behind it like a curtain, then Sépulcre couldn't see him. And then, what if it wasn't what he'd been expecting — what he'd been expecting for the last

329

twenty-five years — and which was now hanging over his head, he was sure of it, since Gaspard's death. What if it was someone poaching in the river? If it was some neighbour looking for mushrooms under the poplars? No. Firing his gun was no solution.

But Didon was uneasy as he worked for the rest of the day. He was on the alert all the time, watching out of the corner of his eye, stopping suddenly, hoping to surprise heaven knows what.

As he descended from race to race and draining trap to draining trap, there were several times when he had the heavy feeling in his back that someone was looking at him (and the worst of it was that he knew whose eyes they were). Once he also thought he heard a quickly stifled cough, which he also recognized. With gun in hand he shouted:

"Qué siès?" ("Who's there?")

As if he didn't know. But the only response was the rain of falling leaves in the birches and the sound of clinking bottles coming from the waters of the Lauzon. He went home feeling very uneasy. He couldn't get the presence that had been prowling around him all day out of his mind. And the fact that it was petrified in a corner of his memory, and as still as a statue in a square, didn't make it any more reassuring.

Now that he'd been able to contain his panic by reasoning with himself, he felt almost calm. The cleaning of the millraces and locks had been completed without mishap. Everything was clean: the reeds cleared away, the dyke reinforced, the channels cleaned out, the sluice gate greased. The only things still to be done were small though quite painstaking jobs, to be finished off inside. He had spent the whole day cutting the chamfered edges of tenons, pins and wedges that he was going to fit on to the pieces of machinery that had some play in them.

What still had to be done now was in the timing mechanism. He had to get rid of all the slack in the linkage between the turn-pins, so that there would be no sudden stoppage along the 150 metres separating the sluice gate on the Lauzon from the lifting beam of the millstones; so that with each movement, the mobile regulator bracket would engage exactly in the following tooth. If not, the slack would become so much worse that after a few days in use, the main pulley would jerk in the regulator until it broke down. And then, good-bye to the whole season!

Didon always did that work at night, alone, far from Térésa's resentful sneers — he hadn't touched her for years — far from ugly Marcelle's whining demands and far from Rose's unanswerable criticisms of everything her father did.

On that particular evening, he left the house only after Rose had returned. Rose in her high heels, always in a hurry. Rose who was always brought home these days by Patrice with the disfigured face. Térésa had had to use all her credit with him (all the weight of her thirty years of conjugal fidelity to a joyless love) to stop Didon from chaining "the apple of his eye" to the bed rails after the first escapade. "Leave the chains alone!" Térésa had said. "Patrice will marry her. She'll be the wife of a Dupin. And now that his father is dead, he's the mayor. And now that his sister is dead, he'll get everything. Everything! Do you understand me? The 500 acres of Pontradieu, the factory, the business, everything! Your grandsons will be millionaires! So just keep quiet and go and clean out the channels!"

He could hardly believe his eyes! He could hardly bear the sight of Patrice with his badly patched-up harlequin's face, and he watched with amazement as his daughter ran to her lover as soon as she heard the sound of his car. Standing there stunned, he saw the faultless beauty of her face, with its eyes wide open expressing all the love in the world, turn up towards that frightful sarcastic face, which was no longer even capable of expressing tenderness or admiration.

And Didon Sépulcre didn't even know all there was to know. He didn't know that his daughter had wrested her future husband from a dead woman. He didn't know that three times during the night and two days when they had kept vigil over Charmaine's body, Rose had had to stop Patrice from going to lie in his sister's coffin with a revolver in his hand. He didn't know that to keep him in this world, she had had to throw away all the bullets from the gun, and that in the end she had offered herself to Patrice a few feet away from the coffin, on the couch with its dust cover, and that throughout this time, he had wet her breasts with his tears. Didon Sépulcre knew nothing of that, otherwise he might perhaps have split "the apple of his eye's" head in two.

At last . . . She had come home at last . . . Didon heard her upstairs, kicking off her shoes, which hit the wall. He heard Marcelle's shrill voice as she asked her if she'd had a good time at least.

Then he left the house and crossed the dark courtyard. The rain had settled in everywhere, falling evenly over the ploughed fields, flattening the furrows and purging the Lauzon basin of eight months' drought. Just a stone's throw away, but sounding as though you were under it, the usually tiny waterfall was roaring like a cataract. Through the heavy, dark rain, you could feel the spray from the falling water rising up from the river bed.

Didon stamped through the puddles as he crossed the courtyard, cursing the good Lord in patois. He was carrying the jute sack full of wedges and tools plus the gun over his shoulder. He was hurrying, rushing in fact, but he scarcely knew where he was going. His arms and legs made rowing motions in the thick night, for the dark courtyard could hide anything. He threw himself against the door of the mill. His hand had trouble finding the latch, even though he had been used to it since childhood. But fear destroys everything, even habit. He opened it, closed the door again and leaned against it, heaving a sigh of relief. Here, more than in his own house, he felt at home.

To get some light, he turned the damp, grating switch that gave electric shocks. Calling it light was rather an exaggeration.

The few forty-candlepower globes here and there were drowned in the oily film that impregnated everything. Here the air, the walls, the ceiling and the paving stones were so saturated with oil that it penetrated through the front wall and turned the whole building a darker olive colour. The smell of the *infers* reigned supreme over all.

The *infers* are deep pits which receive the pulp residue after the oil has been extracted. Those who are tight-fisted come and take it away in buckets, and after a fortnight's exhausting work with coffee spoons, they manage to get another half-litre of oil out of it. Those who are open-handed leave it with the miller. The residue is then thrown into the *infers.* These left-overs increase and reform from year to year as they ferment. They consist of large lumps of spongy matter as thick as beef liver and as oily as mother of vinegar. When you press down, it exudes a noxious fatty substance with a mysterious odour (half truffle, half decay, but not an offensive smell). Some of these cakes have been lying in the bottom of the pits from the time the first Sépulcres began making oil. In the old days, the poor — and the priests for their procession altars — came to collect the small amount of oil there to impregnate the wicks for the small lamps that lit their stables.

Térésa always said that these *infers* were unworthy of a clean mill like theirs, and that if Didon had the slightest sense of shame, he would have had them filled in long ago. She had said the same thing to him today, as she always did at the beginning of each season. Didon shrugged his shoulders as he remembered her words. Even Térésa's constant quarrelling was welcome in the anxious state he was in. It was reassuring, like the smell of the *infers.*

He put his gun down carefully on a pile of pressing mats. He hung up his cap and his damp jacket on the pegs where the workers changed clothes. He tipped his tools out on the ground and began to work.

He worked for a long time, feeling quite calm, all his apprehension dispelled. Nevertheless, it seemed to him that several times when he happened to glance up at the small dim window, there was a change in the sound of the pouring rain that was overflowing the guttering, as if its flow was being stopped by hitting canvas or an umbrella . . . But if he was going to stop for everything . . .

Now everything was in place, tightened, greased, balanced, but Didon still had to make sure that he hadn't forgotten anything.

To do that he had to put the whole machinery assembly into reverse.

Grumbling to himself, he went to look for the big lever with the iron shoe that was only used for this purpose, but it was not there. He found it, not in its proper place, but behind the stove, leaning at the same angle as the pipe, well hidden in a dark corner, probably by a journeyman last year, so that Didon would take a long time to discover where it was . . .

Armed with this tool, he stepped over the wall of the vat and wedged the shoe of the lever under one of the millstones. Leaning all his weight on the lever, he managed to move the two circular stones weighing a ton each centimetre by centimetre. At the same time he listened attentively to the movement of the gear-wheels, which he was driving slowly, right down to the smallest, turning at great speed. Now there was not a single grinding noise, a single sigh: the season could begin. Didon jumped lightly to the ground and went to put the lever back in the usual place, where he could easily find it next year.

All he had to do now was to pour a litre of olive oil into the stone bearing where the steel spindle of the millstone's pivot turned. This bottom part of the pivot, at the end of the chain, took all the force of the work. It absorbed all the jolts a hundredfold. The reason it was greased with olive oil is that it wouldn't take anything else. With any other lubricant it would screech like a baby at every turn of the millstone, so much so that the customers' conversations couldn't be heard.

Didon came back towards the crushing vat with his bottle full. He had a moment's hesitation before stepping into it again. He looked over towards the lever controlling the two coupling pins on the gear-wheels. It was half-way pushed down to the ground. "You really should disengage them," he said to himself, "now that everything's ready to go . . . If ever the sluice gate gave way . . ." He shrugged his shoulders. He had been doing the same thing for thirty years. Why should he change this year? The sluice gate had held good for so long. Between its deep grooves and mortised oak panels, it had never ceased or even weakened in holding back the stream with all the old, robust dryness of a piece of family furniture. It's true that the Lauzon rarely roared as loudly as that particular night. But if he was going to stop for everything . . .

He jumped nimbly into the millstone basin and crouched down in front of the spindle. He took a hollow reed from his pocket and put it into the groove in the stone. He tipped the bottle and slowly, slowly sent the oil down the groove. It was a long, uncomfortable job, under the shadow of the overhanging millstones. This meant that Didon had to twist around and stay crouching on the balls of his feet, trying to keep his balance because of the slope of the vat. Didon was concentrating so much that his tongue stuck out, and he thought of nothing else.

It was then that the person who had been watching him behind the skylight moved away from the wall, beneath the water that poured over the guttering. He went up the stairs cut into the earth and walked along the millrace in the darkness at the same pace as he would have done in broad daylight. The Lauzon growled as it flowed towards him. It drummed against the bulge of the sluice gate. The man steadied his feet on each side of the race. Without a moment's hesitation he seized the two rods of the sluice gate in both hands, then in one rapid movement pulled it straight up. He held it up with one hand, groping around with the other for the bolt, which he plunged into the hole. When he had completed these three actions, the heavy water of the torrent reached out like an arm of steel into the newly cleaned channels. It ran along as silently as a snake.

That was the moment when Didon heard the noise, that noise through all the others: the waterfall, the beating rain, the host of leaves falling from the trees in the surging of the sea wind. It wound its way through them like a little tune played by all the wooden instruments which made up the mill's tablature. It was this supple, sinuous water, held in on all sides, being transformed into solid energy by the walnut-wood chutes, submerging the draining wells, striking the rack paddles, making the counterweights click like castanets, pushing the great cog-wheel with tiny vibrations so that it turned slowly — spoke by spoke, you'd have thought — but transmitting the raw energy of the Lauzon, at last, to the square larch-wood spindle, as broad as a man's torso, to which the one-ton millstones were fixed. Didon was between these stones doing two things too many: wiping the reed pipe, which would do for next year, and putting the cork back on the bottle of oil. Yet he had been doing them every year in exactly the same place and under exactly the same conditions for more than twenty-five years. Why would he have changed? Why would he have got out of the vat to do them?

He was stunned with surprise for a second too long. He definitely saw the gear lever jolt in its groove over on the other side of the vat, but at that moment one of the millstones already cut off his retreat and the other, off centre, pushed him in the back. The force of it made him lose his balance. With the sound of a squashed insect, his body spurted out in all directions under the mass of the millstone.

There was the dark, heavy rain, the miserable little waterfall transformed into a cataract, the Lauzon which could be heard a kilometre away, and deep down below, the grinding of the millstones.

The two buildings — the mill and the farm — were joined by the foundations and the sheds, stables and barns. In spite of the din made by the waters, the droning of the millstones travelled from one building to the other.

Relaxed and cosy in the warmth of love's smile, Rose Sépulcre opened her eyes to this familiar sound. This sound that maintained them had been part of autumn nights for the whole of her life. She could never expect anything bad to come from it. It was like a horse feeding in a stable.

She turned over to go back to sleep and pounded her pillow. Marcelle moaned in her sleep on the other side of the double bed. Rose was suddenly wide awake.

"But . . . what am I thinking of? It's not St Catherine's Day yet."

"What's the matter?" Marcelle said.

Rose gripped her hard by the arm.

"Listen!"

"To what?"

"The millstones . . ."

"Well?"

"What's the date?"

"I haven't the faintest idea. Leave me alone!"

Rose shook her urgently.

"Can you hear it?"

"It's the millstones. Papa must be testing them."

"Nonsense!" Rose said. "You never make them turn with nothing to grind. It damages everything!"

"Well then, it must be . . . must be . . ."

Marcelle's limp arm flailed the air and she fell back face first into the pillow.

Rose threw the eiderdown on to the floor and pulled back the bedclothes.

She jumped out of bed and began pulling Marcelle by the feet.

"Wake up, you trollop! Something's happening!"

She put on her slippers, wrapped herself in her dressing gown and held Marcelle's out to her.

"Ow! What on earth could happen? Are you mad?"

But Rose had grabbed her and was pushing her into the corridor, then down the stairs. The heavy rain made them hesitate a moment on the threshold of the house. Further away in front of them, through the cracks in the door and the dirty panes of the window, a feeble light could be seen filtering through the oily vapour coming off the *infers.* The two sisters ran across and rushed at the door, which they opened wide. The pelting rain had woken Marcelle up completely.

They didn't realize straight away what the heavy glistening red drapery around the moving millstones was. In the poor light it looked like a ruby cope.

A sound broke their stunned surprise. Didon's right arm had been extended beyond the reach of the millstones. It was broken at the elbow on the side of the vat. The stones had so ground the flesh and bones that they had finally severed it completely and its own weight had just made it fall on to the stone floor. This was the sound that turned the

343

girls' bulging eyes towards the sight. The screams they both let out dominated all the noise, piercing the cataract, bursting through the rain, shaking Térésa out of her heavy sleep and precipitating her into the corridor, having just managed to grab a dressing gown as she passed. The screams rushed at her once again with the same intensity, coming from the direction of the mill. Térésa saw the open door, her daughters in front of it, Marcelle rushing forward and bracing herself on the coupling lever and pulling it towards her with all her might.

"Ma! Don't come in! Ma, you mustn't come in!"

They stood there trying to push her out into the soaking rain again. The three women's heads already made them look as though they were drowned. Térésa hit out blindly at her daughters, pulling them along as they grabbed her clothes, and thus arrived at the mill door.

She looked. The millstones were still. Didon's arm on the flagstones with its hand open wide seemed to appeal for help like a drowning man's. Then Térésa gave a long agonized cry, and she continued screaming from then on. She ran off into the rain, up the earth steps leading to the bridge, slipping and dirtying her clothes as she went.

She crossed the bridge yelling for help, then hesitated as to which path to take, still screaming for help in all directions at the top of her voice, her face distraught and her fingernails digging into the palms of her hands. The girls took up her cries as they ran along the path, which could scarcely be seen under the rain, holding on to their mother's skirt as if they were still four years old. There was no hope there, not a gleam of light on the whole horizon, except for that oily glow down below in the mill, to which they could not possibly return.

That night there were three women abandoned by God on the Lurs plain, between Sigonce and the Planier valley. Three women terrified and alone, howling at the moon like animals. The wind swept masses of dead leaves into their faces, while the Lauzon lowed in its sandy bed, deepening the drop of the waterfall as it flowed. And the rain continued to fall.

The three women, guided by instinct, climbed the Lurs hill towards the village. They screamed and bellowed in front of the seminary and nearly broke the door from banging it with the great bronze knocker. But everyone behind the metre-thick walls went on sleeping the sleep of the just.

Then, still shrieking and walking three

abreast, stumbling over the paving stones in their bedroom slippers, they started down the steep village street. One single light two hundred metres further down in front of them shone a bar of gold across the path.

Célestat Dormeur was shaping the loaves of bread with a damp cloth to brown them when the noise reached him from way outside in the rain. He heard the stammers, the cries, the screams, the shrill entreaties, the groaning of worn-out pain which surged like piercing thunder. And this wild chorus of sound was coming towards him with the speed of an avalanche. Célestat immediately believed all the legends he'd ever heard. From the wailing and moaning he built up the vague image of a beast that the Lurs street could never contain. He leapt for his gun, crouched down in a corner between the oven and the sacks of flour, facing the curtain of rain that spilled over the guttering in front of the open door.

But what loomed up then out of the night was more frightful than some foul beast.

Was it three women? They seemed to be three swollen faces with open mouths gurgling with terror and rain water, and with wildly dilated pupils in their red eyes. Their bodies ran with water so that they seemed to have been melted into one by disaster.

For more than three minutes — the three minutes it took for him to recognize them — they just stood there with their mouths open to scream, but without a sound coming from them. All they could do to make him understand what had happened, was to imitate the movement of a wheel turning with their exhausted arms.

XVI

Séraphin Monge followed Didon Sépulcre's coffin. Well . . . what they had been able to recover of him with a bucket, spade and cloth.

Séraphin wondered whether he was going mad. For the third time, someone had done his work for him, and in such a horrible manner that he wondered if he would have had the courage to do it himself. But who? During all those evenings when he had been prowling around the mill, searching for a way to do what he needed to do, he had been aware that an unknown presence was creeping about everywhere in the dark or the mist, almost as elusive, furtive and quick as a squirrel running through the branches of a tree.

Why? Who besides himself, Séraphin Monge, could bear enough ill-will against this man to crush him under a millstone? And besides, who could have wanted to do away with both Gaspard and Charmaine?

Séraphin watched the hearse advancing slowly ahead of the crowd, as the road leading from the mill to the Lurs church and cemetery was steep. They had had to harness an extra horse to the four-wheeled dray.

Séraphin watched Patrice, who was holding Rose Sépulcre in full mourning close against him, sheltering her under his umbrella. For rain was falling on the funeral procession. Up above, Lurs was smoking under wispy patches of mist. A miserable November had finally settled over the countryside.

Séraphin felt shivers run down his spine. Gaspard was dead, Charmaine was dead, innocent of any crime — the crying injustice of it stirred his conscience —, Didon Sépulcre was dead. And now the word whispering its way down the length of the cortège was that Marie Dormeur would die soon.

Gendarmes holding their bikes were in close file around the trembling crowd, where the murderer could be lurking, perhaps surrounded by friends, perhaps talking business down there at the end of the cortège. How could they know? They had found the sluice gate up and the bolt in the hole, but the rain had washed away any clues. On these dark, foggy nights anyone could have left home and dashed off through the familiar darkness to raise the lock while Didon was testing the machinery. Anyone could have put soap on the rim of the pool for Gaspard. But . . . not just anyone could have opened the door wide for the savage dogs at the risk of being torn to pieces.

Séraphin made his way through the crowd without an umbrella. There was always a respectful distance maintained around him. He always walked alone. People moved away from him. They didn't want to be in his shadow.

Several times he had to resist the urge to cut through the crowd, hold out his wrists to the gendarmes and say: "Arrest me . . . I haven't killed anyone, but I did plan to kill those who have died. Arrest me, take me before your magistrate. He's more intelligent than you or me. Perhaps he'll understand it."

Yet, perhaps the reason why Séraphin remained within the cortège as far as the church, and then as far as the cemetery, where he helped slide the light coffin to the back of the vault, was precisely to be sure that no one would understand.

The slow, relentless rain swept down on Lurs and the valley. The waters of the Durance howled at the woes of the world.

Marie could not get out of bed. Her arms and legs thrashed about wildly. She kept repeating the same thing:

"I should tell them . . . I must tell them . . ."

"The doctor is here. He says we've got to wait for the illness to develop. He says that he doesn't know what it is."

"Is she eating?"

"Scarcely a thing. And sometimes she's delirious."

"What does she say?"

"Oh! Just nonsense. What do you expect?"

"What sort of nonsense?"

"That she's forgotten something. That she's seen something. That she's got to get up to go and explain to someone . . ."

Clorinde collapsed on the counter, her hair dishevelled. She was crying: the apple of her eye . . .

"You should get her to drink some St-John's-wort in warm goat's milk. That brings out the illness."

"I've had her drink everything!" Clorinde moaned. "Hyssop and henbane — just one seed — and sarsaparilla and dog's tooth grass and meadowsweet and rampion, everything I tell you!"

She began crying harder than ever.

"She won't take anything! You have to get it in between her teeth with a coffee spoon. My mother gives me a hand and my sister comes, but I'm exhausted! How could you expect me to be in any fit state to serve in the shop?"

The cortège of the deceased Sépulcre passed under Marie's window in the narrow street on its way to the church. The hearse jolted along, each of the four wheels grating in a different key, the horses neighing quietly and discreetly, the mourners walking with slow, silent tread, some whispering to each other, some with heads bent in a final meditation. The priest and the choir boy had been asked to cease their responses as they went down that street, but there is no mistaking the puffing and panting of a funeral cortège.

Marie stopped groaning and seemed to be listening for something. Her feverish eyes darted from side to side. She sat up.

"Who's being buried?"

"No one. An old man. Be still or you'll make your temperature rise."

"I must go and tell them . . ."

She pushed back the bedclothes, put a foot to the red floor tiles, then swayed.

"There, my poor girl. You can see that you can't stand up! You can go and tell them when you're better . . ."

"It'll be too late," Marie said.

She threw herself back on her pillow, shaking her head from side to side like someone who can't make anyone understand.

Clorinde and her sister were worn out when they came down from the bedroom, which was so pretty with its pieces of Dresden china, its nice marquetry writing desk and its sewing kit in the nest of tables.

"And she keeps feeling the place where her ring ought to be . . . And she asks for her aquamarine. Misery me! We'd have to go to Aix to get another one . . . Well, how can we? With business the way it is! And Marie so sick! How can we?"

Tricanote came when she heard that news, and walked around the bedroom three times. Her goatherd's steps rang out on the tiles. She sniffed. Was it disdain? Was it suspicion? Whatever it was, she changed the old piece of blessed boxwood stuck like an arrow across the crucifix of a pink Dresden holy water bowl adorned with a little angel looking more like a winged cupid than one of the Eternal Father's exterminating soldiers.

And Tricanote said, but not straight away:

353

"*Ah vaï!* Typhoid fever, indeed! I know what's wrong with her . . . But God forbid!"

Whereupon she became even more thin-lipped than usual.

Misfortune had struck Lurs once again. The old Marquise de Pescaïré, who nursed her aches and pains amid the winds of the Lure mountains, in the loftiest house of the region, brought all the strength of her faith to the task of warding it off. She dragged her walking stick from oratory to oratory on the Promenade des Évêques, which her infirmities, the stone stations and the chapels that composed it transformed into a calvary.

"Dear Lord, after all these novenas," she repeated, "you surely won't allow that to happen." For she was passionately fond of her goddaughter Marie. She went to see her every day, and if prayers alone could do it . . .

Very late one evening, so that no one would know about it, she ventured out into the street with its uneven paving stones, all bumps and holes, and up to the narrow house, as thin as its owner, the woman who looked after the goats. The smell of fresh grass being peacefully chewed wafted out from it like a perfume. The Marquise gave two discreet knocks on the dilapidated door with the knob on her cane. Tricanote came rushing down the steps and clapped her hand to her thin chest with astonishment.

"Yes," said the Marquise, "it's me. What is so surprising?"

She did not give her time to reply. She took hold of the thick rope that served as a handrail and climbed up the steep steps. She sank down on to the wooden seat in front of the three-legged stove.

"The fact is," she said, "I must have your support."

Tricanote was standing there flabbergasted, her mouth still open. The Marquise took off her mittens and undid her kerchiefs.

"Well, Tricanote, what do *you* think of my goddaughter's illness?"

"The worst," Tricanote said.

This direct approach had immediately restored her equanimity.

"Ah! . . ." the Marquise responded, shaking her head. "Ah! . . ."

Silence reigned for ten seconds between the two old women. They gazed at each other calmly and gravely. There were many silent questions and answers in the swift glances that passed between the two of them.

"Of course," said the Marquise, "I have a strong faith and therefore . . . Nevertheless . . . if you think . . ."

"Oh!" Tricanote said. "I don't just think so. I'm sure of it."

"Well then, if you're sure . . ."

The Marquise took a silver purse from her bag and was about to open it. Tricanote stretched her hands out in front of her. They were as black as her shawl.

"No, *pardieu!* Not for all the money in the world! It would break me body and soul. And," she said, with finger raised, "the strength I have would only increase the way things are."

"Well then, what's to be done?" the Marquise groaned. "I don't want her to die! She's so beautiful, so proud and she loves life so much!"

"God . . ." Tricanote replied.

She said nothing more.

So, during those nights when the north wind blew, the old Marquise could be seen offering her infirmities as redemption. She knelt for novenas at the foot of every oratory of the stations of the Cross on the Promenade des Évèques. Sometimes the sad tolling of the bell at Ganagobie calling the two remaining monks to Tenebrae gave the response. Every time she got up, her knees cracked as if they had just broken.

At Lure, the wind she liked so much gave

her no quarter. A dismal sky rolled low on the horizon over her solitary acts of charity, offering neither mercy nor consolation. But the Marquise de Pescaïré knew for certain that this world is only appearance, not reality. Neither the terrible night, the bitter wind nor her aching bones could affect her strong, sensible faith.

Meanwhile, the man who held the key to the mystery was making his way towards this part of the country, which he felt an urge, albeit a morbid one, to see once again.

The man was unhappy. He was in mourning. A wide crepe band encircled his hat. The wife he had loved had just died. He was lying back against the padded seat of a limousine, his face still pale with tears recently shed. He was coming from Saint-Chély-d'Apcher, in the Auvergne, where he had become a rich man during the four years of the war by supplying knives to the army.

His three children, anxious to try standing on their own two feet, had strongly urged him to use the sad occasion to take some time off. He was going to Marseille, en route for the West Indies, where he had business to do. He could have taken the good road directly down the Rhône valley, but at Lyon he had said to the driver, "Keep on towards Grenoble. We'll go via the Alps."

He owed this detour to his wife, the only person who knew his past. While she was ill, she had made him promise to do it. And that is why this rich, unhappy man in his expensive car found himself going up the bad road between Le Monestier-de-Clermont and the Croix-Haute pass, along the last of a thirty-kilometre stretch of maple trees ablaze with autumn colour.

The weather was clement in Trièves in November. The man's gaze pensively followed the hills, forests, distant mountains, and the villages with their grey steeples waiting for Christmas for all their welcoming fires to send out their smoke from under the snow. He looked at this countryside that breathed peace and happiness at every turn of the road; this poor countryside that didn't need to be rich; this countryside that he had never seen.

He had never seen it and yet . . . twenty-five years earlier he had been through it on foot, going in the other direction, with fear at his heels.

All he could remember was the rain, the darkness, the grim ruined barns on the edge of the deep woods where he had hidden away in anguish and hunger — especially hunger. Three days and four nights with hardly a thing to eat until he reached the Savoie border, where he had finally been able to come out into the full light of day again, more than 250 kilometres from that accursed spot, where he should never have been on a certain night in September. Oh! That smart journeyman's outfit, now in a glass case in his château de Saint-Chély: he had worn it everywhere in fear and trembling. The black flock coat matted by the rain . . . The stovepipe hat, so jaunty worn to one side . . . He had dragged it around with him during those terrible nights, its finish ruined and its shape changed into a battered accordion by the rain that fell constantly from the sky. His big ceremonial stick, with its soaking-wet ribbons stuck to the carved serpent wound malevolently around it, had only been used to push aside the sodden brambles of the thickets into which he crept, trembling with fear. Good Lord! Had it ever rained so much in the twenty-five years since then? He sat there remembering that incessant rain and those endless nights.

It was 29 September 1896 . . . twenty-five years ago, and he was running away down these roads. When he heard the jingling approach of a dimly-lit post coach, he threw himself into the ditch. As it passed, above the steady trot of the horses, he could hear the sound of men joking and women laughing under loosened bonnets. He could smell perfumes, leather and cigar smoke in the wake of that brief glimpse of life. He, on the other hand, was fleeing with the dreadful sound of the guillotine in his ears. There was no doubt that it would fall on his thin, twenty-year-old shoulders if he let himself be caught.

For who would have believed him? Who would have given credence to his statements? That is what he said to himself once again, sitting back against the soft upholstery of his car, watching the crimson maples go by, the smoke from peaceful farms rise into the air and the Croix-Haute pass emerge out of the mantle of pine tree tops. It was here that he had felt for the first time, as he took his first step up that slope — the rain still pouring down — that perhaps he was going to get out of his predicament. But it took an iron will to do it and not succumb to the invitation of brightly lit windows and village squares where cows drank around the fountains. He had to live hidden by day, and walk by night, never laying himself open to suspicion, never stopping at any shop, even to buy a bit of bread. He couldn't allow someone to say, "Yes, we saw a vagabond pass by. We gave shelter to a journeyman. He came from the Basses-Alpes. He looked as though he was afraid of something." Fortunately that very fear had provided his unfailing tenacity. He had walked and walked and walked. Each painful step took him closer to safety.

Once again he remembered that store-room smell that sometimes came at night from providential apple trees that fed him so liberally.

The man passed through the gateway to Dauphiné at Sisteron at exactly midday. He had the driver stop in the rue Saunerie to buy a newspaper. Spread over three columns was this headline: "Another Murder in the Basses-Alpes. A miller crushed by his own millstones. Undoubtedly a murder." There was a very dark photo in which you could still make out the millstones. The man sat frozen on his seat. He felt as though those twenty-five years had not passed at all, and that he was still trembling with fear as he fled in the rain.

However, he pulled himself together. He said to himself that these days murder was nothing unusual. Yet the fact that he had twice come back to this part of the country to find it each time afflicted by spilt blood seemed a bad sign. Fear lurked within him as strongly as before. He should tell the driver to turn around and go back, but the promise he had made to his dying wife, as well as a strange feeling of anguish, made him go on. He felt he had entered the orbit of a tragedy that was drawing him towards it, forcing him to confront it.

He stopped at Sisteron so that the driver could have lunch. He scarcely touched his own meal and went for a walk around the streets. The town hardly looked any older. He thought of the night he had passed through it and all the trouble he had taken to avoid the street lights. He remembered that he had taken his shoes off to deaden the sound of his footsteps. The confusion he felt then took hold of him once again. It stripped him of over twenty years' quiet life.

From Sisteron on, he sat huddled in the back seat of the limousine as though he feared being recognized. Les Bons-Enfants, Peipin, Château-Arnoux, Peyruis . . . At Peyruis the man asked the driver to slow down. He feared he would not recognize himself. At Pont-Bernard, the big farm with the pigeon loft by the side of the road, he stopped the car and got out.

"Wait for me here," he said to the driver.

His anxiety had passed. He went down the road like a real journeyman, bursting with youth and free as the breeze. He even found his lips, this time with a moustache, whistling again in the carefree way he had done so many years ago on his trip around France.

He recognized each rock, each culvert, each clump of willows. He had stopped to drink at the spring coming out of the ground, with its strangely worn stone. Night was falling. The stopping place he had been told about was not far away. La Burlière . . . "La Burlière," they had said to him. "And the owner is called Félicien Monge. You'll get a good reception there, you'll see . . ."

The former journeyman recognized everything, except the railway track which had not existed then. Suddenly, for he thought he had only been walking for five minutes, the lulling sound of the wind in the tall cypresses let him know that he had arrived. He had also heard that sound then. A path, which he had never forgotten, led off to the right. As it was nightfall, he had stumbled over the deep ruts formed in the rounded paving stones by the cartage of goods over several generations. He could feel once again his former joy, energy and self-confidence. He had given his shoes a good rub with grass pulled from the slope to make himself presentable. He had made sure his fancy stovepipe hat was set at a cheeky angle. He had fluffed up the festive ribbons on his stick. He had pushed open the door crying, "Evening everyone!"

That door? Which door? The wind still made the four cypresses sway in its path and give out a long, heart-rending moan.

The man looked ahead of him in surprise at the wide, white open space strewn with gravel dotted with an occasional tuft of new grass. He walked forward on to the space and as soon as he had put his foot on it, he had the fleeting impression of having just gone through a wall. The past grabbed him by the throat, as if he were only separated from it by a single stride. The smell of baby clothes drying, of breast milk, hot soup and soot, which had greeted him as soon as he crossed the threshold, rose up into his nostrils as if the vast empty space he was walking on had been saving it for such a long time just to give it back to him today.

He could picture the scene again perfectly: the pretty young woman sitting on a chair, the red-haired man pacing about the room with his hands behind his back, the old man in front of the hearth, the children's laughter coming from under the big table, the clock, and on the ground in front of the clock, a cradle containing a squawking new-born baby.

It certainly was there. It was between those four waving cypresses which, high above his head, soughed in the wind, whispering of faraway places.

He hurriedly stepped back out of the white area as though he had unwittingly stepped on a grave.

It was then that he saw the well. It shone white under the winter sun as it had in the moonlight. It had not changed; it was not very old; almost new in fact. He thought of the image of that well in the moonlight, which he had kept in his memory from that time when he was young and afraid, with his teeth chattering and the rumbling Durance blowing mountain air at his back.

A sudden gust of wind blew a column of leaves up in front of him from the pool at the washing-place. It swayed and twirled for quite a while, slender and insubstantial, before collapsing in a shower. The cypresses high above seemed to be telling a story.

The man heard the tinkling of little bells among the holly-oaks and went in that direction. An old lady with piercing eyes, in charge of some goats under the oaks higher up, watched him approaching. He went up to her and took off his hat.

"Perhaps you may be able to help me," he said. "I'm right in thinking there was a farm called La Burlière here, aren't I?"

"There was," the goatherd said.

Her jaws clacked when she spoke, like a woman with no teeth.

"And tell me . . . What happened? Was there a fire?"

"No. A murder. A horrific murder. A murder everyone still remembers today."

The woman settled her thin flanks against the rocky slope.

"Five people, sir! They killed five of them!"

Five . . . The man closed his eyes. He hadn't been able to count how many bodies there were in the room. His eyes had been bulging with horror. He could only remember that trickle running towards him, twisting like a snake, then flowing over the edge of the trapdoor, showering down the ladder, falling with a dull sound, splashing his shoes and dirtying the bottoms of his trousers. Who would have believed him, with all that blood on his clothes?

The goat woman told him about the discovery of the murders, the burial of the victims, the arrest of the guilty men, the trial with the courtroom filled to overflowing, the reassuring guillotine. The blade which fell three times. The memories: the shivers of horror on stormy nights.

He kept his hands clenched at the stream of words coming from that black mouth. Ten times he wanted to stop her, and ten times he held himself back. He wanted to shout, "No! No! You're wrong. It didn't happen like that. That's not right! The three guilty men you're so proud to have seen decapitated were innocent! Do you hear me? Innocent!"

He was appalled at the idea of those old executed criminals whose bones lying in a common grave probably no longer even existed. He was appalled because at that time, one word from him could have saved them. But it would have been his head in exchange for theirs. For who would have believed him?

"Why sir, have you turned a bit pale? What I've been telling you is not very cheerful, I must admit. Still, luckily there was one survivor. The good Lord didn't want them all to die."

She pointed towards the empty space with the end of her twisted crook.

"He did that . . . ," she said. "The whole lot! He didn't want a stone to be left standing to remind him."

A survivor! How could anyone have survived in that blood bath? The staggering, glassy-eyed journeyman had only seen people who were dying. He could still see — even more clearly now that he was there — the mother's raised hand with fingers outstretched falling back lifeless on the floor. A survivor . . .

Three weeks . . . So it was the cradle in front of the clock. A man who must be twenty-five now . . . A man to whom he could perhaps finally tell the truth and salve his conscience . . .

"Is he . . . is he still alive?" he asked.

"Good Lord! Is he ever alive! He's as tall as Peter the Brave's tower. And handsome with it!"

She clapped one hand against the other, raising her eyes to the heavens, as if to vouch for that beauty.

"You'd think the good Lord wanted to make amends by making him so hand-some."

"And . . . does he live in this part of the country?"

Tricanote's eyes looked more piercing than ever. While she was speaking, some-thing in her subconscious warned her that she should be wary. So many strange and horrible things were happening in Lurs. And where was he from, this fellow in full mourning, looking inconsolable with his black suit and tie and his hat with the crepe band around it? Warnings of misfortune had often come in such dismal guises, Tricanote thought. He reminded her of the *assavoir* during the war, who came flanked by two gendarmes to report someone missing or killed. The cries from the mothers and wives behind those doors . . . A man in mourning never bodes any good. Poor Séraphin Monge. He'd seen enough of them. Why send him another?

"Madame," the man said gently, "I feel you know where he is, but you hesitate to tell me. If your survivor has razed everything to the ground, it's because the murder which took his whole family still haunts him. Perhaps he's not sure about anything. Well, I'm here to bring him a piece of the truth, and I think it will do him good to know it."

"The truth?" Tricanote whispered.

She leaped to her feet.

"We already know the truth!" she exclaimed.

"No," the man said softly.

Tricanote stood there stock-still without saying a word for almost a minute.

"He lives in Peyruis," she said at last, "in the square where there's a fountain with filthy carvings on it . . . A narrow house with a narrow door and three steps leading to the door and a shed down below . . ."

He thanked her with a bow and put his hat back on his head.

She listened to his footsteps fading away. She listened to — she listened for — the wind in the cypresses. Two favourite goats came and laid their heads on her forearms, letting her know that it was time to get under cover. Tricanote gathered her animals together with a sharp whistle. She went up to the village again, puffing and perspiring, holding up her skirts so that she could move more quickly. Soon she would drive her goats up the street in Lurs calling, "Clorinde! Come out here! You know La Burlière? You don't know . . ." But she suddenly slowed her step. No. She should keep all that to herself. Poor Clorinde. How could she be in any state to listen to tales of woe, with her little girl so sick!

The man had no trouble finding Séraphin Monge's house. The West Indian driver parked in the little square, but not without complaining as it was not easy to manoeuvre the car there. The man got out, went up the three steps and knocked on the door three times. He pulled it towards him and found that it was open. After hesitating for a moment, he shrugged his shoulders and went up the staircase leading directly into the kitchen.

He stood for a minute looking at the humble domestic interior where he had not been invited to enter. The floor clean and shining, the stove cold, the dishes stacked by the sink. He noticed the table out of alignment with the chairs and the shape of the room. He went into the recess where the bed was made — well-made in fact — with clean sheets and one pillow. Meticulous order reigned in this poor dwelling, the meticulous order of someone who did not wish to give any hint of his character to anyone through the look of the place where he lived. There was no smell (except perhaps for a slightest whiff of bergamot) to help break the anonymity of this refuge: not a newspaper, not a book, not even a scrap of paper. The man had to tear a page out of his own notebook to write the words he wanted to leave for the survivor of La Bur-lière.

When that was done, he looked for a prominent object to put on top of the note in the middle of the table, so that attention would be drawn to it straight away. He found nothing. But yes! On the shelves over by the frying pan, that sugar tin would be just the thing. He took hold of it with both hands and found it unusually heavy, but did not wonder about it at first. He slipped the note under the edge of the object so that it could be easily seen. It was only at that moment that the weight of the box intrigued him. He raised the lid and lifted up the papers without unfolding them. He looked inside, sighed as he shook his head, closed the lid again and left.

His heart overflowed with pity for the man who lived so humbly, because a person with four kilos of gold coins who leaves his door open could only be a man full of misery.

When the limousine reached the road that went up towards Mallefougasse, before the Saint-Donat knoll, the sun was bouncing off the great holly-oaks, making them look like ocean waves. These woods were as thick and compact as a fleece. The slow swell of their foliage surrounded the ten-centuries-old church, which now looked like an enormous pile of stones. It was a ruin taking an extraordinarily long time to die. It had been plundered and stripped; its roof stones and valleys had been ripped out; the carved capitals on the columns depicting the saint, who lived as a hermit in a sinkhole on Mont Jura, arriving at his rock hollow had been knocked down at the entrance.[15] Yet the truncated cross with its short arms made to resist erosion still stood out against the fleecy green of the forest.

This citadel stood ten kilometres from any inhabited location, in the midst of woods, which it towered over and kept at a distance. It was high and massive, with that silent, vaguely threatening, enigmatic feel that all religious fortresses seem to have. Who had built it? Where were the crowds who had formed a human chain passing stone after stone, singing hymns in praise of the saint? Now it was besieged by the woods, hemmed in by the holly-oaks and lifted above them by the twisting of their roots.

It had not changed in twenty-five years either. Since that night when it had appeared to the journeyman in the last rays of moonlight, just before everything went dark again and the rain began to come down once more. It was no more ruined now, and the same self-sowing weeds were already growing on the shapeless roof.

The man told the driver to wait for him

15 Saint Donatus, born in Orléans, lived as a hermit on Mont Jura near Sisteron in Provence. He died c.535.

and then began to go up the rise to the sanctuary. He walked in step with the slim, agile young man to whom fear had given wings. Fleeing in any direction, he had been tempted by the black porch, wide open to the huge empty nave, where the rain splashed noisily as it fell on the beaten earth floor. It was here that he had recovered his wits a little and convinced himself that there was no refuge for a man who was the last witness to a murder, and that only by running away . . .

Today, in the November evening, the top of the nave could already only be seen through a veil of mist. Families of bats high above were already wheeling around the thick round pillars reaching up to fifteen metres into the air.

The man looked at his watch. Would he come? Was it a mistake to arrange to meet him here rather than just wait for him in his house? Yielding to the desire to include the church in his confession, he risked saying it into empty space.

He kept his eyes on the porch, where the light was fading.

A dark shape suddenly cut out that light. Someone was climbing in the entrance, as the four steps that led to it had also been stolen, and you had to pull yourself up as he himself had done.

The new arrival slowly straightened himself and moved forward. Fascinated, the man watched him walk, watched him stare with expressionless eyes that seemed to go right through him. He looked at that impressive, large but light figure, which made no noise walking and blended into the squat column behind him, becoming an extension of it, as though he were carrying it on his shoulders.

He held out the piece of paper that the man had left on the table.

"Did you write that for me?"

"Yes" the man said.

"My name is Séraphin Monge," Séraphin said.

"I know. The first time I saw, or rather glimpsed you, you were lying snug and warm in a cradle and yelling because you were hungry . . . I was there," he said quietly, "on the night of the massacre . . ."

"You were there?"

"Yes. I'll tell you about it. Listen to me without interrupting. You can judge what I have to say afterwards."

"I'm not a court."

"Yes, you are. You should be. You're their descendant. Yes, I was there. I'd just arrived. I'd opened the door — I even remember that I hadn't knocked — so sure that I was as welcome as the messiah, because I was a journeyman. Oh! I saw straight away that I'd arrived at the wrong time. Your father frowned like someone who is thinking, 'That's all I needed!' He had a hunted look and was walking up and down. Your mother had hastily covered up her breast. I suppose she was about to feed you. So . . . I saw right away that I wasn't wanted. But, well . . . I'd just done a hundred kilometres in the rain from Marseille, where I came from. And then, I was only twenty. I was so exhilarated with the freedom of it all and so eager to grasp the future. I was rather full of myself. I saw others as figures in a tapestry and myself the only one moving among them."

The man sighed.

"You must be wondering why I got you to come here?"

"No," Séraphin said. "Go on. You were in the kitchen. My mother was going to give me the breast. My father was walking up and down . . ."

"Yes. He grabbed me by the arm, then lifted up the trapdoor. How can I say that word without trembling? He sent me down the wooden stepladder to the stables below. He brought me some home-made bread, sausage and cheese — without saying a word or asking a question. He had a furrow in his brow, which never disappeared."

Séraphin was drinking in everything he said. Old Burle had arrived to find the dead bodies. This man was talking about living people. He was bringing his father back to him alive, going down the stepladder carrying bread; his mother alive and, taken aback by the stranger's intrusion, modestly covering her chest.

"He settled me on some postal sacks," the man continued. "I remember. It smelled of wax. There were large seals on the jute flaps. It was rough, but warm and, above all, dry. I stretched out and ate my food. I must have dozed off from being so tired, with some half-chewed food still in my mouth. (You can see how well I remember it.) It wasn't long! I think there was a dull thud, which shook the beams. I stood up. I was thirsty as they had forgotten to give me anything to drink. There was a dim lantern on a little table. I looked at the horses' buckets. I'd often made do with that. But they were empty. So I said to myself, 'That's too bad. You'll disturb them, but you've got to drink . . .' "

He paused for a moment, then repeated:

"You've got to drink . . . I walked towards

377

the ladder, which was in the shadows," he continued. "Oh, I was aware that the horses were stamping a bit, that they were restless, that they were stretching their necks down towards their hooves and that they were snorting at them. But . . . when you're twenty, you don't take too much notice of such signs . . ."

He sighed before going on.

"There were twenty-two rungs on the ladder. I've had ample time to see them all in my memory . . . I also know that I didn't complete the action, that my arm stayed outstretched holding up the trapdoor for maybe two minutes. Oh . . . I didn't realize immediately . . . And you understand, I saw everything at the same time, in less than two seconds, and it's taking me five minutes to describe it to you . . ."

He sat down heavily on the altar step, which was strewn with rubble, as if his legs already felt weak from what he was going to say.

"Everything at the same time," he said once again. "There was a kind of red roll coming slowly towards me, gathering no dust, as if borne along by its own weight . . . How can I describe it to you? Rolling along in the cracks between the flagstones on the floor, the thing reached the edge of the trapdoor, then burst and spilled over and suddenly my trousers were splashed with it . . . God forgive me . . . Some drops fell on my shoes. I felt . . . It was warm . . . But I didn't have time to pay more attention to that . . . I saw — oh, not a metre away! — a tangle of skirts and bodice, a tangle of hair, all of it crawling, making a terrible sound like a broken bellows, and at the end of it was an arm outstretched, with fingers wide apart, straining towards the cradle — where you were. It nearly reached it, but fell to the ground just before it got there."

"My mother," Séraphin said softly.

"But at the same time I also saw — but through a red haze . . . You see the lamp had been knocked over, and the only light came from the flames in the hearth. I saw two men fighting. One was your father. He was holding something in his hand . . . Something that was also red . . . And in the other he had a weapon which shone in the dim light. And they were trying to cut each other's throats, in silence, without a word. Then your father got the upper hand. He gave the man a sharp blow with his knee, pushing him towards the fireplace and making him lose his balance. The other man fell backwards, but as he fell he managed to catch hold of the larding pin on the spit,

379

which came unhooked. He had it in his hand when your father threw himself at him. He ran himself through on the larding pin . . . and then . . . with this spit through his body, your father took one step, two steps more. He leaned with both hands against the wall of the fireplace. And then, the other man . . ."

"One man?" Séraphin said, his breath quickening. "Are you sure there was only one man?"

"Yes. Only one. One man who now had something shiny in his hand. He went up to your father and he pulled back his head and he cut his throat . . ."

"Just one man . . ." Séraphin repeated.

"Yes. There was another in the room, but he was an old man. He was in the armchair in front of the hearth, with his hand flat on the armrests, his eyes turned heavenwards, with a big red beard."

"The other man on his own," Séraphin said, "did you get a good look at him?"

"No. I saw black. I saw an eye gleaming. I saw two solid legs; I saw hands, a bit like yours . . . I saw shoulders, a bit like yours . . . that rolled . . . The lamp had fallen over. I told you. And then, I was frightened. I'm telling you all this now, but it actually happened in a flash. I shut the trapdoor again

380

straight away. It squeaked as it came into contact with the rivulet of blood, which was starting to coagulate. I've never forgotten that tiny sound. I said to myself that if the man heard it, I was done for. I was afraid, you understand, so afraid! I was just a young man then — as green as grass. Haven't you ever been afraid?"

Séraphin raised his eyes towards the top of the pillars, which were now invisible under the nave.

"Oh! yes . . ." he said quietly.

"Well then, you'll understand. Fear affected my reason. It stayed with me for months, perhaps for years. I went down the stepladder again and back to my corner. It was then I realized that when the man up above left, I would be alone with these bodies, with the blood that had splashed over the trapdoor and on to my shoes, proving that it had been raised. My story about an unknown man I hadn't seen properly, a man who might never be found . . . Who would believe it? A journeyman, that's easily said. Papers can be made up. At that time there were journeymen responsible to no one, who travelled the length and breadth of France. Merry fellows, nuisances, girl-chasers, who took fifteen leisurely years to learn a trade and who felt the world owed them a living. They would arrive without warning, starving hungry and exhausted. A journeyman — whatever was said about him — gendarmes and the law often looked askance at him. And if the gendarmes had looked askance at me the following day . . ."

Séraphin felt that, even today, a shiver of terror went through the man when he described it.

"The fear I felt then had nothing in common with the shock I felt when I lifted up the trapdoor. What gripped me now was fear of society. It was fear of the scaffold. Who would have believed me?"

The man paused for a moment, then continued.

"I took my stick, my hat and my haversack. I picked up my bit of bread, which was very useful later on, collecting every crumb. I plumped up the postal sack where I'd been lying, then went out through the postern in the coach entrance to the stable. I ran out like a madman — like the madman I was at that moment! Then I found myself in the moonlight. I could see the well about fifty metres away, and there in front of the well was the man! He had his back to me, but I had the impression that he had heard me, that he would see me. I dashed behind a cart. I saw him bend down and pick something up . . . I saw him doing something with his hands. It seemed to me he was doing up a parcel. Then I saw him move his arm. He threw something into the well, something heavy . . . No, I wasn't fifty metres away . . . It was more like thirty . . . I heard a plop . . ."

"Only one man . . ." Séraphin repeated.

"Yes. He was quite alone. And I didn't see him. The moonlight played with the shadow under his hat. I knew that he didn't have a beard. His chin was pale. He walked hunched over, rather heavily. I couldn't swear to it but . . . He seemed to be groaning; he seemed to be crying."

"He was the same one you saw stab my father with the spit?"

"Yes. The same. I'm sure of it."

"And there was no one else?"

"No. No one."

"And he threw something into the well?"

"Yes. And then he left in the direction of the railway works, his shoulders drooping. That's when I began to run, through woods and hills, heading directly north with the smell of the mountains to guide me. I walked and walked . . . I came across this church. I've never known its name."

"Saint Donat's," Séraphin replied automatically.

383

"I looked for guidance by praying," the man said. "I received only one answer: 'run!' And that's what I did."

"Only one man . . ." Séraphin murmured. "And you don't know what he looked like . . ."

"It's twenty-five years," the man said. "I've made a life for myself. My wife has just died. No, I don't know. Even if I could describe him to you, what could you do with the information? What would that man be like after twenty-five years? On the outside! And on the inside? And then there's the war. Is he even still alive?"

"If he was dead," Séraphin said, "I'd feel it here."

He put his hand flat on the centre of his chest. The man looked at him, still standing in the same place in the shadows, his back against the pillar as though he were carved into it.

"A quarter of a century . . ." the man said wearily. "You're too young to know what that is . . . and . . ."

He was taken aback and stopped speaking. He had the impression that Séraphin Monge was laughing heartily over there in the shadows. In any case, he was standing up and turning away from the former journeyman. He walked in silence towards the remains of the day which lingered beyond the porch.

The man followed him.

"Isn't there anything I can do for you?" he said hesitantly. "You see . . . How can I say this . . . I'm wealthy . . ."

"For my part," Séraphin said, "I'm poorer than you think. I was weaned from my mother when I was three weeks old. I've been without her for twenty-five years. All I have of her is a bad dream . . . which controls my actions . . . You say twenty-five years is long? Even though she has been dead for twenty-five years, she hasn't aged. Her throat is still cut and . . ."

He was going to say, "And the last two drops of milk she was going to give me . . ." He stopped in time.

"She has not forgiven," he continued. "And I don't forgive. And you, with your one man, perhaps you've come too late. Perhaps," he repeated, "perhaps . . ."

Then he left, without a gesture, without a look, without a word of thanks for that weak man who was now rich.

Rain dripped from the dead leaves on the trees around the church with a sad, dull sound. Night had completely fallen.

XVII

"I should have suspected it," Monsieur Anglès will say later, "it was the first and last time he asked me for a day off. I can still remember. It was a Monday."

Séraphin slept lightly, still on the alert, still wary, his mind full of incoherent thoughts. One man. The well. He had thrown something into the well. And been responsible for this carnage all alone. What about the two others? So he'd been on the wrong track from the beginning. He'd wanted to kill three innocent men . . . Or two innocent and one guilty . . . Only one person knew the truth now: the one who was still alive. The Lurs baker, Célestat Dormeur. Well then, he killed the other two? But why? The well . . . The man the journeyman saw parcelling up something. He'd thrown it in the well. So it was something that could identify him . . . Some personal possession . . . In the well that he, Séraphin, could never go near without being assailed by his mother's ghost. What's more, there's water in that well. How much? One or two metres? He'd never been able to lean over it. How do you look for something at the bottom of a well? And after twenty-five years . . . What would be left of it?

He lay there with his hands under his head in the Peyruis night, with the clear sound of the fountain in his ears. He thought of Marie Dormeur, Marie who was so ill. It wasn't fair. She had so much vitality. He said to himself that — too bad — he would go and see her. Perhaps it would do her some good to know that he was worried about her. That didn't commit him to anything. She knew now that he could never love anyone.

Suddenly he sat bolt upright. The image of Marie sitting on the edge of the well, when he had almost pushed her in, had just made him remember something essential. One day Monsieur Anglès had been standing close by, talking with a colleague who was working on geodesy. Séraphin never forgot anything that Monsieur Anglès said, and that day he had said, "The wells around here are almost all dry. When the company that owns the mines at Sigonce expanded their programme, the new galleries they dug in 1910 damaged quite a lot of water tables and especially sumps. As a result, nearly all the wells have dried up."

That morning, Séraphin asked Monsieur Anglès for a day off and set out along the Forcalquier road on his bicycle. At the market he bought twenty-five metres of thick rope and, at the ironmonger's, an acetylene lamp.

The people waiting for the bus who saw him that morning with the coil of rope across his shoulders and chest, couldn't resist calling out to him.

"Hey! Séraphin! Are you going to hang yourself?"

"Maybe . . ." Séraphin replied.

He was at La Burlière by midday. Tricanote, who was looking after her goats under the oaks, later said that she too had wondered whether he was going to hang himself. She said that he had stayed under the cypresses, looking at the well at a distance, for nearly a quarter of an hour. From that moment on, she had never taken her eyes off him. She had hidden behind a big rosemary bush and had watched what he was doing from there.

"He sat down on the seat under the cypresses," she said, "and unwound the rope and started to make knots in it, one after the other. He made them about every fifty

centimetres and pulled them tight with a
sharp tug. Oh! I watched him make a good
job of it . . . It took him some time, I can
tell you! When he had finished that he went
off down to the road. He was away, oh,
about ten minutes. I could see the bicycle, I
could see the rope, and now that he'd
moved, the carbide lamp on the seat. When
he came back he was carrying a railway
sleeper on his shoulders. He must have
found it left somewhere along the track.
Well, my friends. How can I describe this to
you? Remember now . . . for a strong man
like him, a sleeper shouldn't be too much
trouble. It'd crush me to death, but him . . .
And yet . . . how far would it be from the
cypress to the well? Maybe fifty metres?
Well, just listen to this: it took him all of
five minutes to cover the distance. He
stopped every three metres. I could see him
well as I was facing him, hidden behind the
rosemary bush. He was watching like a
hunter lying in wait for game. He'd stop
with one foot still raised. Then he'd start off
again. When I could see him fairly close up,
I noticed he was looking sideways. It wasn't
the well he was looking at; it was the
washing-place. You know, the one that's full
of dead leaves now? Well, my girl! He looked
at that wash trough as though the Antichrist

was about to come out of it! He looked frightened . . . Well, he got to the edge at last. He put the sleeper down against the rim. He waited a bit longer, still on the alert, ready to leap backwards — he really did! And then he picked up his beam — Oh! No effort at all — almost as though he was lifting a dead branch, and put it over the well. I was watching him and he was staring at the wash trough. He looked . . . surprised. And then . . . what can I say? He went up to the wash trough and put his arms in amongst the leaves and started to move them around . . . Why? How would I know? Perhaps he was looking for something . . . Anyway, he worked away at that for about three minutes . . ."

That time, in spite of any fears he might have had, Girarde did not rise up from her leafy coffin to remind her son what she expected of him. Nothing disturbed the air, as if this evil place had been exorcised at last, as if the path he should take was now clear and all he had to do was to go straight ahead.

Séraphin checked the sleeper on both sides of the well wall. He knotted the thick rope securely around it, then threw it in. He lit the acetylene lamp which he attached to the end of another rope. He adjusted it, then leaned over the rim and, metre by metre, let down the lamp. The white flame lit up the circle of yellow zaffre stone, sometimes catching on a clutching stem of chokeweed or the pale green frond of a cave fern. Séraphin let the rope out between his fingers more and more slowly, peering at the darkness below the flame. The whole shaft of the well was now lit up. Suddenly it revealed the bottom just below it. Séraphin continued to pay out the line, centimetre by centimetre, until he felt it slacken. The lamp had reached the ground. It did not go out and the flame was high and clear.

Séraphin tied the end of the rope to one of the branches of the iron arch above the well. He put his leg over the edge of the wall, took hold of the sleeper and then put his hands around the rope. He took his time and went slowly down the well, knot by knot. He estimated that it must be about ten metres deep. After a certain level, he discovered concentric circles that the water must have left in earlier times. The circles were more or less defined, higher or lower. They indicated the good and bad seasons, the years when water had been in good supply and those when it was scarce.

When he put his foot on the hard white rock, the first thing Séraphin saw in front of him, starkly lit by the white acetylene flame, was a dead man's skull looking at him with its hollow eyes and laughing with its full set of teeth. The body was crouched in an attitude of meditation. It was wedged under an arch of rock, which continued like a grotto over two or three metres of the nodule of sparkling rock that made up the foundation of the well before it narrowed like a funnel. A rivulet of water flowed under the skeleton's legs, drawn up at right angles, then gurgled away through the neck of the grotto's narrow funnel.

The skeleton was quite intact, because it had been petrified by the limestone deposits that had welded the joints together. He must have been a young man, as he had all his teeth. The straps of a cross-belt, also petrified, lay over his ribs and collarbones. A wide belt with buckles hung on his hips. There was a kind of cartridge pouch attached to it.

Séraphin looked at it with the calm seriousness of those who have been so constantly in the presence of death that they are used to looking it in the face. He wondered about the rough calcified ribbon that snaked over the ground and twisted around an enormous round pebble. He bent down to break the limestone shell around it. He discovered a whip leather still intact underneath. He followed it back to the petrified bundle of the dead man's feet. It was then he realized that the body had been thrown into the well feet first, weighed down by the stone and with its hands tied behind its back. But was he even dead when that happened?

He looked up at the opening at the top of the well and above it the blue circle of sky with its wisps of clouds. Around it was La Burlière. La Burlière, the cradle of his family. La Burlière, where the Monges had always lived . . . One of them, one day had thrown that man in feet first, or else, if he hadn't done it, he couldn't have been ignorant of the fact that it was being done . . . The sword of justice, which had kept Séraphin so keyed-up since he discovered the acknowledgements of debt, suddenly broke within him. He was descended from murderers or accomplices to murder. What right had he to set himself up as a righter of wrongs?

He wanted to know more. He pulled the petrified cartridge pouch off the belt with the sharp tug. The skeleton collapsed on him with the dry crack of branches being broken by the wind. The skull, propelled by the weight of the calcification, rolled away to the neck of the narrow funnel where the rivulet disappeared. Séraphin, still holding the pouch, took out his penknife and tried to prise off the limestone deposit over the tongue of the buckle.

The case still looked like leather. It was empty apart from a shapeless mass of something still soft and sticky, which smelled of wax. Séraphin dug into it, not really knowing what he was looking for. The blade grated on a metallic surface. Having completely forgotten that he was actually looking for something else, Séraphin began scratching it then cleaned it. It was a coin. He held it up to the light, examined the edge and the profile of the bourgeois king, Louis-Philippe. It was identical to those that filled the sugar tin discovered in the wall of La Burlière. So, this murder, this robbery, this whole business was more than seventy years old. Two wars had come and gone. His father, who hadn't even been born under Louis-Philippe, couldn't have committed it, although he had profited by it. And his mother Girarde was not part of that family of murderers. Yet it was she whose throat had been cut and whom he was born to avenge.

Séraphin, still kneeling, turned around and forgot the skeleton. Under the roll of surplus knotted rope lying on the ground, he pulled out two flat stones also tied by a leather thong. But here the calcification had not yet encased the leather strap. It was black, hardly worn and still supple. Séraphin severed it with one cut of his penknife. The two stones slid on the sloping floor. Two objects were released from it and went tumbling towards the rivulet. Séraphin caught them and bounced them in the palm of his hand, looking at them closely in the light of the lamp. Then he rolled them in his handkerchief and put them in his pocket.

He got up and slowly and deliberately, knot after knot, he climbed up to the surface again.

"I saw him get out," Tricanote will say later. "And neither more nor less hurried than before he went down. And he left the thick rope and the other rope with the lamp still lit on the edge of the well. It was a strange light, what with the sun still shining. You'd have thought it was a candle . . . And then he went over to his bicycle and slowly rode away . . . But now that I come to think of it, I think he knew where he was going . . ."

He knew where he was going. The house could not be seen straight away as the cart track twisted and turned among the olive trees. It was not used very often. Hedge hyssop, horse-tail and shepherd's purse had sprung up again in the ruts, under the sea holly and native couch grass. The ground on the path was soft underfoot and then, quite suddenly, the house loomed up at the last turn.

It was a big square house with a four-sided sloping roof, two storeys of tightly closed shutters, giving the impression that they had been like that for a very long time. To the left of the building, growing out of a thick clump of yuccas, a cypress as old as those at La Burlière rose up higher than the roof.

The only sign of life was the ground floor where the shutters opened on to three large half-open windows. An acanthus leaf carved in freestone decorated the pediment of the door, which was at ground level. There was an old bicycle with a luggage rack against the wall, almost lying on the ground, as though someone had just got off it in a hurry.

Séraphin leaned his bike against the trunk of the cypress. He stood there, looking at the front of the house. The door was hidden by a jute curtain waving in the breeze. Anyone safely placed behind it could see everything arriving on the path. On the other hand, for the person approaching, this veil was as impenetrable as an oracle's mouth.

Séraphin went over and lifted it up. The door was open behind it and you felt that it was never closed, as a clump of dandelions had grown up in the corner of the door frame. A dark, musty-smelling staircase rose up opposite the entrance. There was a closed door in the main wall to the left of the vestibule. Séraphin raised the latch and pushed the door, which opened reluctantly, scraping against the tiles and groaning at the hinges.

Séraphin found himself in a huge, cold room. It was in a mess, but a mess obviously organized so that all the necessary objects of life were within hand's reach. Light came in through the three windows with open shutters on the front of the house. Some sort of heavy hanging had been drawn across the third, so that it was hard to see the end of the room. The dominant feature of this shambles was a fireplace with a coat of arms. On the canopy — and it was one of the first things you noticed — stood a single picture hidden by a black veil.

Séraphin slowly looked around, taking everything in. He saw a cold, lifeless kitchen corner. He saw a large desk table surrounded by piles of everything that must have fallen off it through the years and everything that had been swept off it to make room for new collections. He saw a heap of ashes in the fireplace that indicated a large fire had been built up and was just dying. In the shadows at the end of the room, behind a tattered curtain, he saw a bed.

This huge gloomy space had an atmosphere of abiding misery. No fire, no matter how fierce, could have banished the cold. The rays of sunlight, dimmed by the curtains at the windows, fell cheerlessly on to the red floor tiles. High up on the walls hung church pictures, but only Christ's red robe was still visible.

Séraphin walked past the fireplace and continued on towards the shadowy end of the room, towards the bed under its canopy. He stood at the foot of it, in the light, so that he could be easily recognized.

He saw a man lying in the bed, the blankets pulled up to his chin and his hat on his head, staring at him in silence. From the small part of the face that he could make out beneath the hat, Séraphin realized that this man too was not far from death. He felt a dull indignation welling up in him at the idea that he could only drag the dead or dying before his mother's judgement. The only two living beings that had confronted his anger were two dogs. He arrived too late. This murder, which was so much a part of him, had faded too long ago for others. Now it was only a story that was told at the end of a winter evening with neighbours, before saying good-bye to each other at the door, shivering with cheap thrills.

Séraphin felt an awful bitterness as he looked at the dying man. What he had been pursuing for months was just a murderer's ashes. But he had to know. A few words, but quite audible ones, burst forth from the tightly-pursed old mouth.

"A bit later and you wouldn't have found me here. I've caught my death. It must have been on the night when I went to open up the sluice gate at Didon's mill. I was soaked to the skin . . ."

Séraphin took the two objects from the bottom of the well out of his pocket.

"A. Z.," he said. "That's you, isn't it?"

"Yes, it's me, Alexandre Zorme. People can laugh at the name now, knowing the state I'm in. But nobody laughed at it then."

His sigh made a sound in his chest like wheezing bagpipes. His hand groped for the objects that Séraphin had thrown on the counterpane. He took hold of one and gripped it tightly in his hand.

"It's mine," he said, "I don't have to look. I can tell just from the feel. Oh! I know the blade isn't there any more. Water and rust have eaten it all away . . . My knife, my *tranchet* . . . After that I never bought another. It's strange, the habit we had of burning our initials into everything with a hot iron. Afraid of being robbed!" he said with a wry smile.

He shook his head.

"Without it though," he said, "I'd be dead. You'd be dead . . . No one would ever have known."

His breathing was making a strange noise, like a valve opening and closing. Now and again he hiccoughed loudly like a man who has eaten too much. His black eyes held Séraphin with their intense gaze while his fingers stroked the bone handle of the *tranchet* thrown into the well twenty-five years ago.

"I never thought I'd see it again," he said. "I never thought anyone would bring it back to me. Certainly not you."

"I had to know," Séraphin said.

"Oh, yes! When I saw you with old Burle, I knew you'd have to know. He didn't take that to Heaven with him . . ." He gave a mocking laugh.

"It wasn't through him that I knew."

"So you think you know now?"

"Yes," Séraphin said.

"Well, you don't! Why do you think I threw two knives into the well. You've looked at the initials on the other one?"

"F. M." Séraphin said.

"Yes, that's right . . . F. M.," Zorme repeated. "Félicien Monge. When I went in, he had just cut your mother's throat. She . . . she was still moving . . . She was crawling with her neck gashed and the blood gushing, sounding as though it was coming out of the neck of a bottle. She was crawling towards you, raising her hand towards Monge, who was already holding you and raising your head so that he wouldn't miss . . . With that!"

He groped about in front of him, seized the other horn handle missing a blade like his own, and brandished it in front of him. Séraphin saw the thing trembling in the dying man's hand.

"I turned him around towards me and struck at him with my *tranchet*. I didn't do a good job of it. We struggled. He pushed me against the wall. I fell. If my hand hadn't come across the larding pin, I'd never have got the better of Monge. Never. That night, Monge was like hot iron. Even when I ran the larding pin through his body, he was still hurling insults at me. You'd have thought that the life didn't want to leave him. I expected it to come out of him, leave his body to die and rise up again beside him, spitting in my face . . . hitting me with invisible arms . . . choking me with steaming venom, and all that for . . ."

"Why?" Séraphin asked.

"Why, why! You're all for ever wanting to know why! How do I know? Fear. We all frighten each other. After that evil deed I was frightened for twenty-five years, I can tell you."

"Why?"

Zorme's eyes slid away from Séraphin's attentive gaze, like the bubble in a water level when you try to get it straight.

"He couldn't stand me," he mumbled. "He thought that I'd done him wrong."

"But why my mother? Why my brothers? And why me, since you say that . . ."

Zorme nodded his head in agreement several times.

"Yes you! I snatched you away from him. He had the blade three centimetres from your little neck. He'd have cut your head off."

"But why?"

Zorme didn't reply straight away. He

seemed wary, looking out of the corner of his eye and listening in that direction. Séraphin thought he could hear a noise of something mechanical outside.

"Don't count on me to tell you," Zorme continued. "I already had my work cut out just extricating myself from all of that. Who would have believed me? All alone there with five dead bodies around me, and my bad reputation and the larding pin and the *tranchet* with my initials. You'd have had to be mad to believe me! They'd have marched me to the scaffold with great ceremony. I'd have heard the whole district gloating . . ."

The bagpipes wheezing in his chest sounded sharper and stopped him speaking. After a long moment he began again.

"And then I went out, I went to the well and I threw the two knives to the bottom. I could have left Monge's. I don't know why I threw that one down as well."

"I've been told that you were crying . . ." Séraphin murmured.

"Who told you that?"

Zorme had suddenly unwound like a spring and was sitting up against his pillow.

"Who told you that?" he repeated sharply, in an almost threatening tone of voice.

"What's that to you?" Séraphin said. "I went down to the bottom of the well and found the two knife handles . . . What does it matter who it was?"

This time Zorme did not try to avoid his gaze; on the contrary, he held it, he even sought it, but Séraphin could see that his fists were clenched.

"You're right," Zorme said. "But as far as crying is concerned, they're wrong. I wasn't crying. I've never cried in my life. I was afraid, that's all."

"Who could you have been afraid of?"

Zorme had difficulty chewing the thick saliva in his mouth. He had begun to look away from Séraphin.

"I'll tell you everything," he announced. "And you'll tell it all to the gendarmes. Now, this is it, no more, no less . . . That night, when I went around the well, I saw three men behind the broken wheels of a timber cart. Oh! They thought they were hidden! But they were shining in the moonlight like the skin of a snake in the grass. Only I couldn't see their faces as they were wearing the hats bee-keepers put on to cover their faces when they collect honey. Yet they must have seen my face as clearly as in full daylight. It's not possible that they didn't recognize me. I ran off like a coward, with fear at my heels. I stayed hiding away here, keeping very quiet . . . waiting for the

404

gendarmes to come. Luckily . . . Luckily . . ."

"Luckily they guillotined three innocent men," Séraphin said.

"Idiots! They must have arrived at daybreak . . . Maybe already drunk . . . They came to pinch some eggs, a ham, who knows? They must have seen the open door, and in the sink was a demijohn of brandy. There was always one to serve to the carters . . . Oh! They must have seen the bodies too! But the brandy . . . The demijohn must have been like a bait that attracted them. Savages . . . They must have walked among the bodies, up to the bottle . . . They probably didn't even notice you. The brandy . . . How could they explain that?"

He waved his arms, muttering something that sent the three executed Herzegovinians to the devil. Séraphin observed his toad-like complexion and the old tendons that made the tics in his face move. The truth that came out of that bitter mouth didn't seem to him to have any relation to the horror of the scene that he carried with him everywhere.

"I said luckily," Zorme continued, "but who knows? Who knows whether it wouldn't have been better for them to take me than to live through all those years of fear and

405

anxiety? I didn't know who those three were. There were so many dangerous situations: in bed with a woman, the drunken evenings, and afterwards pissing happily into the nettles: 'Ah! *vaï!* La Burlière . . . *I* know what happened there. And it's not what everyone thinks . . .' It was so easy to say . . . I felt as transparent as rice paper. Luckily, the people around here make a detour when they come across me. Luckily, they avoid looking at me. No one has ever stared at me as much as you have . . ."

He stopped talking. Once again he had pricked up his ears. In the silence, you could hear the cypress softly moaning in the wind. Zorme relaxed, his head falling back on to the pillow.

"It's getting late," Séraphin said.

'Ah! yes," Zorme said, "you're straight and strong. You want to know. You think I won't have time to tell you everything, do you? When I saw you pounding your hands against the stones, I thought that you wouldn't give up, that you'd lift up every stone to know what was underneath. From then on, I never left you. I was in the copse of bay trees the day you spoke to . . . you spoke to . . . Célestat Dormeur's daughter. I was there the night Brother Calixte came to fetch you. And it was that night that I understood that everything would combine to lead you to a false truth."

"You were the one who called to me from below?"

"Yes. It was me. And I followed you to the Sioubert spring and saw you run your hand over the spot where the scythes were sharpened. I realized that you had found out something . . . I spent agonized nights and days watching you demolish La Burlière . . . I went walking around the rubble, the night you broke up the fireplace. I saw the hiding-place that you'd discovered. I had to know what you'd found."

"You were that black shadow? It was your presence I could smell in my kitchen?"

"I said to myself, 'When he takes the others by the throat to strangle them, they'll scream my name like stuck pigs. They'll shout until he hears it. And he'll come. And then . . .' "

"I've come," Séraphin said.

"Too late. I'm going to die and now you know the truth. But I couldn't risk not having the time to tell you the real truth . . . And then again, perhaps you wouldn't believe me."

"That's still possible," Séraphin said.

"Wait, if you want me to finish. I couldn't run that risk. I didn't know when or how you would attack them. When I saw you go to Pontradieu, I went too. I began with Gaspard. He had it coming to him anyway. If they hadn't killed Monge that night, it's because I'd seen to it before them . . . I'd done them a real favour."

He suddenly stopped dead. He shot a look out of the corner of his eye towards one of the half-open windows with its curtain waving in the breeze.

"Who's spying on me?" he growled. "I wasn't expecting anyone else but you."

"It's the wind in the cypress," Séraphin replied.

"You're the one . . . who gave me the idea. I saw you run your hand over the edge of the pool as though you didn't find it smooth enough . . . And one foggy morning, I also saw you go and stand deep in thought beside the sluice gate on Sépulcre's millrace, then go back towards the mill and look through the window."

"I did all that . . ." Séraphin said quietly.

"Yes," Zorme said, "but I did the rest."

"You've forgotten Charmaine. Because of course it was you who opened the gate to let out the dogs, I suppose?"

"Ah!" Zorme sighed. "Dogs, nature, men . . . I knew everything there was to know about them . . . I could speak to owls, to badgers . . . The badgers now! They'd sit up there on their back legs listening to me for hours . . . All the more reason for me to be able to speak to dogs . . ."

"Charmaine hadn't done anything to you."

"She'd seen me. Oh! Just for an instant. In the garden at night, she mistook me for you. She called out, 'Séraphin!' "

Séraphin felt his heart stop, for Zorme had used Charmaine's voice to call out his name.

"Only, she'd have remembered it," Zorme said. "She could have described me . . . run into me, recognized me. Who knows? I couldn't risk it."

He gave a cynical laugh.

"To think that you go to so much trouble to avoid death, and now look . . ."

Séraphin turned his eyes away, then turned away from the bed. He wandered aimlessly around the huge room, not knowing what to do or think. So that was the truth that had given him so much trouble. A man who goes mad and kills his family. Another man who has to kill him too in order to save the baby in its cradle — himself, Séraphin.

He had stopped in front of the table-cum-rubbish dump, which took up a large corner of the room. He looked at it absent-mindedly, saying to himself that being the son and descendant of criminals, he hadn't the right to judge. The skeleton at the bottom of the well weighed on his shoulders, as though it were not only its dust that had fallen down on him; as though he had brought it up into the daylight with all the rest.

He stood there vaguely staring at the mess of that desk, which had nothing but strange things on it. The flat part was strewn with objects, some dusty, some clean, which must have been piling up there for decades; objects that had something to do with the passage of time: hourglasses, heavy watches with cases worn from having been handled by rough fingers. Various engravings depicting human bodies, which made you feel uneasy because although their eyes were open, you knew that they were dead. Dog-eared photos of overbearing women or cunning old men. Penknives, collar studs, worn wedding rings, little lady's mirrors, locks of hair in a medallion, mittens, monocles. It was as though dozens of people had emptied out their pockets before going to bed. Most prominent amongst this jumble of objects were a compass rose engraved on a pottery tile and a sextant that had long ago been removed from a ship's binnacle.

In contrast to this disorder, a large, clean empty space had been left in front of an armchair with a sagging cane seat. It was easy to see that in more normal times someone would have spent a lot of time deep in thought there. A few murky-coloured iridescent bottles were lined up according to size on this meticulously dusted space, and in front of them was an unexpected object here, an object that was out of place in the house of an old man who lived alone. It was a doll's bed with wooden rails, meticulously copied in walnut from a real bed: a luxury toy that must have been more than a century old. It was high off the ground, with shiny scrolls at the head and foot, and stood on a plaque of dull metal, probably lead.

In the bed lay a doll, more than thirty centimetres long. It was a roughly made clay statuette, with a long torso, thin legs and long arms like a monkey's. But on this torso, someone had taken the trouble to fashion two round little dishes for breasts. Between these breasts, seven tie-pins with cabochon stones of different colours, crossed in a bundle, had been pushed into the clay figure in a star pattern. The head leaned a little to one side, and the only

411

feature that made it look like a human head was its oval shape. There were no eyes or mouth. You could see that it was a head because another pin — just one this time — had been stuck into the middle of the forehead. Someone had hung a ring on the part of the pin that was still protruding. It rested on this shapeless forehead like a diadem, its weight making a slight imprint in the soft clay. An aquamarine set in the ring caught the scattered rays of the setting sun that streamed into the room and sent them into Séraphin's blue eyes in a single beam of light.

Where had he already seen that ring? Under what circumstances? Had he ever been interested in a ring? And yet, it wasn't the first time he had been dazzled by this one, and it wasn't the first time it seemed to be sending him a message. Charmaine? No. Charmaine never wore rings. Charmaine, all her life, had always wanted her identity to remain essentially impersonal.

"Marie!" Séraphin exclaimed softly.

She had just flashed into his mind, fresh and pretty, sitting on the wall of the well that he had wanted to push her into. She was holding on to one of the supports of the wrought-iron frame over the well, and on that hand she was wearing that stone, which was now sparkling on the dun-coloured clay of the doll stuck with pins.

"Marie!"

Séraphin thought he could vaguely hear around him the frightened whispers of the people he had seen in the last few days and even this morning (yes, it was only this morning) in the market place at Forcalquier; words of ill omen about Marie. "Poor Marie . . . The daughter of the baker at Lurs." — "She has typhoid fever." — "They've put ice on her head." — "They've tapped her lung." — "She hasn't long to live." — "Such a beauty! My dear, what a tragedy!"

"Marie!" Séraphin whispered.

He took off the aquamarine and put it in his pocket. Then he seized the clay doll and crushed it with his two enormous hands. The clay squeezed out between his fingers. The pins stuck into it pierced his flesh, but he didn't feel them, just as the dogs' teeth had done and he hadn't felt the pain either. The same destructive rage had just taken hold of him and the strength to finish off the dying man surged in him at last. He threw the pitiful doll on the ground and stamped on it furiously. He began walking towards the bed, knocking over the stool on which he had sat down without thinking.

He heard someone running swiftly and lightly. Someone suddenly appeared there in front of him. It was Rose Sépulcre.

"No!" she said. "Not you! You mustn't kill him!"

"Get out of my way!" he growled.

He tried to grab her by the wrist to get her out of the way. She escaped him, running, dodging, spinning round. With lightning speed, she reached the spot between the wall and the side pillar of the hearth where, in all the houses in this part of the country, you only have to reach out your hand and your fingers will feel the butt of a firearm, even if you can't see it. Rose took down Zorme's gun and knew it was loaded, from the weight alone. She pointed it at Séraphin's chest, pressing the barrel into his ribs. She retreated step by step as he continued to advance, breathing heavily.

"Stop!" she said. "You mustn't. You'd regret it all your life."

He put his hand on the barrel of the gun to push it aside.

"At least listen to what I have to say!" she begged. "Afterwards, if you still want to, you can kill him! I won't stop you! You don't understand. He's a liar. What he told you is all wrong! Patrice and I were there behind the open window. We heard everything.

We've just come from your place. We found the papers. Now we know. Almost everything. But you don't! It's more terrible than you think. You mustn't kill him!"

Séraphin had stopped moving forward. He felt the gun barrel digging into his stomach, but that wasn't what stopped him. He knew that this was Didon Sépulcre's daughter who was speaking — Didon who had been crushed to death by the millstones. Since she had been listening, she also knew now who her father's murderer was. If *she* asked him to stop . . .

Rose heaved a sigh of relief and lowered her gun.

"You love truth so much," she said. "You've been searching for it for so long! Well then, here it is!"

"Don't tell him!" Zorme cried in a quavering voice.

He had sat up on his bed, throwing back the covers, and, looking at him there in his nightshirt, you could tell that death had already hewn him down to size for a coffin.

"Why shouldn't I!" Rose muttered. "He wanted the truth, so he'll get it!"

She walked towards the fireplace. With the barrel of the gun she raised the black crepe hiding the object on the canopy, where it stood alone. It was an old photograph in a frame — the blurred, sad face of a woman from many years ago, but a young woman. She had pale eyes, and the one on the left was very slightly turned upwards.

What he saw made Séraphin do what the gun could not: he took three steps backwards. A kind of shiver spread all around his skull. The whole of his great body began to tremble like a tree being felled. He drew his hands across his face three times, but the portrait with the bright gaze and with the slightly squinting eye was still there. It was an object: it could be held, turned around, kissed on the lips. And it was the face and the lips that had so often materialized in front of him; it was the mouth, slightly open and showing little white teeth, which so much wanted to tell him what he refused to hear. It was the little head which rustled the leaves beside the well.

"My mother . . ."

Séraphin could scarcely pronounce the words that terrified him. Rose looked at him with astonishment.

"How do you know?" she said. "*You've* never seen her."

Séraphin just shook his head. He was hardly listening. He could not share the mystery that had allowed him to know his mother's face with anyone. He was beginning to understand what she wanted so much to tell him and what he wanted so much not to hear.

"*I* have," Rose said. "She made her first communion at the same time as my mother. When my mother told me about the crime, she went and got a photo of both of them at about the age of sixteen . . . She told me a lot about Girarde . . ."

Séraphin looked at the crepe which had fallen by the side of the hearth, making a large black spot on the red tiles.

"My mother . . ." he repeated.

"Do you understand?" Rose said gently.

Zorme had fallen back on to the bed. He sounded more and more like bagpipes with a hole, losing all their air.

"She loved me before him . . ." he said. "And I loved her. By the time she realized what a brute he was, it was too late. Just once," he panted, "just once we consoled each other . . . One single time. I never . . . never looked at another woman."

"Everyone knew," Rose said.

"I wanted her still to be considered an honourable woman," Zorme said.

"Everyone knew!" Rose repeated vehemently, "and not honourable! My mother told me often enough, 'A love child!' It was the midwife, talking deliriously on her deathbed. My mother said that she gave us the key to the mystery of four or five strange resemblances . . . But you . . . no one suspected . . . You didn't look like anyone. It took the midwife who said — oh, maybe two hours before she died — 'And there's Séraphin, the poor little thing. Even him! When he was born, the living image of Zorme! The living image! I didn't know how to hold him so that l'Uillaou wouldn't notice!' "

With the sound of a wine skin losing all its air, Zorme wheezed,

"One single time! I wanted her still to be an honourable woman. I didn't want people talking about her. And later, when I saw you, when I saw you . . ."

"Tell him, Zorme, now that you have nothing more to lose, tell him why you murdered my father and Gaspard Dupin. Tell him the truth."

"I didn't want you to become a murderer. When I looked in your kitchen and discovered the papers you found, I realized what you were going to do . . . So *I* did it instead. If I'd told you the truth, you'd have despised your mother and she made me swear . . . I wanted you to keep her memory intact. I wanted you at least to escape destiny."

"Charmaine . . ." Séraphin said.

418

"No. She didn't recognize me that night in the garden. But I saw her go into your house. I saw her through the window looking into the sugar tin. She had you in her power. You were at her mercy."

"And Marie?" Séraphin said quietly.

"Marie's not part of it."

"And Marie?" Séraphin shouted.

He went towards the bed, his open hands dripping with clay and bleeding from the needles that had stuck into them.

"She got herself involved," Zorme said. "She'd seen me, the day I discovered Charmaine in your house. She's delirious and keeps repeating, 'I saw someone . . . I must tell them . . .' And then . . . instead of her father, who's too careful . . . I thought that the daughter would do . . . that when death and ruin had descended on the three families, you'd be satisfied at last . . ."

He raised himself up on his elbows with one last effort, which dragged a great moan of escaping air from his chest.

"Are you satisfied at last, angel of justice?"

"He's raving," Rose said.

"Already too late . . ." Zorme wheezed, "for Marie. She'll die. I can't go back on it."

He mumbled something else as he fell back on the pillow with a look of indifference on his face. Rose will swear later that she heard him say, "I'd have on my hands . . ."

"Father or not . . ." Séraphin said.

All he thought of now was Marie. He pushed Rose aside, causing her to take several steps back. Then he leaned over the big bed.

But someone had got there before him. Zorme's mouth hung open and his nostrils were pinched into a pyramid on the bridge of his nose. The flesh had collapsed under the features of his face and spread out over the bony skull, more or less concealing the triangle. His eyes were focused on other visions.

"You see," Rose said gently, "you weren't born to punish."

Séraphin turned away. He felt much more bereft and poor in spirit than when he came back from the war, dragging so many dead behind him. But Marie's name gave him his bearings.

He looked at the portrait of his mother on the canopy over the fireplace as he passed. He raised his hand as if to stroke her face, but that was as far as it went. He was starting to love her less.

Patrice saw him come out looking stony-faced. Out of a sense of propriety Patrice had not shown himself until then. He couldn't help being happy, for he was beginning to see his face with Rose's eyes. She was slowly curing him of his self-loathing. Séraphin, deeply distressed, looked at him without really seeing him, but Patrice wouldn't have been able to console him anyway.

Séraphin got on his bicycle. Bending over the handlebars, he went off without a backward glance.

XVIII

The people of Lurs had been eating badly baked bread for a week. Célestat could not concentrate on his work. They forgave him. They said, "What can you expect, with his daughter so sick . . ." — "She's no better?" — "Oh! Worse. She asked for the clock and the cradle to be brought to her bedroom." — "What cradle? What clock?" — "Oh! It's no use trying to explain it to you! You wouldn't understand!"

When Séraphin appeared at the door of the bakehouse, the ill-fated sugar tin held tightly under his arm, he took up the whole doorway. Célestat was slumped at the table that held the shovels. His arms, white with flour, lay there in front of him, still and useless. He did not even have the strength to begin kneading. He felt the same fever as the one consuming Marie running in his veins.

When he became aware that someone was

blocking the last of the daylight, he raised his head a little. He reached for the gun, but what was the use? Saving his life seemed pointless now that Marie was going to die.

Séraphin bent double to get under the low door. He saw the firearm in front of him, aimed at his stomach.

"It's not worth it," he said. "I know who killed my mother."

"Oh . . . You know?" Célestat said without conviction.

That old story seemed outside of his life, as though it had happened to someone else, as though it had been told to him and he had listened with indifference.

"Zorme is dead," Séraphin announced.

"Oh . . ." Célestat said.

He ruminated briefly on this piece of news, but it had come too late. Only a week ago he might have rushed out into the street wild with joy, scarcely able to check the desire to run around shouting, "Zorme is dead!" Now he was so miserable that it hardly impinged on him.

"Well," he said, "if Zorme is dead, perhaps I can tell you the truth?"

Séraphin shrugged his shoulders.

"I didn't come for that," he said.

Célestat looked straight in front of him at the arch of whitewashed stone above the

423

bakehouse.

"You wouldn't have a cigarette, would you?" he said. "I'm in such a daze that I've left mine on the counter in the shop."

Séraphin rolled one and lit it for him. The combined smell of tobacco, flour and the pine faggots piled up in the loft revived the poor baker a little. "When we were creeping up to La Burlière," he said, "Zorme was coming out. His face looked terrible and his hands were red. And there we were . . . with our *tranchets* trembling in our hands. He went to the well, came back, then went off on the line-inspection car. So we went in. It smelled of blood, just like when we kill the pig . . . We saw everything in a haze of blood . . . We left without waiting to find anything more. We left along Ganagobie. Every man for himself. We never saw each other ever again. If our paths happened to cross, we'd go down a side street. Never . . . As far as I'm concerned, I've never stopped being afraid since then. Same, I think, for the other two, till the moment they died . . . We were afraid of Zorme."

"On the subject of deaths," Séraphin said. "It was Zorme who killed them. He was afraid of you too."

"Zorme! It wasn't you?"

"No. I wanted to, but he did it for me."

424

"There wasn't only Zorme. There was the law. Even after they'd guillotined the three, I felt the blade on my neck. I used to wake up with a start. I heard it falling with a noise like a scythe."

Célestat was silent for a few seconds.

"My poor father," he continued, "said to me on his deathbed, 'Célestat, remember this: if you need *anything at all,* go and see Félicien Monge. He can't refuse you. Do you understand? He can't . . .' Then he mumbled something about some business between the grandfathers years ago. I don't know what . . ."

"*I* do," Séraphin said.

"Oh! You know? Then I can tell you. I heard something about it from a very old man from Villeneuve who was almost one hundred years old when he died, and he told me . . . But I didn't believe him at the time."

"Go down the well at La Burlière," Séraphin said. "You'll understand."

"Ah? Do you think so? Well, in those days, in families like ours, if you wanted to get ahead, you had to give chance a helping hand."

"You can be sure of that," Séraphin sighed.

"Oh! When I needed it," Célestat said, "Monge didn't say no . . . Nor to Gaspard or Didon. Only every year on St Michael's Day, the three of us would be there at the door of La Burlière. Twenty-three per cent! One day we finally had enough . . . We couldn't take it any longer. We'd had to marry ugly girls to get a bit of money! But . . ." he added nodding his head, "we were well prepared, but we weren't up to it . . . We couldn't have done it. When we saw all that blood, we clung on to each other as though we were drunk . . . We couldn't have done it . . . Especially with you screaming in your cradle."

"Did you know that Monge wasn't my father?"

"Yes, unfortunately."

"I don't even have a right to my name," Séraphin said.

He stretched out his arms and pushed the tin with the Breton calvary on the lid across the table towards the baker.

"The papers you signed for Monge are inside," he said. "Burn them. Underneath you'll find some gold coins, a heap of them . . . They're for Marie. Give them to her when she's well again . . ."

"Well again . . ." Célestat said. "Well again . . ."

He slumped down on the table, his head on his arms, and began to sob.

"There's no hope!" he groaned. "No hope! The doctor said she can't last more than a week!"

Séraphin got up and came and put his hand on Célestat's shoulder.

"Give it to her when she's well again!" he repeated firmly.

Then he added sadly, "So that she'll forgive me, if she can, for having come into her life."

Célestat raised his head with surprise. He could feel Séraphin breathing beside him: Séraphin, the person he had been so afraid of, who reminded him of the worst moments of his life. He was breathing over him, and the hand on his shoulder felt like protection. Célestat opened the box without thinking. There it was, the stamped piece of paper that had made his life a misery, that had made him old before his time, that had — in any event — killed the other two. Under it, he could see the bed of warm coins lying there innocently glistening, as though nothing was wrong.

"They're more steeped in blood than the papers," Séraphin said.

"But . . . what about you?" Célestat asked.

"Me? What would I do with a heap of gold coins?"

"You could . . . What are you going to do?"

427

"See Marie," Séraphin said.

He turned away from Célestat and bent over to get out the door. He walked down the empty street. Night had well and truly fallen. He lifted the bead curtain at the bakery and found Clorinde slumped over the counter with her head in her arms, crying.

"I'm going to see Marie," he said.

Without waiting for a reply, he slowly and deliberately climbed each step of the narrow stairs leading to the bedrooms. He saw a door half-open and the glow of a nightlight. The strange heat and unpleasant smell of a sickroom emanated from it. Séraphin pushed the door open.

"I was watching over Marie," Tricanote will relate afterwards. "I turned round and saw him there. How can I describe it? Anger was all around him like a halo. I could see him trembling with indignation like a branch shaken by the wind. He smelled of the hills, the bowels of the earth, dead leaves, the waters of the Durance — of everything but man. I got out of the way. I left them alone. It was like their wedding night."

He stayed there alone with Marie.

Marie was fighting the sickness. Weak and delirious though she was, it seemed that a

428

mighty strength was concentrated deep within her, refusing to be dragged out, refusing to be won over by death, wrestling it while she had a breath in her body.

There was nothing left of her: she scarcely made a bump in the counterpane on the bed where she lay. Marie had lost her hair. What could be seen of her face was her white forehead and her ears, which stood out a little from her head. Her eyes were not closed. Two blue pupils were turned to the side, watching elsewhere, ready to slip out of their orbits in one last glance. Marie's mouth was half-open; you couldn't hear her breathing, but each breath filled the room with an unbearable smell. Her hands were now like those of a miserly old woman, clawing at the counterpane with the rapid movements of a spider at work.

Séraphin looked intently all around the room. He saw the Dresden figurines set out on the marble top of the chest of drawers. He saw — but with no surprise — his own cradle at the foot of the bed, and inside it, like the head of a deformed child, the workings of the clock she had snatched out of his hands and taken away at La Burlière.

At the head of the bed was one of those yellow and green straw-bottomed bedroom chairs, which are the luxury of the poor in this part of the world. Holding his breath, Séraphin sat down on this chair, which he turned perpendicular to the bed. He reached out his hands towards those misshapen claws that seemed to be scrabbling in the earth. He imprisoned them between his palms. They were burning under their cold, loose skin. At first he felt them put up an almost spiteful resistance to his hold. They seemed like cats' claws digging into his flesh. But little by little, he felt that they ceased attacking him and became just poor, weak hands. Her hands told him humbly what Marie, gagged by sickness, could not.

He too raised his eyes towards the Dresden china crucifix and its holy water bowl with the blessed box twig in it. With an intense, questioning anguished look, he kept his eyes fixed for some time on this knick-knack.

Lurs was sinking deeper into the darkness, and Séraphin alone in that room with Maric felt like a wisp of straw, scarcely more alive than the dying girl. But he never let go her hands. He never stopped thinking only of her, feeling compassion only for her, concerned only with her breathing, which he had finally detected: an infinitely fragile movement, painfully raising the counterpane, as though it weighed as much as a marble slab.

Through the casement-window with its shutters facing north to the Lure mountains, the passing hours were registered in the black sky by the Great Bear slowly moving backwards until it gently came to rest against the mountain. The hills and villages, where an odd light shone here and there, slept peacefully in the distance beyond that window, and would wake smiling in the sun . . .

The china crucifix was on the same level as the window. He never took his eyes off it. He had confidence; he did not doubt. What would he have been had he doubted? Yet he was filled with anguish at the idea that the whole weight of his silent prayer was carried by the intermediary of that pathetic crucifix.

He fought with death through all the miserable hours of the night with the weapons at his disposal. Sometimes the air stopped smelling foul above Marie's mouth and he said to himself that she had gone. Sometimes the pulse under the pressure of his palms became wildly irregular and seemed to be trying to escape, to run in answer to an urgent call. Then he would increase his pressure on those poor claws within the warmth of the nest he had made for her with his hands, supporting Marie's struggle with all his might. Through all the miserable hours, until the chariot of the Great Bear began to rise on the right above the la Graille pass, over by Jabron. It was then that Séraphin's head drooped on to his chest. Prostrate on his chair, with Marie's hands still lying in his, which had opened up like a flower, he was now just a man exhausted by fatigue, falling asleep, forgetting.

He was awoken — and it was still night — by the alarming sensation of a new presence in the room. Marie's hands were still in his and it was in them that the new presence was moving. The irregular pulse that jumped everywhere had been replaced by a lovely clockwork beat, muted but with that interval of still silence which accentuated its majestic rhythm.

Séraphin looked up at Marie's face. Her eyes were open and she was smiling at him. Life was flowing back into her at an extraordinary rate. She was filling out again; her colour was coming back by the minute. All the air in the room was scarcely enough for her lungs, now relieved of the weight that had pressed on them.

Séraphin then went to open the shutters a little to the morning air from the Lure, so that she would not breathe the smell death had left behind. Marie thanked him with a long drawn-out sigh.

He returned to her bedside. He took the aquamarine from his pocket and put it on her index finger. He then put a finger to his lips and tiptoed backwards out of the room. He went down the stairs. Clorinde was still in the same position, huddled on her chair with her grey hair dishevelled about her head. Séraphin touched her shoulder.

"Go up," he said, "she's alive."

He went out. The morning sun was shining in the street. Of course he didn't notice Tricanote by the side of the last step of the stairs with the Marquise de Pescaïré, both of them with hands clasped, kneeling on their ancient knees, gazing at him in wonder from behind the half-open door as he passed.

He picked up his bicycle and went down Lurs' steep paved street. He looked at the four doleful cypresses waving in the morning breeze. For the last time he crossed the clean, empty site where the house he had never had once stood. He glanced at the well and the washing-place. His mother would never visit it again. Love had fallen from him like autumn leaves from a tree.

He now had to complete the hardest part

of the journey among men: everyday life.

He got on his bike and began to pedal. He did not once look back.

XIX

I crossed the Durance, now gagged with dams and no longer able to sing. I entered this village, which continues to age gently under the protective shell of its roofs, sheltering the narrow streets from the sun.

I asked the first old man I came across for Marie Dormeur. She had had another name, but that old man should know her first one.

"Just go under the bells, past the church. The first street on your right hand. You'll see it. It's a green house with an arbour and a balcony. At this time of day, Marie should be coming out to take the air . . ."

The house was half-hidden under mauve fuchsias, begonias and geraniums. It was all freshly watered and breathed tranquillity of mind. Marie was holding a green watering-can and had almost finished carefully sprinkling water over her flower pots. When it was done, she took her folding chair and newspaper under her arm and went down the stairs step by step with a heavy, cautious tread, watching where she was putting her feet. She sat down half in shade and half in sunlight.

I knew she was almost eighty-two, since on that fine morning when I had left her after Séraphin's departure, she must have been eighteen or nineteen.

I knew that she had married an average sort of man who had had a happy childhood like her own. She had had some beautiful children who had scattered throughout the world, as was the fashion. And now she was there alone in front of her doorway, sitting on a folding chair, her ankles bulging over her slippers because of troubles with her circulation, watching the world go by through the thick glasses worn by people who have had cataract operations.

The past, when she was full of life, has sunk deep into the silt of time. Does she still remember it? How could you tell? Eyes that have lost their crystalline lens can no longer express regret or melancholy: they are perpetually smiling.

She was happily knitting a bed jacket and watched me approach. I saw the aquamarine that Séraphin had put on her finger sparkling in the sunlight. The flesh around that ring had weathered more than sixty years of living, but the stone and the setting were the same as when Célestat and Clorinde had chosen them in secret for their little girl's eighteenth birthday.

"Ah! Monsieur. So that's what you want to see!" she said.

She put her knitting and her newspaper down on the chair. She went up the stairs in front of me, hobbling a little but still agile. She pushed open the fly-wire door. Then she went up another handsome flight of polished-wood stairs. Sounds echoed in that perfectly kept house, which smelled of walnut liquor and wax.

Marie ushered me in front of her into a dining-room full of heavy furniture. I saw the clock straight away. The mechanism had been set into a handsome case of light-coloured wood decorated with a large sheaf of painted flowers. The letters of the maker's name still stood out in elegant script on the dial: *Combassive, Abriès-en-Queyras.*

"It never varies a minute," Marie said proudly. "It never goes too fast or too slow! Well, there it is!" she said.

Her short arms were pointing between the foot of the clock and the heavy Henri II table, to a cradle on rockers, polished to within an inch of its life. It held two pots of

437

splendid aspidistras. The star of the Hautes-Alpes, the rosette symbol that reigns over all those stark valleys, still shone at its head.

"I'm sure, Marie, that your heart is never a minute fast or a minute slow either. I'm sure that it has never had the slightest scratch, just like that aquamarine that suits you so well. So tell me — because you know — who was Séraphin really?"

"Ah!" she exclaimed.

She left a long interval between this "Ah" and the rest of her reply.

"Is that what you wanted to ask me? And that's why we had to be alone?"

I nodded my head.

"Did he even know himself what he was? At times . . . At times . . . It seemed to me that he was lost on earth and that he was crying out all the time. He had a look . . . like a tethered animal, looking at you, imploring, 'Set me free!' That was Séraphin. Poor us . . . How could anyone have thought I could hold on to him? He left, he left . . . As for me, I was married at twenty to a man whose better you couldn't find anywhere . . . As good as the bread he made . . . At thirty I had my four children. What could be done about it? Oh! I found out in the end. By dint of playing the toreador with pine trees thirty metres high, Séraphin finally got what he wanted. Giant versus giant, and it's the tree that won. It crashed down on him. At least that's what I was told by someone from up there who sells pears, who told me one day when I was buying some for the winter. And he told me, 'He's buried at Enchastrayes, under the brambles in the old cemetery. At least I think he's there. At least, I think it's him . . .'

"And then, when my poor husband died, I wanted to go to Enchastrayes. I wanted to have a gravestone put there for the poor wretch, so that at least people would know that someone remembered him. Afterwards, I would have gone there every year on the first of November to bring flowers. It would have been an outing for me. You don't know Enchastrayes? It's magnificent, especially in autumn.

"And so I searched, in the old cemetery . . . in the brambles . . . indeed I did . . . In the end I came across two very old people who were looking for mushrooms. They had always lived around there, from father to son. I outlined Séraphin's size with my arms and my words, and his head with my hands and my eyes (they were still good at that time). They searched their memory; they consulted each other; they went through all the strong men they knew who had died. No. I was mistaken. If it was the one they thought, well, in that case . . . No, he wasn't buried in the old cemetery. Your Séraphin would more likely be the one who was in the forest during the landslide of '28. We think he was under it. We think so! Because, well, you can just imagine! Hundreds of thousands of cubic metres! What use would it have been trying to find something under all that? Since then, pine trees twenty metres high have grown up again on top of the landslip. There's not even a sign of it any more, except for a big gash in the shape of a cross on the mountain. If your giant is anywhere, he's under there. And he doesn't need a stone to mark his grave! He's got quite enough of them on top of him as it is!"

"But Marie, you're talking about a time when you no longer knew him. What about before that? When he was living and breathing within your reach?"

She looked at me as though I were an unfathomable oracle, as though I held all the mysteries of the world. She looked at me to convince herself that she could speak as though she were alone and said to me:

"The night he saved me . . . And remember, you who know, that the same day he had gone to Forcalquier, he had climbed down the well, and he had been there when Zorme died — all in the one day! And then he sat up all night on a chair conquering the sickness that was in me. And then, suddenly I woke up. Cured. It was the feel of his breath on my face that woke me. He wasn't snoring. He was breathing like a blacksmith's bellows. The air coming down on me from his nose and mouth, well . . . it was like breathing the mountain wind . . . And there he was, with his head drooping and his back bent and . . . I still had my hands on his, but he had let his fall open, defenceless! They were open like two halves of a pomegranate! Remember how he always obstinately kept them closed, even when the dogs' teeth had pierced them! And then, that night, I gently withdrew mine and looked at his palms. And then, the truth . . . the truth is that his hands were smooth: they had no lines! And that's why, my dear man, he had no proper life!"

Marie was still breathless, sixty years later, when she told me about this mystery.

"Oh, but don't think that . . . After my illness," she said, "I went around calling his name everywhere. They thought I was going mad. Where could they go to find him for me? When he put the ring on my finger and left, with his finger to his lips, I thought he

441

was coming back . . . What would you have thought, if you were in my shoes? Tricanote would run after me and shake me like a plum tree: 'Forget him, you silly girl!' she would shout at me. 'His body is ashes!' And one day I answered her: 'I know that better than you do! What difference does it make? Do you think that can stop me crying?' "

. . . Marie told me, among many other things . . .

Then, so that no one but me should ever hear the truth, all that remained now was for me to kill her, which I did. She died peacefully that same night, in her comfortable bed, with no one at her bedside.

Her children, anxious to return to the Americas, sold off the good furniture in the market square at Les Mées. An antique dealer who has a shop in the Place Saint-Michel at Forcalquier acquired Séraphin's clock and cradle. The shop is still there. The window is still as evocative of the past. As for the clock and the cradle, I believe they are still there too.

ABOUT THE AUTHOR

Pierre Magnan is an award-winning French crime writer who publishes his novels to rave international reviews. *The Murdered House* is his third mystery to be published by Minotaur Books; previous titles include *The Messengers of Death* and *Death in the Truffle Wood.*

We hope you have enjoyed this Large Print book. Other Thorndike, Wheeler, Kennebec, and Chivers Press Large Print books are available at your library or directly from the publishers.

For information about current and upcoming titles, please call or write, without obligation, to:

Publisher
Thorndike Press
295 Kennedy Memorial Drive
Waterville, ME 04901
Tel. (800) 223-1244

or visit our Web site at:

http://gale.cengage.com/thorndike

OR

Chivers Large Print
published by AudioGO Ltd
St James House, The Square
Lower Bristol Road
Bath BA2 3BH
England
Tel. +44(0) 800 136919
email: info@audiogo.co.uk
www.audiogo.co.uk

All our Large Print titles are designed for easy reading, and all our books are made to last.